"When go Vicky?"

The question caught him like a kick to his stomach as he cinched the saddle buckle tighter under his horse's belly. Surely she didn't expect to ride a full day and a half back to the hacienda if she hadn't even been in the saddle once since her accident.

"You need to take things easy still, Vicky. If we try to take you back to the hacienda right now, you wouldn't make it more than an hour or so."

"I no ready go hacienda. I ready to ride. When Chris make horse take Vicky in corral?"

A breath of relief filled his chest. "You want to ride?"

"*Sí!*" She clapped her hands together. "*Gracias*, Chris!" In an instant she had all but thrown herself at him, squeezing him around the middle. His arms caught her and held her without his permission.

She belonged there. Right in his arms. She fit. As if Chris had been made to protect her and hold her within the shelter of his own arms. Of course, that was nonsense. Thinking that way only spelled disaster.

As soon as she healed, he'd take her back.

Bonnie Navarro lives in Warrenville, Illinois. She and her husband, Cesar, will celebrate twenty-four years of marriage this year. They have four beautiful children, two still in high school and two college age. Cesar has often called their children Amerikicas—a mix of American and Inca. Bonnie works as a trained medical interpreter for a hospital close to home and when not at work, she is either reading, writing or knitting.

Books by Bonnie Navarro

Love Inspired Historical

Instant Prairie Family
Rescuing the Runaway Bride

BONNIE NAVARRO

Rescuing the Runaway Bride

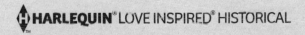

HARLEQUIN® LOVE INSPIRED® HISTORICAL

Recycling programs for this product may not exist in your area.

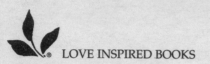

LOVE INSPIRED BOOKS

ISBN-13: 978-0-373-42509-9

Rescuing the Runaway Bride

Copyright © 2017 by Bonnie Navarro

www.Harlequin.com

Printed in U.S.A.

For if thou altogether holdest thy peace at this time,
then shall there enlargement and deliverance
arise to the Jews from another place;
but thou and thy father's house shall be destroyed:
and who knoweth whether thou art come to
the kingdom for such a time as this?
—*Ester* 4:14 (KJV)

To my own princesas. Liz and Gaby. You make your mother so proud of the beautiful women you are becoming, both inside and out. I pray daily for you.

And let's not forget my guapos (handsome men). CJ and David, it makes my heart sigh to see God's hand in your lives.

I stand in awe of the way my babies are all growing up and how blessed I've been. May God continue to bless you.

And none of our darling children would exist without my own hero, Cesar. Te amo and thank God that He placed you in my life so many years ago. Your encouragement to learn Spanish and submerging me in the Latino culture has given me a rich life, a career I never dreamed of and fodder for a few more stories… And when you cook dinner and see to the kids so I can write… I realize, how truly blessed I am.

Chapter One

Mid-January, 1842
Alta California, Territorio of México

Tightening the strap under her chin, she pushed the old wide sombrero back on her forehead as she looked out over the swift stream. Vicky tried to ignore a growing sense of foreboding. Or at least she attempted to as she refilled her canteen. She had never seen this stream before. The fact that she didn't recognize it could mean only that she had somehow wandered off Hacienda Ruiz land.

Rubbing a gold crucifix between her numb fingers, she tried to pray once more to a God she wasn't convinced listened. An icy shiver sent fear up her spine and made her tremble as she hauled herself back onto Tesoro's back. She'd had the chills most of the morning as she had tried to find her way out of the woods. Papá would be furious with her when he finally made it home, not to mention José Luis, who had made her promise to come back by midday if she didn't catch up with Papá. But she had bigger concerns at the moment.

She'd chased after Papá, attempting to go with him to the secret meeting of the noblemen of the territory. She had to convince him to stop the plans for her wedding to Don Joaquín on her birthday. But the snow started to fall before she caught up to him and his men, and she was forced to take shelter in one of the rustic cabins on the outskirts of the hacienda, almost a full day's ride from the main buildings. Somehow her journey brought her here, three days later, off hacienda lands and sick with a fever and no more provisions.

Tesoro, her best friend and true companion, shifted underneath her. *"Que pasa, Tesoro?"* Vicky asked the horse what she sensed, even as she patted Tesoro's neck and urged her on downstream a few more feet. When Tesoro stopped and pawed the ground, a shudder passed through her, as well. They were no longer alone. Pulling her rifle out of its scabbard, she listened. Nothing. No sound. No bird singing or squirrels chirping. Utter silence. The wood's way of warning about danger. Predators. Or strangers.

Then she saw him. An Americano from the looks of his dress and his hair, which she caught a glimpse of just before he shoved his hat back on his head. She'd never seen anyone with such golden hair before except for pictures in books. Even her mother, the fair-complected Crilloya, had dark brown hair. Vicky's own dark skin came from her father's native mother instead of his noble father's lighter hair and skin.

Tesoro snorted and pawed the ground, but she didn't

turn away from the man downstream. Maybe he was lost, as well. Vicky sat straight in the saddle and watched him closely. Was he friend or foe? Considering she was off hacienda lands and not sure how to get back, she didn't dare make contact.

Should she flee? She wasn't sure she could stay in the saddle at a gallop. The fatigue she had felt all morning pulled at her like a millstone. She needed to find a place to stay for the night.

Vicky forced her attention back on the stranger. He might not be alone. Searching the area, she didn't see any movement, but the spooky silence kept her frozen in place.

The man downstream crouched to examine something just as his horse shied away. A branch in the tree right above the man bowed. Crouched and ready to pounce was one of the world's most magnificent and deadly creatures. Without much thought to her own safety, she dropped the canteen, pulled her rifle up and sighted in a blink of an eye, her knees communicating to Tesoro to get closer even though wisdom would dictate she escape as fast as she could. Her movements caught the predator's attention, and its orange eyes fixed on her as it made ready to leap.

Chris couldn't believe the size of the paw prints on the bank of the creek just to the east of his farm, or ranch, as they called it in Alta California. They were almost as big as his hand. A few years before, he had killed a cougar trying to get into the barn, and its paws had been about the size of this one's. That beast had weighed about three hundred pounds and taken down a yearling. No wonder the horses had been skittish the past two weeks.

"Thank You, Lord, for Your protection once again," Chris heard himself say aloud. If the cat had found its way into the barn or come across him or Nana Ruth unsuspecting, it would have been bad—very bad.

Knowing was only half the battle. Last time he and Nana Ruth's husband, Jebediah, had taken turns watching and caught the cat in the act—returning for a second helping of tender horse flesh. But Jeb had been killed last summer, and now protecting Nana Ruth and the ranch was all on Chris's shoulders.

Years before, back on the plantation, his father would send the foreman and a hunting party of the slaves out to chase down anything that threatened the well-being of the livestock or the fields. Chris had lived his entire life as the spoiled son of the plantation owner, "preparing" to someday be the future master. He'd learned to do the books, barter the cotton, tobacco and peanuts, and see to a host of other responsibilities, but never did he have to get his hands dirty or risk any physical harm. That's what the slaves had been for, until his father died and Chris gave them their freedom.

He would never again benefit off the labor of another man held in bondage. Nana Ruth and Jebediah had accepted their freedom but refused to leave him. Instead, they traveled west with him, not that the end result had turned out well for them.

As he bent down to inspect the prints, Comet shied behind him. Chris cocked an ear and noticed the silence was…too silent. In the six years he'd lived in Alta California, he'd learned to read the signs of the woods, and he knew that either his presence—or something else's—was making the inhabitants of the area uncomfortable. He lifted his rifle and looked around closely.

Suddenly something heavy splashed into the creek. A few hundred feet to his right a young Indian boy, maybe fourteen or fifteen years old, rode into sight on a golden mare. With a fierce determination written across his face, the boy stopped his horse in the icy water and aimed a rifle at Chris. Indecision cost Chris valuable seconds while his mind fought the idea of shooting a boy, even in self-defense.

The decision was made for him when the boy fired. Chris ducked instinctively. It seemed as if time stood still, and he wondered if he were truly ready to meet his maker. His thoughts flew to Nana Ruth as the ground came up to meet his face. How would she survive on the ranch alone?

Just as his body tensed to take the bullet, he heard another sound, as if the tree above him were crashing down. Something large fell from above and knocked the boy off his horse, submerging him in the flowing creek. Chris was on his feet and in the water, his gun ready, before his mind could process what he had seen.

As he stepped closer, his gut twisted at the sight of blood turning the water red as it flowed with the current. Neither the boy nor the cougar came up for air. The mare, prancing close by, neighed in distress but didn't run off.

Chris kept a careful eye on the cat, its orange eyes

unblinking as he moved closer to the boy. Just under the surface, the boy thrashed but the big cat, almost as long as Chris was tall, pinned him down. Chris quickly shoved the cat to the side with his boot while aiming his rifle, should it regain consciousness and come at him. He plunged his arm into the frigid water and pulled the boy away as fast as he could while still keeping watch on the cougar. It was then that he noticed the bullet hole in the chest of the magnificent feline. Awed and humbled at the true shot, he looked down at the boy, who gasped and started to cough.

What was the child doing out in the woods alone? Chris hadn't heard of any native people living close by. Even the men from the Hacienda Ruiz rarely came anywhere close to his ranch. Had the boy gotten lost or had something happened to the rest of his party? Had they been hunting the cat?

He looked down at the boy and prayed that this young hero hadn't sacrificed his own life for Chris. With each minute that passed while the boy still didn't open his eyes, Chris's unease grew. He needed to get the boy out of the cold. Nana Ruth would know what to do.

He whistled for Comet, but the mare came over instead. Noting the saddle was of the finest leather, he hesitated before mounting up. Something about the horse was familiar, but now was not the time to figure it out. The stirrups were way too short, but he didn't have time or a hand free to adjust them with the boy in his arms. They needed to get home as soon as possible. The sun still shone in the January sky, but the trees shaded most of the ride, and the wind cut like a knife through his wet clothes. As Chris lifted the boy with him onto the horse, he was surprised to discover that he weighed even less than expected. Maybe ninety pounds at best, an even hundred with the waterlogged serape.

It took less than an hour to get back to the cabin, Chris carrying the boy on the mare with Comet following close behind. As soon as the cabin came into view, Chris started yelling. Nana might be slow moving, but there was nothing wrong with her hearing. She'd appreciate the advance warning that they had a guest. Especially since no one had come by in over four months.

"Nana Ruth!" His second shout brought Nana to the door of their wooden cabin just as he rode up.

"Land sakes, child, what's all the hollerin' about?" Nana Ruth paused only a second at the threshold, her work-worn hands resting on her ample hips. Her big brown eyes widened, and her ebony skin bunched into a thousand wrinkles crisscrossing her forehead as she hustled out into the yard as fast as her arthritic knees would allow.

"I need your help here, Nana Ruth."

"Now, just what have we here?" She leaned closer as Chris dismounted with the unconscious boy in his arms.

"I don't know, but I think we'd better find out. Can you get the door?" Readjusting his hold, he headed toward the cabin. The horses would have to see to themselves for a while.

The interior of the cabin was darker than outside, even with the windows he had built into the walls. He passed Nana's bed next to the hearth and nodded to his larger bed. "Nana, could you turn down the bedding?"

"But Master Chris, it's not right for you to be out of your bed on account o' no stranger. You can stretch her out on my bed." She stooped with effort to ready her own bed, but he shook his head.

"You won't be able to see to his wounds or take care of him on your small bed, and you'd have to bend down all the time. No, Nana, the boy will rest in my bed until we can find out where he came from and how to return him there."

"If that there's a boy, he's about the prettiest boy I ever seen, Master Chris. And I still say you ought not be putting her in your bed."

Her words stopped Chris in his tracks. Of course the child was a boy. True, even with dirt and blood on his face, he could be considered "pretty." But this couldn't be a girl. Preposterous! Not even an Indian girl would be out riding all on her own in the middle of the wilderness. It was true that some of the haciendas enjoyed relative safety because of their numbers and the way the hacienda señors or dons led their communities like feudal lords, but it was still dangerous in the wilderness. Chris himself had discovered his greatest enemy wasn't the wildlife or even the harsh weather of the higher altitudes but the lawless men who sacked and plundered and then melted back into the forest.

And then there was the shot that killed the cat. No girl could have made that shot. No, their guest had to be a boy, and he hoped to get some answers from the boy if the Good Lord willed the child's eyes open again.

"Nana. Help me peel this serape off first so we don't soak the bedding."

"Poor child, out in that cold all wet." Nana Ruth's gnarled fingers fought with the sombrero before it fell away. "I think she's got a knock on the noggin, Master Chris. There's a lump back here. Now looky here…" Nana Ruth's hands came away with hairpins. A braid cascaded down and swung like a pendulum. It wasn't the first Indian boy Chris had seen who had long hair worn in a single braid.

But he'd never seen a boy pin his braid into a bun.

Misgiving settled like a stone in the pit of his stomach.

Nana Ruth slid the thick fabric of the serape over the child's torso and head before Chris adjusted his grip to let the garment fall to the floor.

"Could you put some toweling down on the bed?"

She did his bidding even as she murmured, "We got to get this child warm soon. Look how dark her lips are."

It might already be too late. The boy was too still. As still as Jeb had been when Chris had finally run off their attackers and carried Jeb back to the cabin the day of the ambush… But he'd do everything he could to keep that from happening to this nameless boy who had saved his life. He couldn't let another person die. The thought spurred him to act faster.

Chris set the boy down. Nana Ruth tried to get the child's sweater undone, but her arthritis wouldn't let her manipulate the small buttons.

"Here, let me get those." He quickly had the sweater unbuttoned, only to discover a rustic wool shirt covering what was clearly a female figure. He turned away from the bed.

The day just kept getting stranger and stranger.

"Nana Ruth, you were right about her being a girl."

"And a right pretty one at that." She cackled.

"Do you think you can tend to the rest of her care?" he asked as he strode to the front door of the cabin.

"Don't you worry, Master Chris. I'll take good care of her. I'll get her all warmed up and better in no time."

Chris headed out the door to take care of the horses and give the mystery girl some privacy. A girl! Who would have believed it? He hoped she'd get a chance to explain her reason for being in his woods and who had taught her to shoot like she had. Was it skill or just God guiding the bullet like David and his slingshot?

Setting foot outside again sent a chill through him, and he debated going back in for dry clothes. On second thought, he'd grab some of Jeb's clothes from the old cabin the couple used to share before Jebediah died and Nana Ruth couldn't live alone. He'd rather wear tattered hand-me-downs any day than interrupt whatever Nana was doing for the girl. The horses would have to wait a few more minutes. He hustled to the long-abandoned cabin, aware both Comet and the girl's horse followed on his heels.

It took only a few minutes to get into something warm and dry, and then Chris headed back toward the barn. A snicker from the stranger's horse was the only warning before the mare nudged him on the shoulder like an old friend. He stopped in his tracks and studied her.

He blinked and resisted the urge to rub his eyes. Could it really be?

"Goldenrod! It is you!"

Four years prior he'd sold her to the owner of Hacienda Ruiz a full day and a half east of him. With his broken Spanish and a lot of gestures and hand signaling, he was able to barter a good deal for her and three of the other horses he had trained that year. Goldenrod still looked agile and well fed. Just as he had expected, they had taken good care of her. So why was a peasant girl riding her out in the middle of the wilderness alone? And why was the girl dressed like a boy? "So what brought you back to me, huh, Golden?" he mused, wishing that the horse could tell him where they had come from and who the girl was. He set the small saddlebag to the side before removing the magnificently tooled saddle and thick saddle blanket.

His fingers itched to search the bag for more clues as to the girl's identity, but chores needed to be done before he could investigate any more.

Taking up the brush, he worked the snarls out of Goldenrod's mane. After feeding and grooming all the other horses in his barn, he returned for the small saddlebag. Inside he found a skirt of silk and many layers of ruffles, a satin blouse of some sort and a pair of slippers. Not the typical clothing he had seen the local native people wear. The cloth itself was of fine quality and the stitching elaborate.

How old was this sleeping beauty, and why had she ended up alone in the woods with two very different sets of clothes? Was she a pauper who had either bartered or stolen this horse and saddlebag, or was she someone of means traveling in disguise? Again with the questions.

Judging by the sun hanging just over the peaks to the west, two hours had passed. Maybe he shouldn't have stayed out so long, but if Nana had needed him, she could have rung the cowbell he had hung on the overhang by the door. He quietly entered the cabin, his gaze falling on the still form on his bed. The girl's face, with a long gash across the forehead, was the only visible part of her except for a few wisps of long black hair against the white bedding. Nana Ruth struggled to stand from one of the stout kitchen chairs he had fashioned during their first winter in the woods.

"Soup's on the stove, Master Chris. You want somethin' to eat?"

"Sit back, Nana. I want to check on our visitor first." He crossed the room to stare down at the girl. "Has she woken up yet?"

"No, sir. Just mumbled and thrashed a few times. She's heatin' up somethin' fierce." Nana shook her head and tsked her tongue.

"She has a fever?"

"Yes, sir. How long was she wet?"

"Less than an hour before we arrived. It's my fault. She shot a cougar out of the tree above me and saved my life. It fell and knocked her off her horse and into the creek." Slipping a hand across the girl's brow, he flinched at the heat coming off her skin. Her cheeks were unnaturally rosy, and yet she shivered. "Poor girl. I wish I knew something about you or where you came from. Maybe I could go fetch your mother to take care of you."

Of course, that would be nearly impossible. Nana Ruth could no longer be expected to tend to the girl on her own, and leaving two defenseless women in the middle of the woods for more than an afternoon was completely irresponsible. If there was one thing Chris had learned well from his father, it was that he was responsible for everyone at all times. The last thing he needed was one more death on his conscience.

Turning from the child before he could dwell on the past, he summoned a smile for Nana Ruth and set about putting the stew on the table with the cutlery and cups of hot tea.

Once he and Nana Ruth were seated at the table, he wrapped his fingers around Nana's swollen and disfigured ones. "Father God, thank You for Your protection and providence. Please bless this food we're about to eat and bless the girl who saved my life. I ask You to heal her and enable us to get her back to her home and family. In Your name, Amen."

Chapter Two

There was that voice again. As if someone on the shore of the river had thrown her a rope, that voice pulled her toward safety. She'd heard it before and tried to open her eyes, but this time, they obeyed. Her body felt like it had been trampled by a stampede of horses. She had no energy to lift her leaden hands and rub her eyes. Blinking in the dim light, she tried to take in her surroundings, but either it was evening or the room had no windows. The only light was given off by a lamp on the table and the glow of fire. Was this a home or a cave?

As her eyes adjusted, details became clearer. The room resembled Berto and Magda's cabin, made with the same rough-hewn logs instead of the stucco and grand slate stones of her own home. Two wooden chests sat to her left. A smaller bed hugged the far wall, and whoever occupied it snored loudly. The hearth glowed with a dim fire, keeping the winter winds at bay. By the foot of the bed Vicky occupied, a figure sat in a chair with a book. His stocking feet were propped on the side of her bed. It felt strange, and somehow too intimate, that a stranger would be so informal in her bedchamber. But as her foggy mind cleared, she remembered that this was not her bedchamber.

Where was she? Who was he? And how did she get here?

The lamp on the table behind the man left his face shrouded in shadow. She couldn't determine his age, expressions or even his coloring. From her vantage point he appeared very large, his long legs like tree trunks and his wide shoulders easily twice her width. He continued to read, oblivious of her scrutiny.

She tried to shift to her right, but her arm wouldn't move. Not only did it feel like it weighed a ton, but it was somehow tangled in her bedding. Suddenly she couldn't breathe. Whether it was the sharp pain stabbing her in the right side or fear, she didn't know. Struggling to sit up, she gasped as the pain became so intense she saw stars. Her movements caught the man's attention. He sat up, his long legs withdrawing from the bed and settling silently on the floor. He laid the book aside and leaned forward, his face coming into the light. He said something—she only wished she knew what.

Concern showed in his eyes and something else… Kindness. His relaxed posture reassured her.

He got up and reached an arm behind her back, holding her up as he plumped the pillows. Laying her back gently, he readjusted the blankets to cover her shoulders and placed a palm gently against her forehead. She felt his calluses as he smoothed back her hair from her face. His tender touch surprised her. He studied her eyes for a minute, his own gaze full of questions. Then he pulled his chair closer to the head of the bed and sank back down.

He said something again, and this time she picked out the English words *pain*, *you* and something else that sounded familiar, but she was too groggy to try to make sense of things.

"Español. No Ingles." She tried to remember more but couldn't.

"My name is Chris." His Spanish sounded funny. His next words were lost to her since he switched back to English.

"My name is María Victoria Ruiz Torres." She answered in Spanish, pointed to herself but couldn't quite stifle a groan, her voice husky and barely audible. Compassion flashed in his eyes.

He pointed to her, but his words blended together, not making any sense. Talking required breathing, and each breath felt like a knife digging into her ribs.

"Pain? *Dolor?*" he asked.

"Sí, much pain... I...no air." Gasping, she nodded her head, only making it throb worse.

He leaned over and sat her up straight, holding her by the shoulders, avoiding contact with the most injured parts of her. When he did, she felt the binding around her ribs for the first time. Someone had bound her as if she had a corset on, but it was different. There were no bones and stays digging into her flesh, just soft cloth wrapped around her and holding her right arm to her side. She was still in pain, but at least sitting up she could breathe.

Who had brought her here? The last thing she could remember was stopping at the stream for water and letting Tesoro drink… Tesoro! Where was Tesoro?

"*Mi caballo?* Tesoro?" she questioned him frantically.

He smiled and said something about "Golden…" Most of the words he used made little sense to her.

"*Mi* horse?" she tried again, wishing the English she had once learned would come back to her.

"*Fine. With my* horses," he answered in his funny accent. She thought he was trying to say that her horse was with his horses. Vicky took a deep breath and closed her eyes to calm herself and drown out the pain.

When she opened her eyes, he was studying her again. Only inches from his face, she could see his eyes. Blue, like the sky on a cloudless day. She had never met anyone with eyes so light before—although they matched her grandfather's in the portrait in her father's study. The Americano's hair color surprised her, as well. Honey mixed with cinnamon that glowed like polished bronze in the firelight. What would it look like in the sun? Then she remembered—he was the Americano who had been by the stream when the puma attacked.

"*You two days,*" he said in broken Spanish, holding up two fingers and then pretending to lay his head on his hands and close his eyes.

"*Two days!*" she exclaimed. What would Papá say when she got home? Groaning again, she realized she couldn't leave tonight anyway. She was too sore, and it looked like it was already dark out.

Who had taken care of her? What would Mamá

think? What would she do? Had she even noticed that Vicky hadn't been back to the hacienda in all this time? Where was this man's wife, and why didn't he call her now that Vicky was awake?

Her thoughts raced around and around in her pounding head, and she suddenly felt very tired. Her eyes became heavy even as she tried to remember something of her English lessons.

"Water," she finally managed.

A tin cup came into view, and he held it for her as she sipped. The cool water soothed her parched throat and quelled the need to cough. But it wasn't enough. She wanted to gulp it down, not take in just a trickle, but he only let her have a sip at a time. "Slowly," he cautioned. Unable to even lift her arms to tilt the cup, she resigned herself to sipping.

Sleep wanted to claim her again—she could feel it like the undertow in the stream. Chris put a hand to her shoulder and gently leaned her back on the pillows. Frustrated at not being able to communicate her basic wishes, much less get up and get her own water, Vicky turned away from the man. What could she do? She wouldn't know what to say even if they had both understood the same language. She knew nothing about him—could he be one of the many bandits who roamed the Sierra and plundered those unfortunate enough to have to travel far from home?

No, he couldn't be a bandit. No man she had ever met would have taken the time to play nursemaid to a sick woman, except for maybe Berto. Her father's groom, who had helped her own grandfather found the Hacienda Ruiz over forty years earlier, had a gentle hand and soft heart, which is why he was so skilled with the horses. He had risked his own life to save Vicky when she was five years old, and she was forever bonded to him. His wife, Magda, was their housekeeper and cook at the main house, and had been since the days that Papá was a mere boy.

If only she had listened to José Luis and waited for Papá to return, surely Berto could have talked Papá into canceling the wedding. If only she were home. And yet, being home would be worse. She'd be preparing for her wedding with Don Joaquín right now, and he was a horrible man. He had been married several times, and all his wives had died. Vicky was convinced that if Don Joaquín hadn't killed them himself, they had taken their own lives rather than live with the fiend. The fact that her father would even consider marrying her off to such a monster was more than she could bear.

Letting her head rest against the pillows, she closed her eyes, surrendering once again to her exhaustion.

Nana Ruth's clanging the cowbell brought Chris rushing into the cabin the next afternoon. Milk sloshed as he dropped the pail on the table. In three quick strides he drew up next to Nana Ruth as she tried to settle Maria. Once again the girl was thrashing about in the bed, her words colored with fear.

"Did her fever come back?" he asked even as he leaned past Nana to touch the girl's forehead. Cool skin calmed his racing heartbeat.

"No Wakin!" Maria called out again, attempting to

push someone or something away from her. He caught her left arm gently in his hand and smoothed her hair with the other hand.

"Maria, you are safe. It's just a dream. You're safe." He grimaced even as the words left his mouth. Who was he to promise safety? His history was filled with failures to protect the people who depended on him.

She quieted. Her arm went lax in his, and then her eyes fluttered.

He set her arm on the blankets covering her and then waited. After a few more minutes, she settled into a peaceful sleep. When she woke, he had a cup of water ready by her side before she could even ask for it.

Chris watched as Maria tried to down a second cup of water as quickly as she had the first. He studied the emotions that raced across her face as she drank. Confusion when she first woke was quickly replaced with greed for the water and then frustration when he gave her only a little at a time. For a small young lady, she had a fire in her eye. If she weren't stuck in bed with broken ribs, having fought a fever for a few days and not taken anything solid, he'd bet that she would have demanded that he hurry up with the water.

"Maria?" She was slow to respond to her name. Odd. Had she also hit her head on the stones that broke her ribs? He hadn't noticed what lay beneath her at the time because he was so focused on getting away from the cougar in case it gave chase. He tapped her shoulder to draw her attention back to his face instead of the now empty cup.

"Why say me Maria?" she asked, her brows scrunching together, creating lines in her otherwise perfectly smooth skin.

Had he misinterpreted their most basic communication? "You said your name was Maria." Not that he could have pronounced all the words that had come after that.

"Maria name for baby when father at—" She stopped, puzzling out the English words. "When baby new, mamá take to padre for to—" Frustrated, she placed her hands together and bowed her head, closing her eyes as if praying.

"Where was your father when you were a baby?"

"No! No *mi* father," she shook her head and then stopped as if the movement pained her. She pointed to her chest and then to the sky. "Father from Dios, you call God. Father come to *hacienda* to say to God, 'be good baby.'"

Unsure what she was trying to say, Chris set the cup back on the table and pondered what to do next. Her English was much better than he had expected, but even so, he wasn't even sure what her name was now. How would they ever get her back to her people if he didn't even know her name?

"Master Chris, I heard tell that some people call their minister 'Father,'" Nana Ruth suggested.

"She's talking about a minister?"

"Ain't most babies christened by a minister?" Nana's question made sense, but then it still left the girl without a name.

Turning back to their patient, he slowly asked, "What is your name?"

"*Mi* Vic-kee-ta." She pointed to herself. "Maria Victoria Ruiz Torres. Vic-kee-ta."

"They call you Vicky?" Her beaming smile completely transformed her face, and for the first time, she looked like a woman, not a young girl. That smile made him want to say the word again just to make her happy.

"So where do you live?"

"Hacienda Ruiz." Her eyes flashed pride and fear at the same time.

At least he knew where that was. He'd be able to take her back to her people without too much problem, once she was ready to travel—assuming she wanted to return. Something in her eyes made him wonder why she had left the hacienda to begin with.

"How did you end up in the forest all by yourself?" The questions wanted to pour out all at once, but the confusion on her face told him that she hadn't understood.

"Master Chris, why don't I get the girl some of that soup you got on the fire. I dare say she's plum worn out, and a little warm soup might just loosen up her tongue."

Nana Ruth made to get up off the chair. "Sit back, Nana. I'll see to this." He laid a hand on the older woman's shoulder until he felt her relax into the chair.

"Now, this just ain't right, Master Chris."

"Nana, you've had your years of serving, and you've done a good job. Now it's my turn."

"It ain't fittin' for you to be servin' me, Master Chris."

"We're not in South Carolina anymore, Nana, and last I checked, God's word said to care for our family. You just about raised me from the time I could roll over in my crib."

Taking two bowls down from the shelves, he partially filled both, set a spoon in each one and then pulled the tea off the hook over the fire, poured it into two tin cups and then added some fresh milk.

"Now, don't let your mother hear you say such a thing, Master Chris! Why, she'd be mighty upset."

He set the first bowl and cup on the table next to Nana's elbow and then returned to the stove. "Good thing she's not here to find out, isn't it?" He chuckled as he returned to his guest's side.

Setting the cup and soup bowl on the chest next to the bed, he sat in the chair facing Vicky.

"You eat and no give me?" Vicky's astonished expression and the disapproval in her eyes made him chuckle. Did she really think he'd be so rude as to eat in front of her without offering? Little did she know about good old Southern hospitality.

"Of course not, Vicky." Nana had left some toweling next to the bed, and he draped it over Vicky from shoulder to shoulder. Picking up the bowl, he dipped the spoon into the steaming broth, ladled out some and blew on it like Nana Ruth had done for him as a child. Somehow, this situation felt very different. He raised the spoon and blew a little more. "Now, let's see how you like my cooking."

"I no baby." Indignation darkened her already jet-black eyes so much that he couldn't distinguish the iris from the pupil. Her jaw tightened, and he actually feared for her teeth.

"I know you are not a baby, but you can't move your right arm. Nana tied it to your side, and the soup is too hot for you to manage one-handed." The furrows in her forehead didn't relax, but she opened her mouth when he lifted the spoon. Sitting back, he waited for her verdict. It wasn't long in coming.

"No tiene sabor." She wrinkled her nose at the food but opened her mouth again for more.

"Is there something wrong with my soup?" Chris asked. He had never bothered to learn to cook until this last year when Nana's arthritis started to act up so bad that some mornings she couldn't even get out of bed. To Chris, making soup consisted of chopping up meat, a few carrots and maybe some potatoes and letting it all boil throughout the day while he saw to his chores. It might not have been as appetizing as something Nana would have made, but it kept spirit and body together for another day. Nana Ruth had never complained, but perhaps that was because of the guilt she felt for not being able to work anymore.

Using the edge of the towel that had kept his poorly aimed attempts at feeding the girl from soaking her, he wiped her chin where some soup had trickled down. Almost as quickly as Vicky had finished off her soup, she fell back to sleep. Thankfully, this time she seemed to rest peacefully. How young and vulnerable she looked as she slept.

He suddenly felt a surprising desire to protect her, and it caught him off guard. He stood up quickly, nearly upending his chair. He'd felt a need to protect others before, and it had never worked out well for him. In fact, it had caused him nothing but pain. The last thing he wanted to do was go down that path again. But he wasn't about to abandon this young woman.

"You'll be safe here, Vicky," he heard himself say. But who was he to promise such things? He had failed to protect others before, and he knew he shouldn't let himself get wrapped up in Vicky's dilemmas. She was better off without his help. If not for saving him, she'd probably be at home, hale and happy and surrounded by those who loved her.

His own baby sister, Nelly, had tumbled right off the porch when they were just tots. His father had taken him to the woodshed for that. He'd been overprotective of her from that day on and so relieved when Matt came along and took the job from him.

The whole reason he'd sold the plantation, left his mother living with Nelly and Matt and sailed months on end around the very southern tip of South America to come to the wilderness territory of Mexico was so that he could be far removed from the horrible way that some humans treated others, be where no one would bother him or depend on him while he built his own farm. He would never again sit around and let the forced labor of others benefit him.

He thought of Ezequiel, one of the younger slaves he'd been so happy to free after his father died. Ezequiel had tried to behave as a free man in a world that wasn't ready for him to be free, and he'd paid with his life. Chris would probably feel responsible for Ezequiel's death until his own.

No, the last thing he needed was to have someone under his care. He clearly wasn't good at it.

Of course, from the start, he had to take care of Nana Ruth and Jebediah because they had nowhere to go when other freed slaves left for the north. They were too old to start over and had no living children who could take care of them in their later years. He had done everything in his power to provide and protect them, but even here, five years after they built the cabins and barn, a trio of outlaws came and killed Jebediah. Chris had managed to fight off the three bandits, but he wasn't able to save Jebediah.

The old slave had been more of a mentor and father to him than his own father had. Instead of enjoying his last years on earth peacefully living in a small town with someone looking out for him and his wife, he'd spent the last of his strength helping to build the cabin, barn and all the other outbuildings plus working with the livestock. Chris should have settled them somewhere safe, then maybe Nana would still have her beloved husband beside her.

Could he do better for Vicky? Did he have it in him to try?

He'd just see to her safety while she healed and then she'd become someone else's concern. He'd get her home…somehow. Hopefully the girl would be missed and someone would come looking for her so he wouldn't have to leave Nana Ruth on her own. Maybe someone would arrive within a few days.

Setting the dirty dishes in the sink, he sat down to nurse his own bowl of soup. The first scalding sip brought his mind back to Vicky's scrunched-up nose. She'd been right. The soup didn't have *"sabor,"* and she hadn't been shy about telling him that.

For reasons he couldn't entirely explain, the thought of her reaction to his cooking made him smile. He allowed himself to enjoy the image of her in his mind before he forced himself to take another bite of his "soup."

Chapter Three

Vicky blinked to adjust to the soft morning light filtering through the windows of the rustic log cabin. A visual search of the room revealed a pallet next to the large stone fireplace had been pushed to the side and the blankets folded and stacked on a chair leaning against the wall.

The large woman whom Chris called Nana Ruth slumbered on, her snores stopping abruptly and then, after a few snorts, starting up again. Her swollen hands lay on the rough blanket, and Vicky had noticed her rubbing her knuckles and her knees the night before. If only Magda were there, she would make a poultice that would work wonders for the arthritic joints. The washer-woman from the hacienda suffered from swollen joints and would visit the kitchen almost every day for Magda's remedies and massages.

Careful not to move anything but her head, Vicky took her time studying her surroundings now that daylight flooded the room. The two wooden chests that stood side by side against the wall gleamed a dark chestnut color, and the woodwork would have made Manolo, the hacienda's carpenter, proud. The table Vicky had taken for rough-hewn the night before was intricately engraved. Glancing at the headboard of the bed she occupied, she saw the same design graced the fine wood there, too. The chair Chris had sat on to feed her also had the beautiful carvings. Who had done the masterful woodwork? Had the Americano brought all this with him when he moved here? The wooden pieces looked like they should occupy a palatial home, not a cabin in the woods. And just how long had he been living in the hills not more than two days' journey from her own home?

The Americano's face hovered in her memory. As he fed her the tasteless broth, she'd seen the compassion and concern in his eyes.

Nana Ruth mumbled something as she shifted in her sleep, drawing Vicky's attention. Pushing up from the pillow sent a bolt of lightning through her and stole her breath away. Tears formed, but she blinked them back.

At least she wasn't injured for nothing—her shot had found its mark. She could be proud of the way she defended Chris, but if just simple movement stopped her breath, how would she ever manage to ride back to the hacienda? She needed to find Tesoro.

Tesoro, fulfilling her name as Vicky's only treasure, was the golden horse her father had given to her nearly four years ago, the day she turned fifteen and the entire hacienda had turned out to celebrate. Of course, a few wealthy landowners and some brave *vaqueros* had attended her Quinceañera with high hopes of winning her dowry that night. Why did the Spanish lords think that when a girl turned fifteen, she immediately left childhood behind and longed for a husband and family of her own?

If only everyone would just accept that she did not want to marry! In all fairness, some of the men were quite handsome and a few were kind, but how could she bear to leave her hacienda and all that was dear to her? To never ride a horse astride again? To never be allowed in the barns, or go hunting and fishing with Berto? Unthinkable.

She shook off her musings and focused on the room. She took in the door at the far end of the wall. There was open shelving built into the wall above the waist-high counter, and more shelving down below that ran the length of the wall. A dry sink sat in the corner closest to the fireplace that took up most of the side wall.

What would she find if she made the trek to the dry sink? What kind of ingredients did the Americano and Nana Rut have on hand? Itching to get out of bed and do something, Vicky slowly slid her legs off the bed, letting them hang down as she caught her breath. She pushed off the covers, revealing the long chambray shirt that hung on her like a tent. Even with all her binding around her ribs and the shirt, she still felt exposed. As she swiveled around to look for a dressing robe or something else to put on, the room turned black and she felt lightheaded. Holding completely still until the sensation ebbed away, she gritted her teeth and swallowed hard.

Turning only her head this time, she spied behind

her, under the top pillow, what looked like piled-up shirts. After two attempts, she finally came within reach without twisting. Snagging one, the pillow fell to the floor. She followed its progress with her eyes. The distance from the bed to the floor seemed like miles. The shirt she had unearthed had a large tear in one elbow and stains down the front, although it smelled clean. It would have to do.

Struggling into it caused more pain than she had expected, and she sat panting, waiting for the black spots dancing in front of her eyes to go away. Reason argued that she should stay in bed and let the Americano wait on her hand and foot like the hacienda *princesa* she was, but how long would any man put up with a woman who did not see to the cleaning and cooking? No man would complain on the hacienda since the servants would see to it all, but here, the man was doing all the work, and she doubted that even in his culture it would be expected of him. If she could only stand and get to the kitchen area, maybe she could find something to make for breakfast. Or at least some water to drink for her parched throat.

Head clear, she stood, forcing a breath out. The room spun twice before it righted itself. With her left hand bracing her right rib, she shuffled one step, then another, away from the edge of the bed. A cool draft raced across the floor and skimmed over her bare toes and up her legs. The shirts were long but only reached past her knees. Scandalous! If Mamá ever found out, she'd swoon right on the spot. Three more steps brought her within reach of the table. Her left leg collided with it, and suddenly she couldn't see anything between the tears of pain and the dancing black spots. A draft of colder air hit her about the same time as she registered the sound of a door opening, then slamming closed.

Seconds later cold arms still smelling of the crisp air outside caught her at the knees and around her back and settled her back in her cocoon. The blankets she had thrown off with such pain were gently tucked back around her, and only then did the room start to reappear, first in the center of her vision and then completely.

"Vicky? Did you need something?" Chris stood hovering above her. He retrieved the pillow from the floor with a frown. "Are you sick? In pain? *Dolor?*"

Panting let the air in without drawing on the muscles that screamed in agony in her middle. "I...*agua.*" He shifted the pile of his old shirts, topped it with the pillow and then, with a gentle hand, leaned her back to rest.

"I will get you water." He said the words slowly, pointing to himself, the water bucket on the floor by the door that hadn't been there moments ago, and then to her. Nodding, she closed her eyes and waited, afraid to move even the slightest bit and bring on the blinding fire again.

"Here." His breath brushed across her forehead and stirred her hair. He held the cup in front of her and once again would not let her gulp it down like she wanted but rationed it sip by sip until she finished. Then he poured more from a pitcher he had placed on the chair next to her bed. This time he let her take longer sips. Thirst quenched, she sighed.

"*Gracias*, thank you."

"You are welcome." His deep voice drew her eyes to his. In the light of day his eyes shone like a cloudless summer sky with flecks of gold like sunlight. His skin, even with the kiss of sun, looked shades lighter than hers. Glancing down at her hand, she saw just how dark her skin was compared with his.

You're a mix between the glorious lords from Europe and the filthy, heathen Indians, Mamá quoted often, reminding her of her father's own mixed parentage. Vicky's grandfather, Don Ruiz, had been a lord from Spain while her grandmother was an Indian who had worked as a housekeeper for Don Ruiz before they fell in love and married. Mamá constantly reminded her that blue-blooded Spaniards like her own family would never look twice at Vicky's Indian skin. What must the Americano think of her? Yet he did not treat Nana Ruth as if she were less human than he. Rather, he had served her a bowl of soup and helped her with the chores.

Was it different where he came from? Did people treat each other without prejudice or concern for their heritage? Slavery had been outlawed about the time she had been born yet not one of the former slaves whom she had met was ever treated as anything other than servant and underling, just like the Indians who also served the noble and not-so-noble-born Spanish. *Mestizos* were looked upon as more Indian than Spanish because of their mixed bloodlines, and they earned the same disdain from the nobles.

"Are you…?" The next word Chris used was unfamiliar to her. He smiled when she gave him a puzzled look. As he pantomimed eating and then rubbing his stomach, she cocked her head to one side.

"Do you want food?" he asked. This time the words were all familiar. Nodding, she patted her stomach with her left hand, and he grinned. His eyes brightened, and she found herself smiling in return. His grin caused tiny laugh lines around his eyes and a dimple in his left cheek. The dimple looked the right size to poke her index finger into. *Silly girl, you'll never touch his face, much less when he is smiling*, she scolded herself silently. After all, as soon as she could stand on her own without blacking out, she needed to find her own clothes and head back to the hacienda. Of course, she'd have to tie herself on Tesoro's pummel to stay in the saddle but regardless, she couldn't stay away from the hacienda too much longer.

"I'll make food," Chris said as he set the tin cup down on the chair and headed to the sink.

"I make food," Vicky offered, unwilling to sit still and do nothing, especially if it meant that she would have to choke down more of the insipid soup she had the night before.

"You can't cook. You can't even stand." He shook his head at her. Turning his back, he set a small cauldron onto the counter and then poured water in, adding eggs. He slid the caldron's handle onto a hook that swung over the fire in the hearth. Then he took a metal bowl out and added ingredients from metal tins he had under the dry sink, and he added water and an egg before rolling the mixture out on the counter and pressing it flat as Vicky would have done with her tortillas.

He formed balls with the dough and set them inside a greased frying pan that he covered with a lid and set directly onto the fire.

Bread and boiled eggs would be a bland but filling breakfast. If they had some salt, pepper, tomatoes and chilies, she could make a salsa and give the meal some life. But the thing was, this man was cooking for her. He was taking care of her, when he didn't owe her anything. He was clearly a kind person, a person of character. He was…different.

He glanced over his shoulder. Vicky was watching him with obvious skepticism as he made breakfast. Admittedly, he wasn't the best of cooks, but even he could do biscuits and boiled eggs. He wondered what she usually ate for breakfast. Was she thinking he was crazy for making her such simple fare? He gave her a quick smile. She did not smile back.

From the paleness of her face when he'd entered the cabin a few minutes before, he could tell she had been about to pass out. Questions he still had no answers to circled around in his head like a herd of horses unsettled by something lurking just beyond the corral fence. Perhaps he'd see if he could get some answers.

"So, Miss Vicky, how did you end up here?" he asked.

Her cute nose bunched up as she bit her lip in concentration. "I look for Papá. No want…*casar* to Don Joaquín."

"You didn't want to walk?"

"No, *casar* to Don Joaquín," she stated. Her chin

and shoulders lifted in an air of defiance, but her little gasp of pain revealed how much even the slightest move still hurt.

"No house? *Casar* house?"

"No, *casa* is house. *Casar* is when man make woman…take to house and live. Have family. *Bebe?*"

She waited while he poured himself a cup of tea, trying to decipher her last statement. "*Casar*…is to marry?"

"*Sí! Casar* is to marry."

"And you were going to get married walking?"

"No, no want marry Don Joaquín de la Vega. Bad man."

He still didn't know what she was talking about, but there was something vaguely familiar about her words. "So you were looking for your *papá*, and then what happened? How did you end up here, away from Hacienda Ruiz land?"

As he quizzed her, he checked the biscuits, feeling more and more uncertain by the minute about this breakfast. He decided the biscuits needed just a few more minutes.

"I look for Papá on hacienda for one day." She lifted one finger on her left hand to clarify. "He not there. *Nieve*, white and cold? Come from—" She pointed to the ceiling and wiggled her fingers in a downward movement and cocked an eyebrow as if to test Chris's ability to play pantomime games.

"Snow?"

"*Sí*, snow. Snow make stay in cabin two day, no go home." Two fingers were added to the first. With Chris's nod of understanding, she continued. "I no know way home. I stop by *rio*, water run. Puma want eat Master Chris."

"Puma?" She must mean the cougar. So she remembered saving him. And she was calling him "Master Chris." She'd picked up Nana's speech.

The smell of biscuits pulled his attention away. Wrapping a towel around his hand, he pulled the pan off the hot coals and set it down on the counter. He poured some cool water on the eggs and set them aside for a moment.

"I need to thank you, Miss Vicky. You saved my life." He tried to forget the sight of her small body half submerged under the cougar's large frame as he pulled three plates and tin cups down from the cabinet. Once the table was set and the image was out of his mind, he turned his attention back to the small slip of a woman. "I was amazed by your shot. Who taught you how to shoot?"

It was clear that most of what he said was lost on her.

"You poor child," Nana Ruth interjected from her bed. She shook her head. "I thank the Good Lord that He done made your shot true like David and that giant in the Bible."

Nana Ruth struggled to sit up, and Chris left breakfast at the counter to help her. Once she waved him away, assuring him that she could manage on her own, he turned his back, knowing she would take a few minutes to dress.

"Who David? And who Good Lord, Master Chris?" The girl's questions froze him in his spot.

"Why, David, the shepherd boy who grew up to be King o' Israel," Nana Ruth answered for him, "and the Good Lord, why He be God, honey child. Don't you know 'bout God?"

"God? *Sí*, I hear Padre Pedro, um, Father Pedro talk about God when visit hacienda. He have big book. Biblia."

"I have a feeling she's talking about the priest who comes through here a couple times a year," Chris called over his shoulder to help Nana.

"I think our little visitor needs to learn 'bout the Good Lord, and He sent her to us so we can tell her," Nana Ruth mumbled as she walked past him on her way out the door to see to her most basic needs.

"Master Chris?"

Turning back to his visitor, he found her once again trying to climb out of bed.

"Miss Vicky, stay there, don't move! You're going to hurt yourself again!" Tossing down the last of the eggs, he strode across the room and leaned over her, pushing her legs once more under the covers and pulling the sheets up to her chin. She turned her head to the side, her left hand coming up in a defensive move to protect her face. Something in his gut twisted. Did she expect him to hit her?

"Miss Vicky." He forced his voice to be gentle even as he fought not to get angry with himself. Of course she would be fearful of him. She had never seen him before, and who knows what was expected or allowed in her family? Stepping back so as to not crowd her, he waited for her to open her eyes and turn her head to face him.

She didn't. She looked toward the door where Nana had left, a deep blush creeping up her neck to her cheeks. "I need—" Suddenly he understood what she needed, but there was no way to get her all the way out to the outhouse.

"Wait, let Nana help you." With a nod, she settled back against the pillows, though she still wouldn't look at him. The last thing he wanted to do was frighten her. He stepped back and studied her from a few feet away. Maybe if he removed the formality in their address. "And Miss Vicky, I'm Chris, just plain Chris. Nana calls me 'Master' because she was my parents' slave and she won't drop it, but I will never be master to anyone ever again."

"No master?" Her gaze finally lifted to his, and he wondered what she must think of him and Nana Ruth out here.

"No, no more master. Only Chris."

"*Bien*, Chris."

He turned to go, but she called, "Chris?"

"Yes, Miss Vicky?"

"I no Miss Vicky. *Mi amigos*, friends, say Vicky."

"Very well, my friend. I'll call you Vicky." With a nod, he forced himself to go back to preparing breakfast.

As soon as Nana returned, he handed her the bedpan and left the cabin without a backward glance. What had happened back there? Why had she flinched as if he were going to raise his hand to her? Did he seem like that kind of man?

His mind busy, his feet took him to the corral. Goldenrod and all the rest of the horses came close, nudging each other out of the way to get some attention and affection from him. If only he could reassure Vicky that she was safe with him, too.

He hated to think that he'd scared her. She was already worried about this "bad man" whom her father wanted her to marry. Actually, it seemed like maybe she didn't want to marry at all. And if she expected the man she married to hit her, he couldn't blame her for her lack of interest.

Chapter Four

In all her eighteen years, Vicky never stayed indoors, much less in bed, for more than a day or two—even her mother's disapproval hadn't kept her from helping in the kitchen with Magda or heading out to the stables to visit Tesoro. She'd now been confined to bed in the small cabin for five days, and she thought she'd go mad. The sun peeked in the windows as if trying to coax her to come out and play. Her right arm was no longer tied to her body, but movement still remained so painful that she didn't dare try to get up on her own.

"Now, you stop…" Nana Ruth's words were harder to understand than Chris's, but her tone was kind and soothing, and she rattled on as if Vicky understood her every word. Today the woman sat on the edge of her bed, though she'd spent most of the last three days in it.

"Nana Ruth?" Vicky interrupted. "You make dress for Chris?"

"Dress for Chris?" The woman's voice rose in pitch

and then she chuckled. "Master Chris is a man, child. Our menfolk don't wear dresses."

"You no make?" Vicky pulled one of the shirts from the pile behind her and waved it.

"Yes, I did. But that was—" Nana rubbed her arthritic joints, which explained enough.

"You have for make?" Pantomiming sewing, Vicky waited.

"Sure do." She hobbled across the room and lifted the lid on one of the chests. The wonders that lay inside almost had Vicky hopping off the bed, pain or no pain. To think she had been lying idly by for the last five days while there were sewing and knitting supplies just a few steps away.

Vicky hated the needlepoint and counted cross-stitch her mother demanded she concentrate on for hours at a time. However, Magda, their housekeeper, had taught her how to knit and mend men's work clothing. Somehow, that kind of sewing had purpose. Vicky loved to sit with Magda, mending José Luis or Berto's clothes for hours. She admired the marriage that Berto and Magda had, and even allowed herself to pretend she could be a normal wife with a family to care for and a husband who loved her like Berto loved Magda. But she knew that she would never be loved like that.

Being born of noble blood, even if only half, she would be doomed to marry for money and political arrangements between her father and some other nobleman. But after seeing what that kind of marriage had done to her parents, she would rather live the rest of her life alone, dependent on one of her younger brothers but not trapped in a loveless marriage where husband and wife at best avoided each other and at worst wounded each other.

She could earn her own keep by helping on the hacienda either with the care of the houses or keeping the books. She had learned bookkeeping when she helped Papá from time to time. It would be better than marrying one of the noblemen she didn't know who had come courting soon after her Quinceañera, or Don Joaquín, who began his courting last year, only a month after his last wife had been laid to rest. Vicky suspected Mamá had encouraged the man despite the many times Vicky had told everyone she would never, ever marry, especially Don Joaquín. He was known for his drinking, cigars and unkempt appearance, but his hacienda had been one of the most extensive of the area, and he had cultivated favor with Mexican officials—mostly by way of extortion and bribery.

The next few hours passed by much more quickly than any since she'd been in the cabin. Once all the worn shirts in the pile were repaired, Nana Ruth arranged some knitting so that Vicky could work without moving her right arm very much while she cast on stitches for a sock for Chris.

"Nana Ruth? You have husband?"

Nana Ruth looked up from her chair at the table, and emotions ran across her ebony features.

"Yes, honey child. I had a good man. His name was Jeb."

Already worried she'd asked more than she should

have, Vicky concentrated on her knitting even though she wanted to ask more.

"We be slaves on Master Chris's father's plantation since we were born. We had a good life for slaves. We had four babies. Two die young, before they could even walk. Another one, Daniel, was sold when he reached eighteen. And our Samson, he grew up to be a good man, just like his father. He married but then died a year before Master Chris freed us."

Vicky glanced up and saw the woman swipe a tear away from her cheek even as she continued her story, a smile brightening her face.

"When Master Chris told us he was gonna move all the way over to Mexico 'cause they had outlawed having slaves, well, Jeb said to me, 'We gotta go with that boy. He's gonna get hisself killed out there on his own alone.' So we came. And Master Chris has been more like a son than a master to us from the day he was born."

"Where Jeb now?"

"He got killed last summer. Some men attacked him and Master Chris in the field." Her breath caught, and she cleared her throat before she went on. "Master Chris got hit in the arm, but my poor Jeb didn't suffer more than a few minutes. Now Master Chris feels like it's all his fault, but it ain't, no sir. The Good Lord just needed my Jeb, and his time was done here. But when my day comes, I worry about Master Chris havin' no one left here to care for him. I do declare that the Good Lord must have sent you for that purpose."

She couldn't claim to understand everything that Nana Ruth had said. Did she mean to hint at Vicky staying longer than a few more days? As soon as she was able to ride, she'd be headed back to the hacienda to face her father's wrath and the arranged marriage that she dreaded more than death.

As Nana Ruth added ingredients to the pot Chris had left over the fire earlier, Vicky found herself thinking about Magda and Berto once again. She wondered what it would be like to look after a husband who hadn't been forced on her by circumstance, a man she truly loved. Even though she knew it would never be possible for her, some part of her couldn't help but wonder…

Chris could tell from the smells coming from the cauldron hanging over the fire that Nana Ruth was up and about and had added dumplings and seasonings, at least. Setting the milk pail on the counter, he shrugged off his coat. "Good evening, ladies." He bent down and tugged off his boots, setting them below where he'd hung his coat. He stood, rubbed his hands together to get the blood flowing again. The snow had melted, but the temperatures were cool.

"Evening, Master Chris," Nana Ruth called out.

As he turned around, his attention snagged on Vicky. Her hands seemed to fly as the needles clicked, her concentration keeping her from looking up at him. She was sitting up without the use of the pillows. Closer inspection proved that her cheeks were dusty rose in color, and her dark eyes glittered in the waning sunlight shining through the windows. Delightfully unaware of his scrutiny, her tongue peeked out from a corner of her mouth, and he couldn't hold back his grin.

"I see you have found a project." Startled, she dropped the knitting. "Sorry to catch you unawares, Vicky. Looks like you've been at it for a while." A tube about six inches long hung off her needles. Her frown of confusion made him wish once again that he had learned more Spanish on the boat.

Pointing to her hands, he cocked his eyebrow in question. She pointed to his feet where one of his toes poked out of a hole in his sock. Nana had kept up with the darning of socks and mending until the cold weather set in last fall. He'd tried his own hand at it with dismal results. The only reason he had any socks that still held together is he'd sold three horses and a few of the farm goods to the Hacienda Ruiz last spring. In exchange he had brought back sugar, flour, salt and tea as well as some knitted socks for himself, Jeb and Nana.

What would it be like to have a wife who could take care of such things? He had decided to move to Alta California on his own. Completely alone. Admittedly he had been young and unprepared for just how isolated he would find the woods. Their nearest neighbors were a full day's ride away. But then Nana Ruth and Jeb had needed someone and he had brought them with him, believing they could make it without anyone else. With Jeb gone and Nana feeling the aches and pains of arthritis, the realization hit hard that he was not self-sufficient and there were increasingly more things that he needed that he couldn't produce for himself.

And what would he do when Nana needed more care? It hadn't come to that yet, thankfully, but it might sooner than he expected.

"You 'bout ready to eat, Master Chris?" Nana called from the stove.

"Yes, Nana. My belly's been kissing my backbone for a while now."

"You always hungry, Master Chris. Been that way since the day you was born." With a chuckle, she filled bowls with the stew, and he carried them over to the table.

"I eat?" Vicky asked. Chris sent a quick glance at Nana.

"If you could get her to the table, I think she'd be just fine."

Pulling out a chair so he had a place to set her down, he crossed over to the bedside and took the offered knitting she held out. Setting her handiwork on the chest, he turned away to give her some privacy while she pushed down the covers and straightened out the giant shirt that hung off her slim shoulders.

"Ya." It was the word he would have used to get a horse to move, but she had just spoken it to him. Seeing as he was to be her beast of burden, at least to the table, it might have been appropriate but a little haughty for a peasant girl. Then again, in the wilds of Alta California, he no longer was the owner of a large plantation and the closest thing to American nobility.

Turning around, he found her bare feet hanging off the side of the bed. His shirt covered her to her calves like an old nightshirt. "Nana, could you come here and help us for a moment?"

Stocking feet were one thing on the rough wooden floors of his cabin, but being barefoot in the winter would send her right back to bed with another fever and, with her ribs already in poor shape, possibly pneumonia this time. When Nana lumbered over, Chris bent down to her and whispered, "I put her stockings over there, with the rest of her clothes after they were washed. Could you help her get her clothing? I'll just step out while you help her get situated."

He didn't wait for an answer as he crossed the room, slipped his feet into his boots and fled. Once the cool air smacked him in the face, he realized he'd forgotten his coat, but he decided he'd rather suffer cold than go in that room for a while. And the slight breeze might rid his cheeks of the telltale heat he'd felt when he'd been close to Vicky. The way his heart beat an extra beat and his pulse jumped in his veins hadn't happened since he was twelve and had a crush on the new schoolteacher who came for only one semester. As a grown man, he'd believed he had left silly reactions to pretty girls long behind. He would never put a wife or family in the peril of being dependent on him. He would fail them like he'd failed everyone else.

The cabin door slammed behind Chris just as Nana Ruth hustled to the side of the bed with a glorious gift. Vicky's own stockings and the peasant pants that she had borrowed from José Luis years ago so she could ride astride. The older woman started to lean down as if to help with the dressing.

"No, Señora, I do." Extending her left arm, she waited for Nana Ruth to give up her clothes. With just one arm the task wasn't very easy, but after Vicky scooted back in the bed a little, Nana could help without having to bend down. The pants were more of a struggle, but eventually they were pulled up, and the nightshirt she wore covered them all the way past her knees. Nana Ruth also brought her the first sweater Magda had helped her knit just before her Quinceañera. It was still by far her favorite even though her skill had improved, and she cherished the warmth and softness as if it were a hug from Magda herself.

Would she ever get home to see Magda and Berto again? Did she want to go if it meant marriage to Don Joaquín?

"You all right?" The older woman studied Vicky as if she could read her thoughts.

"Eat?"

Nana Ruth nodded. "Stay, child." She painstakingly headed to the door and then returned with Chris right behind her. He stepped out of his boots and crossed the room once more. He slipped his arm around her shoulder, careful to not bump her sore side, and then caught her legs up at the knees with his other arm. His movements were slow and steady, but even with his consideration, her breath caught and her eyes teared up. She had to grit her teeth against the pain. He took all of four steps before they were at the table. He set her down as if she were made of porcelain like the dolls her mother had on display in their home.

Funny, for the first time in a long time she remembered that Berto called her *muñeca*, doll, almost as often as he called her *princesa*. Fighting a sudden wave of homesickness, she forced her thoughts on pleasant

things. Namely, dinner. The smell of food was entic-
ing as she leaned forward and scooped a spoonful from
her bowl, blew on it and then sipped it.

The sigh that escaped her as she closed her eyes
didn't sound loud in her own ears, but when she opened
her eyes, both Chris and Nana Ruth were sitting across
from her, staring wide-eyed as she went after her next
spoonful.

"Vicky." Chris cupped his hand over her own, keeping her spoon still buried in the stew. "We say *gracias*
to God." He took his time, clearly trying to convey the
message.

She dropped her spoon quickly and crossed herself,
kissing her index finger as it curled in when she was
done. Chris lowered his head, closed his eyes and began
speaking, mentioning "Jesus" and "Lord" often. Finally he said "Amen" like the priest did at the end of
his prayers, and then both Nana Ruth and Chris picked
up their spoons. Only after they had taken their first
bite did she pick her own spoon up and savor the thick,
rich broth.

If only she could understand more of the words he
spoke or know more of what was expected in his home.
Working for him as a housekeeper would be a much
better alternative than becoming Don Joaquín's wife.
Would the Americano hire her, a *mestizo*? His treatment
of Nana Ruth made her think that maybe he just might.

Chris smiled often while he spoke with Nana Ruth,
and even when they didn't understand each other, he
had shown patience with Vicky, something few men on
the hacienda would have done. Having been born the

daughter of Señor José Manuel Ruiz González, owner of the Hacienda Ruiz deeded from the very king of Spain, everyone expected her to marry a man of noble Spanish descent and take on the role of wife of a nobleman. Riding horses and taking care of livestock were not part of her future, yet it was what she enjoyed more than anything. Many times she was tempted to question God's plan for her. Why had He given her this life when she could have been content as the wife of a simple ranch hand?

But could it be that God had finally answered her prayers to get away from a forced marriage to Don Joaquín? Surely Chris would soon need more help on his small ranch and with Nana Ruth.

For the first time in weeks, Vicky felt the stirrings of hope in her heart. Maybe God had heard her prayers and had brought her here. Maybe Chris was a priest and could tell her more about the Bible. After all, the only person she had ever met who had a Bible was Padre Pedro. The priest read out of it in Latin when he performed Mass at their chapel each time he visited the hacienda. If she could learn enough English to communicate and show Chris that she could cook, clean and sew, maybe she could convince him to hire her and she would be safe from Don Joaquín. Maybe she could have the life she wanted or at least avoid the life she feared after all.

Chapter Five

Dipping his spoon back into his bowl, Chris studied his houseguest. What must she be thinking? Emotions ran across her face—fear, concern, frustration and then something like hope. He'd never been so frustrated by an inability to communicate with someone in his entire life.

"You feelin' all right, Master Chris?" Nana Ruth's gaze bore into him as if she could see what he was thinking. "Was sure you was gonna down that whole bowlful in a blink like you normally do."

"I'm fine, Nana. I just wonder what she must think of us or how much she understands. How I'm going to get her back with her family." He plunked his spoon back into his soup with more force than necessary, and some sloshed out the other side. Grabbing his handkerchief, he cleaned up his mess.

"I been thinkin' 'bout that myself, and I do declare the Good Lord must have had a good reason for sendin' the poor thing here to us. He'll let us know when

He's good and ready." She patted his hand like she had when he was just a kid.

"Well, I'd appreciate it if He'd see fit to show us sooner rather than later."

"You always was mighty impatient, Master Chris." She chuckled good-naturedly. Wasn't the first time she'd made that observation, and he'd stopped trying to deny it long ago. "Of course, the Good Lord just might have sent her along to be your helpmate. Seems to me you could use one."

His glare was answer enough. She knew exactly what he thought about ever bringing someone else into his life. No way was he going to take the chance with someone else's welfare—especially not a wife and children. For all the longings in his heart to have children himself, he could not take that risk, or the strain of feeling constantly responsible for their safety. And the idea that he could possibly marry Vicky? Impossible. She was a young girl, still years from marrying.

"Chris?" Her almond-shaped eyes, dark as strong coffee, nearly stopped his breath. Pure foolishness. He would never take a wife. He'd proved that he couldn't take care of those entrusted to him. Forcing his face to hide the hollowness the last idea had left inside, he ignored Nana's quiet chuckle and faced Vicky.

"Yes, Vicky?"

"*Mas?* More *soopa*?" She tipped her empty bowl so he could see the insides.

"Would you like more soup?" he asked, already assuming the answer but hoping to help her learn some

English. He hoped she retained more of his language than he had managed to of hers.

"Yes, please." She smiled shyly. "More soup." This time her pronunciation was on target.

"It would be my pleasure." He stood, bowed gallantly and swept her empty bowl into his hand, turning to refill it from the pot that still hung over the fire, and then set it down in front of her with a flourish. She watched him with wide eyes as Nana made a tsking sound between her teeth.

"That poor girl don't know if you just plain out of your head or if that's the way you white people serve the table." She shook her head once more and then started to laugh.

Chagrined at his silly behavior, Chris sank back into his chair and concentrated on finishing off the rest of his now cool meal. A quick glance at Vicky revealed a wide smile.

"You make Nana Ruth, um…ha, ha, ha?"

"Laugh. Yes. I made her laugh."

"I like hear laugh." He had to admit, he liked hearing Nana Ruth laugh, as well. There hadn't been as much laughter in the cabin in the last year, but since Vicky came, Nana had started to smile more—and he'd found a smile on his face more often, too.

Silence filled the room as they finished eating. With the last spoonful of soup, Chris's gaze found Vicky's across the table again. Had she been watching for very long? He noticed that she had eaten very properly, like an elegant young miss from back home, despite having to use her left hand. No slurping or dripping like he had accidently done a time or two. His mother would have cuffed him on the head for his poor table manners. As he looked at her, curiosity shined from those dark expressive eyes. She probably had as many questions about him as he did about her.

"So tell me, Vicky, what do your parents do at Hacienda Ruiz?"

"*Mi papá* is Don Ruiz, José Manuel Ruiz González de Jacinto, España, son of Don Juan Manuel Ruiz González de Jacinto España, *el rey*, king of España say to *papá* of *mi papá*, he come to América and make new hacienda. Hacienda Ruiz." Her eyes glowed with pride and her chest rose, her shoulders straight as if she were nobility. Then her words clicked. If he understood her right, that's exactly what she had just claimed to be—nobility.

"Your father is Don Ruiz? Hacienda Ruiz is your family's hacienda?"

"*Sí*, Señor."

The thought of having a nobleman's daughter staying in his humble cabin gave him a start. Why hadn't someone come looking for her already? Surely they had missed her by now. Would they think he had abducted her?

For the last four years he had bartered a couple of horses each year for many of the products they could produce in the hacienda's village instead of having to go all the way over the mountains to the west and to the nearest port, but he had not ever had anyone visit him. On the first encounter, he indicated that he was not interested in socializing with anyone, and with the exception of the traveling priest and the bandits who had attacked last summer, his lands had been left alone. The closest Indian village was a two-day ride to the north, the Hacienda Ruiz a full day to the east and nothing but mountain peaks to his west for miles. To the south, the next hacienda's main buildings were three days of winding trails in the foothills away from him.

"Where is your family?"

"*Mi papá* go talk with dons from haciendas *de* España. Many do not like Mejico take taxes for *presidente* but no have vote. The *gobernador de* Alta California bad man."

"Your father is meeting with other hacienda owners?"

"*Sí.*" A shadow passed behind her eyes as if something had frightened her.

"Are you worried about your father? Is the place he is going to dangerous?" Were the noblemen considering revolting? It wouldn't be the first time something like that was attempted. The Mexican government had forcibly taken the missions over and given them to the natives and peasants. The outcome had not been good from what he had seen during his last visit to the coast—just another reason why he hadn't made the effort to go a week's journey there for supplies.

"Worried?" she queried, her brow furrowing in concentration.

Chris turned to Nana for help. How did one explain worry? She shrugged at him. "Worry means you think about something, upset, nervous."

"*Nerviosa.*" The frown lines smoothed for a moment

as she smiled with the success of understanding, but she said, "*Sí*, I worried. I *nerviosa*. I worried *mi papá* talk with Don Joaquín about marry."

"But you're young yet. Surely your father will not make you marry until you have come of age," Chris reassured. "After all, you can't be much more than fourteen."

Nana snorted as if she knew a joke he didn't.

"I...what?" Vicky said.

"Fourteen. You are fourteen." He raised all ten fingers and then left four up while he lowered the others.

"Not fourteen." She counted under her breath until she reached the number she must have been looking for. "I have eighteen."

"Vicky, you can't be eighteen. You barely measure five feet." He started counting again out loud, holding up his fingers as he went. But when he reached fourteen, she continued counting on her own hand until she reached eighteen.

"I have *cumpliaños*...how you say, day of Santos?"

"What are you asking about?"

"Day baby new. Day I *bebe*, I get nineteen."

"She's talkin' 'bout her birthday, Master Chris."

"Birthday. The day you were born?"

"*Sí*, birthday. I have birthday in six weeks. I get nineteen."

His gaze skimmed her from her messy hair, still tangled and dirty in places, to her smooth forehead and dark eyes, following the line of her straight flat nose to her lips and then down to that enormous-looking shirt Nana Ruth had put on her, now only half covered by her woolen sweater. The shirt had been too small for him to wear for a few years now. The heavy work of clearing land and then keeping wood chopped for the fire, feeding horses and general farming had bulked up his shoulders and arms to the point that all of his clothes from South Carolina no longer fit him. Returning his gaze to her eyes, he wondered how she could possibly be nineteen.

"You'll turn nineteen, Vicky. We don't 'get' an age, we are an age in English."

"I no understand."

"You say, 'I will turn nineteen on my birthday.'" To his surprise she repeated his words perfectly.

"And you turn how many on you birthday?" she asked innocently.

"I will be twenty-eight in August."

The answer gave him pause. How differently his life had turned out from what he had envisioned when he turned nineteen. Most of his schoolmates were married and starting to take over the reins of their family plantations back home now. Even his younger sister, Nelly, had two children already. In fact, Nelly had married at age eighteen after a two-year courtship that had started on her sixteenth birthday when their family had presented her to society. The ball had taken months of preparation, rivaling the effort that went into putting the wedding together two years later. Matthew had swept Nelly off her feet despite his Yankee upbringing. It had taken two years to wear Father down to the point of consenting to the marriage, but they were happy. Chris had seen true affection reflected in Nelly's and

Matt's eyes. His brother-in-law had been supportive about Chris's decision to sell the plantation, taking their mother in to live with them. Mother would never have survived the primitive surroundings of the ranch, and Chris could never have left her if Matt hadn't opened their home to her.

Thinking back to his interactions with Hacienda Ruiz, he suddenly remembered the first year he had sold them four horses from his stock. Goldenrod had been chosen by the foreman who ran the stables for Don Ruiz's daughter's birthday party. The girl had been turning fifteen at the time, and they had invited him to come for a celebration. Had that been Vicky's birthday party?

"Vicky, how did you get Goldenrod?"

A glance at her face forced him to look for another way to ask the question. "Your horse, *ca-bey-o?*"

She lifted her left hand to her hair and winced. "It need clean."

"Your horse needs to be cleaned?" Chris was puzzled. He had been taking care of Goldenrod himself and knew that she was well groomed and bedded down for the night in the barn.

"Mi ca-bey-o." She pulled at her hair. "I need *say-pi-yo."* She pantomimed brushing her hair.

"I do declare, watchin' you young folk sure does make me smile." Nana Ruth chuckled. "Somehow you got her talkin' hair instead of horse."

"We can get you a brush as soon as we clean up from dinner."

"Brush?"

"Brush. To brush your hair. *Ca-bey-yo*?"

"Sí, ca-bey-yo."

"If *ca-bey-yo* is hair, what is horse?"

"Horse? *Ca-buy-yo.* Neigh." She blew air out her cheeks like a horse would.

"She done a right fine imitation, Master Chris. She's one smart gal if ya ask me."

"Ca-bey-yo is hair, *ca-buy-yo* is horse. Well, they are close." Too close. How was he ever going to keep these new words straight, much less learn more?

"How did you get your horse? Neigh." He mimicked her, and she giggled. Her laughter made him smile and made all this tedious and sometimes frustrating communication suddenly worth it.

"Tesoro is *mi* horse. *Mi papá y* Berto say '*Feliz* birthday' and give me Tesoro."

"I sold Goldenrod to Berto. I raised her."

"What Goldenrod?"

"Goldenrod is Tesoro. I call her Goldenrod and you call her Tesoro."

"I see Tesoro?" She leaned forward in her chair as if by straining in her seat she would be able to see the horse out the window.

"Tesoro is in the barn for the night." Chris shook his head. Already Vicky had been up at the table for the better part of an hour. Any more excitement would slow down her recovery.

"When see Tesoro? She eat? She…?" Her words fell away, and he saw the affection the girl had for her horse. He understood. Golden had been one of his favorites, and it was only because he could tell Berto would treat all the animals well that he had been willing to sell her to the hacienda. Now he could see that girl and horse were well matched—kindred spirits.

"Tesoro is good. She's in the barn with my horses. I fed her and took care of her earlier. As soon as you are able to stand up on your own without too much pain, we can make a visit to the barn to see her." The blank look on Vicky's face told him that his words had not been understood. He was about to try again when a yawn caught the girl unaware, and she grimaced when she accidentally tried to move her right arm in an attempt to cover her mouth.

As Nana Ruth stood and picked up the empty bowls, Chris bent to pick up Vicky. "But for now, I think you've been out of bed long enough today. Let's get you tucked back in."

Lifting Vicky up in his arms, he couldn't help but notice how little she weighed. She settled against his chest as if trusting him not to hurt her.

Did she feel safe? He suddenly realized he wanted to protect her. The thought materialized with a force that nearly halted his steps. He needed to get her back to her people. His cabin in the middle of the woods could be safe for only so long before someone else showed up and tried to run him off or take what was his. He'd already failed at keeping Jeb safe here. What made him think he could take care of Vicky?

Quickly he set her back on the bed and left the room, feeling the cold air steal her warmth away when he let go of her. The cold felt even colder than it had a few minutes before, penetrating not only his clothing but his skin as well, almost as if it were seeping into his heart. He shut the door behind him and headed off to check the corrals while the women prepared for bed. As he stared up at the night sky, it seemed that he would always be alone with just his land and his horses. For the longest time that had been all he had wanted. Was it still?

As Nana Ruth adjusted Vicky's bedclothes, Vicky tried to run her fingers through her tangled hair, which made her wince.

"Nana Ruth?" she asked. "Can you hair? Brush?"

"Do you want me to brush your hair, child?"

"*Si*! Yes." She nodded, showing Nana the tangles in her hair.

Nana nodded and shuffled over to the cabinet near the sink and came back with an ornate brush. "Turn to face the wall, girl." The kind woman pointed, and Vicky moved carefully. Nana pulled all Vicky's hair over her shoulder, but when she tried to pull the brush through, it snagged and then fell to the floor. With a groan the woman bent and then attempted brushing again. After four failed attempts, she sat back. "These here hands don't serve me for diddly-squat."

"Diddly-squat?" That was a word the British teacher had never taught her.

"Nothing."

"No…thing?"

"Not a thing."

"Hmm…" Before she could confirm the meaning of all the strange words, the door opened and closed with a creak. Cool air drifted across the room as if announcing Chris and his return.

"Master Chris." The older woman stood up, the chair squeaking as she moved. The two conferred over by the table, but Vicky couldn't turn enough to see what they were doing. Heavy footsteps crossed the room, and a shiver ran down her body from her head to her toes. She couldn't imagine what Chris might want with her. Nana had said she was going to help her with her hair. Had he been angered when he saw his slave doing extra work for Vicky?

A hand lifted her hair away from her neck, and she held her breath. She had heard of some men pulling a woman's hair in a fit of rage, but she had seen no evidence of rage in Chris. He had been nothing but kind to her, and because of her injuries, he treated her like she could break at any second. She told herself to relax.

Without warning the brush started to detangle the ends and then worked its way up slowly. His ministrations were gentle. Even more so than Nana Ruth's had been. A strange comfort wrapped around her, almost as if Magda had hugged her tight. The only time she had ever seen a man brush hair before had been in the stables as the grooms brushed down the horses. Did Chris see her as a horse that needed to be curried?

The idea stole some of the pleasure from the moment. After all, she didn't know what he thought about her, or her trespassing on his land. Was he biding his time until he could send her on her way? Would he send her packing on Tesoro tomorrow? She hoped to be better soon, but just having sat through dinner left her feeling worn out. Riding Tesoro for days to get back would be impossible for at least another week. Would the Americano's patience and hospitality wear out by then? Did he have other reasons for keeping her here?

Did he know Joaquín? If he had sold horses to her father's hacienda, maybe he had sold animals to others in the area, as well. If he did know him, was he keeping her here until he could get word to Joaquín so that the vile man could come for her? Again she wondered how Papá could ever think that she should spend her life with a man like Don Joaquín. At the very thought, a shudder shook her shoulders.

"Did I hurt you?" His words were soft, and his breath blew across the crown of her head like a warm summer breeze, causing a tingling to spiral down her spine.

"No, no hurt."

"This next part may be more difficult. You have blood and dirt mixed into your hair. *Ca*... Which one is it again?"

"*Cabello*, hair?"

"*Sí, ca-bey-yo.*"

"I know dirt." She pointed to the clump of it that had already been knocked loose and lay on the bedspread beside her. "What is 'blood'?"

"Blood, red water inside you and me."

"You blood red? Not blue?" Even with the sun-kissed glow on his skin, when he sat at the table she could see the thick blue veins running up and down his muscular arms. The veins were bluer on his wrists, whereas most of the cowboys she had grown up with had dark skin that didn't show veins. The few people she knew with visible veins had dark purple ones.

"No, Vicky, if I were to get a cut my blood would run red just like yours or Nana Ruth's. Inside our skin, we are all the same. Now, I'm going to wet your hair here a little."

"You clean hair?"

"I'm going to wet it with water." He stood closer to her right side. A wet warmth surprised her as he rubbed a towel into her scalp close to her temple. Turning slightly, she could see only his profile as he concentrated on her head. "Don't move, Vicky."

"No *jabon*?"

He spared her a glance before turning back to his work. "I don't know what 'ha-bon' is, Vicky."

"Use to make no dirt in hair."

"Soap?" He shook his head. "No, I don't want to wash your hair tonight. It's too late, and you might catch a chill."

A snarl caught the brush, and he froze as a gasp escaped her. She closed her eyes so he wouldn't see her tears of pain. "Sorry, Vicky." He paused to touch her shoulder before he untangled the brush and started to work at the snarl. The brush moved smoothly through her hair, and she closed her eyes again, trying to relax into the feeling of such gentle care. When had anyone taken time to do a task like this for her in the past years?

The last time Magda had been in her room to brush her hair had been for her Quinceañera. Mamá and Magda had both fretted about her clothes, hair and presentation. Of course, Mamá's concern was that she look as white and sophisticated as she could so she could catch a Spanish nobleman with money and land, while Magda cooed about how beautiful she had become.

In the end, she had let down both women that night. Her mother never wanted anything for her other than an advantageous marriage, and while there were a few offers the first year after her presentation to society, her penchant for riding astride, helping with the cattle and insisting that she have a say in conversations about the ranch had driven all those would-be suitors on to more delicate, submissive prospects. For almost two years, no suitors had visited the hacienda, and Vicky had relaxed, hopeful that she could stay there, a recluse and old maid but happy with her lot in life. Until last year, when Don Joaquín showed up only a few weeks after his latest wife had died.

And as far as disappointing Magda, Vicky understood she would never be the beautiful girl Magda claimed she saw. Her dark skin would be considered uncivilized and too Indian to be acceptable in the finest society anywhere other than rural Alta California. Not that Vicky necessarily wanted to travel and see bigger cities. Her beloved little villa at the hacienda was all she needed. It was home. Most of the landed families in the area made trips to Mejico every couple of years so that they could keep track of the latest styles and news from Spain and the rest of Europe. But after her parents' very public fight about her grandmothers when she was just a girl, Papá had declared that he would never take Mamá off the hacienda until she apologized to his mother. The fight had been the culmination of years of insults and feuding between her parents about their mothers.

As a pretty young girl from a Spanish upper-class family in Jalisco, Mamá had set her sights on the land-owner nobleman who had come to the city to study for two years without asking too many questions about his parentage. Mamá had all but left Papá when they arrived to the hacienda for the first time. She had treated Papá's mother like a servant because of her native blood. When Mamá's mother had come to visit and actually insulted Papá's mother to her face, Papá had sent his mother-in-law packing, and they had never had contact again. Abuelita had passed away five years ago, and Mamá had never uttered a word to her in all the years Vicky could remember. And true to his word, Papá never took her mother anywhere.

"Vicky, you're not falling asleep on me, are you?" Chris's words were whispered close to her ear.

"I no sleep. I remember."

He continued to wipe away dried blood and dirt from her head. How awful she must look. Surely Mamá would faint at the embarrassment that a strange man was seeing her like this.

"Were you remembering something good?" Chris set his rag aside and began brushing out the last of her knots.

"Magda brush hair for Quinceañera." For once not having the words to express herself was a blessing. Only Magda had witnessed how disappointed Mamá had been when Vicky managed to run off the last of the suitors.

Vicky could hear her mother's words in her mind. *You must hate me, Victoria, that you choose to humiliate me in such a way. Not only are you just as black as your grandmother who bewitched your grandfather, but you choose to behave like a heathen Indian. Why did God punish me by sending me here? Why did you live and Angelica die?*

With her mother's words that cold winter day, something inside her had died. The willingness to try to earn her mother's affection had been slowly waning for years, but that day it was gone. She would never be anything other than a bane to her mother. If only she had been born white like her little sister, Angelica, who had lived only a few hours, she could have made Mamá proud.

"What is Quin-sin-era?"

His pronunciation made her giggle. Counting in her head, she answered, "Quinceañera is when girl have… she turn fifteen."

"Did you have a party to celebrate your fifteenth birthday?"

"Yes, a party and a *misa*."

"Misa?"

"In chapel. Father of church come and say, 'Dios, God be good to you.'" The brush paused in its downward path.

"They done had a ceremony for her blessin', Master Chris. Jest like for Miss Nelly."

"Did you like your Quin-sin-era?" He resumed his brushing. His standing so close, running the brush through her hair, was the nearest thing to being cared for that she had felt in a long time. It took her a moment to realize that all the knots were out, but he was still brushing her hair. She figured he must not have noticed.

"*Sí y no.* I like food and dance and Tesoro. No like men."

The brush froze, his hands coming to rest on her shoulders. "Did a man do something to hurt you, Vicky?" His words sounded slow, and almost forced. Tension that hadn't been there a moment ago radiated off him like heat from a fire.

"No, no man hurt me. I no let them. I no want leave Hacienda Ruiz. No want leave Tesoro, Magda, Berto." After a moment, Chris stepped away. Vicky missed the warmth of his hands on her shoulders immediately.

"Is *Magda* your word for *Mother*?" Nana Ruth asked. "Are you missin' your mother, child?"

Vicky took a few careful breaths and then turned her body, leaning on her left arm to support her weight as she readjusted her legs under the quilts. Shifting around hurt but not as bad as it had earlier in the day. She raised her head, and her gaze found Chris across the room. He watched her carefully, his emotions unreadable as he waited for her answer.

"Magda is cook. I miss Magda. I no miss *mi mamá*. And she no miss me."

Chris looked surprised. "Vicky, I'm sure that's not true—"

Vicky raised her chin and cut him off, running a hand through her hair. "*Gracias.* Hair."

Then she looked away, hoping he wouldn't ask her anything else about her mother. She probably couldn't explain her mother to Chris even if she spoke perfect English. After all, she'd never understood why her mother hated her, so how to explain that to someone else? There was no point in even trying.

Chapter Six

As he looked at Vicky, wondering why she was so reluctant to talk about her mother, he realized his hands were tingling. He rinsed out the cloth and hung it on the back of the dry sink, poured himself a cup of coffee and tried not to think about what had just happened.

He'd picked up the brush thinking that he'd plaited and combed the manes on all of his horses for years. Surely brushing out a woman's hair would be the same, especially since it was just as tangled as that of some of the wild ponies he had caught when he first came to Alta California.

What a mistake. Her hair slid through his fingers like silk, not at all coarse like a horse's mane. He'd felt her tense when he first started to fight the snarls into submission, but after a moment she relaxed. How could something as mundane as brushing her hair feel intimate?

Had she been as affected by his closeness as he had been by hers? His reaction when she had said she didn't like men almost bordered on madness. The party had been four years ago. Even if someone had mistreated her, what would he be able to do about it now? Yet, if she had said yes to his question, he would have tried to avenge her reputation or her pride.

The silence in the room grew awkward. Clearly she didn't want to talk about her mother. So he'd make other inquiries.

He cleared his throat. "You have brothers or sisters, Vicky?"

"I have two brothers. Juan Marcos *y* Diego Manuel." She held up two fingers as if to clarify the number. "I have *mi papá*, Señor José Manuel Ruiz González." With all those names, they sounded like a dozen or so, not just three people. After a pause, she added in a sad voice, "Mi brother Juan Manuel no live. He die when I ten. Angelica, mi sister, no live more than three hours."

"Do you miss your brothers and father, child?" Nana Ruth asked, reminding him that she was still in the room. How could he have forgotten her? Yet while he had talked with Vicky, all else was forgotten.

Nana's words brought a strange expression to Vicky's face.

She turned her attention to Nana. Stirring sugar into his cup, he watched their interaction. Not for the first time, he noted that she spoke to Nana like she spoke to him. No air of superiority or discomfort like most young woman of his acquaintance would have had interacting with a Negro woman, slave or free. Were the Mexican people more accepting of others? It had been his greatest hope when they picked up and traveled from

South Carolina to come to a new land, one where no man could own another.

"I want be with them, *sí*. Juanito *y* Diegito fight and no be good. Papá love horses *y vacas*—no time for ride with me. I miss Magda *y* Berto. They miss Vicky."

"Sure they do, honey child, sure they do."

Vicky's response resonated in his heart. Did he miss his family? His father had been dead almost nine years now. Yet the closeness he shared with Jebediah as the older man had taught him how to breed and raise horses, perform carpentry and to take care of tools had been far more influential than any lessons his father might have tried to beat into him.

Did he miss his father? He missed the chance to prove he was just as much of a man if not more so for following through on his beliefs even if it cost him everything. But did he miss the man?

He'd stood over his father's grave a few weeks after the funeral and prayed that God would allow his father peace, even though the man had never given peace to anyone on this earth. Then he'd shouted to the wind that he had released the slaves and they had all decided to stay on the plantation and work for meager wages. Work that had been accomplished in mere days by freed men and women who wanted to see the plantation prosper far surpassed all the work the foreman with a whip and rod had ever managed to deliver. Of course none of that mattered now. The other plantation owners in the area had forced him to sell out and leave or face being responsible for even more deaths.

He set his mug down on the table and turned to go

outdoors. He needed to release some anger, and this cabin—in the presence of two ladies, no matter what walks of life they had come from or how much English they did or didn't understand—was not the place to let loose. Snagging his coat off its hook, he pulled his boots on and headed out the door. He grabbed an ax out of the barn and lost track of time splitting firewood as he felt the anger slowly draining out of him. When he felt somewhat normal again, he set the ax back in the barn. Closing the barn door and checking the latch, he walked the edge of the corral with his rifle tucked in the crook of his arm.

The horses had been calm this last week now that the cougar was gone. Amazing what Vicky had done. She looked so fragile and weak. Then again, the first time he saw her he thought she was an Indian boy about to shoot him. He'd not mistake her for a boy ever again, not after the way his fingers tingled with just the touch of her hair. Or the surge of anger and something else, something unnamable, akin to possessiveness that flared to life in his chest when he thought someone had hurt her.

Nope, no mistaking Maria Victoria Ruiz Torres for a boy now. Unfortunately.

Nana Ruth thought that God had brought Vicky to them for a reason. God probably brought her to them for her own protection while her ribs healed.

"Thank You, Lord," Chris whispered as he headed back toward the dark cabin, the sound of a lone wolf howling high up in the mountains. "If she had died in the woods, I wouldn't have known her and so wouldn't be missing her. But someone would be. Despite what she says, I'm sure her whole family is missing her. Please help her to heal quickly so I can get her back to her home and her family."

The white vapor of his breath rose like a tangible prayer toward the sky speckled with stars. The night sky always made him feel small compared with all of God's creation. It made him lonely, too. If he walked into the woods tonight and came face-to-face with a bear or another cougar, who would miss him? Nana Ruth and now Vicky. For so long that had been what he had wanted. To just disappear from "civilization" and live without worrying about anyone else or having anyone else worry about him. Prove he didn't need anyone else to be "successful" or to make money.

Now that "freedom" didn't seem so freeing. It felt empty. Could it be that he needed more than the woods and his horses for companionship? If he had been living closer to a settlement, he could have already sent word to Vicky's family. What if being out here someday cost him Nana Ruth, either because he couldn't get medical care or they came under attack again? The questions started to spin in his head as he stood outside his own door.

"Lord, I don't know what you're up to by bringing Vicky into our lives, but you've got me questioning things I thought I had settled. Can't say that I'm liking it right now, but You're the boss. Guide me to do Your will, even if I don't like what it is." He sighed deeply, knowing God heard his prayer and would answer in His own time. "Amen."

Chapter Seven

"Can I cook?" Vicky asked as Nana Ruth worked at the dry sink. Being a burden on the older woman chafed. Vicky had always been independent—to a fault, according to her mother. Magda's girls had grown up helping in the kitchen, and Vicky had silently watched with longing for the camaraderie and sense of belonging they had.

When she was old enough to wield a knife, she attempted to chop her first onion. The experience had caused a lot of tears, both before and after she had cut her finger. Somehow, in the days that followed, Magda's girls started treating her like their younger sister. When they had married, she felt the loss almost as much as Magda did, and she stepped in to do what they had been doing. Now maybe she could earn her keep in Chris's cabin.

"You want to eat now, honey child?" Nana Ruth asked.

"*Sí*, I want to eat." Repeating the words helped her remember them better. "But I cook food?" She stood slowly.

"Now, settle on down, honey child. I be movin' slow with this here…" Nana shuffled toward the counter and dry sink.

"No, Nana no cook. Vicky cook." Pointing to herself and then the large fireplace, she tried once more. "Nana rest." She'd heard that word so often from Chris that she hated it.

"I can't have you cookin' for me, child. Bad enough Master Chris seein' to so much 'round here."

Without waiting for permission, Vicky pulled the canister in front of her and peeked in. *Excelente!* Flour. Looking around, she cataloged the ingredients that she had on hand. No chilies, no tomatoes, no lemons, no cilantro, no garlic, but the stems of an onion stuck up from a basket on the countertop. Flour, water, salt and lard were all that she needed for tortillas.

Within minutes she had the ingredients for the tortillas assembled, but it hurt to stir it all together. Tears escaped, but she refused to give up.

"Here, how 'bout I hold this bowl while you mix it up," Nana offered. She held the bowl firmly while Vicky struggled to pull the fork through the mixture. An eternity later, she stood back and nodded. It wasn't as perfectly mixed as she would have liked, but it was the best she could do under the circumstances.

"Where for cook?" she asked.

"Skillet's under there, child." Nana pointed to the cloth hanging under the wet sink. When Vicky pulled the curtain back, she found three shelves, two stocked with canning jars and the lowest holding an assortment of cooking equipment. Kneeling in front of the shelves, she started to inspect the new treasures she had found. Green beans, jelly and some unidentifiable greens were closest to the front.

"Que rico!" Tucked in the back corner was a jar that looked like Magda's salsa. Finally! Something to put a little flavor and spice into the bland foods.

"What are you doing?" Chris's question caught Vicky by surprise. She hadn't even noticed when he arrived. Standing so quickly caused another fire to blaze through her ribs.

"I…" She paused to find the words again. "I cook for you, honey child." The words slipped off her tongue easier than they would have just a few days ago. Chris's eyes opened wide for a moment, and then he laughed. A full belly laugh. Any other time she would stop to listen because she had never heard him laugh like that. But not when he was laughing at her.

Did he think she had no cooking skills? It was true that she had let them wait on her hand and foot because she had been too injured to see to even the most basic of her needs, but now that she was on the mend, she would show him.

Nana Ruth laughed, too. Well, she'd prove it to both of them.

Straightening her spine, she dragged the jar up to the counter and stared at it. Yes, the food would taste better with a touch of salsa and some tortillas, but a small part of her wanted to taste Magda's cooking again. Living at the Americano's ranch made her feel as if she were cut off from her life on the hacienda. Holding a jar of Magda's salsa wasn't nearly the same thing as getting a hug from her dear friend, but it was the closest she'd come in days.

"Don't be mad, Vicky." Chris set a pail of milk on the counter and then squeezed her arm slightly as if he wanted her to turn around.

"I cook. I make tortillas," she barked over her shoulder, unwilling to face either one at the moment. If they laughed in her face, she wasn't sure she could keep the tears under control.

"I'm sure you can cook just fine, Vicky. I just don't want you to hurt yourself by doing too much too soon."

"I cook now. Go there." She pointed to the table next to Nana, still refusing to look at either one.

"How about if I help?" he offered.

"I no want."

"I know you don't want help, Vicky, but I have a feeling you still need it."

"You no think I cook." Her statement came out more of an accusation.

"I believe you are an excellent cook," he retorted.

"Oh, *sí—excelente*! No, you 'ha, ha, ha, ha'..." she argued, unable to keep her words from spilling out.

"I laughed? I guess I did, but not about you cooking." He pulled on her shoulder again. "I laughed that you said 'honey child' just like Nana does."

"*Sí*, I learn English. I learn talk Nana." She thought it sounded very close to Nana's English. And he had no right to tease her about her English. He had learned only a few phrases of Spanish, and he didn't use those very often, while every day she conversed with them in English.

"What're we gonna do 'bout that girl?" Nana started to laugh again.

"You certainly learned to 'talk Nana,' but some things she says you probably shouldn't say. She can call me 'honey child' because she's my Nana. She took care of me when I was a boy. But you can't call me 'child.' I'm older than you and…not your honey." His voice dropped a bit on the last words.

"What honey?"

"Honey is sweet, from the bees." He reached around her, into the cabinet, and came out with a jar with a piece of honeycomb. "This is honey."

"*Miel*—honey. *Bien.* But why Nana say me honey?" She finally turned to look at him. His closeness mixed her up inside. When he was near, she felt safe and protected and yet nervous at the same time.

"Because you're sweet." He ducked his head and turned to study her work. "What are these?" Chris pointed to the dough she was flattening into tortillas.

"It *masa*…dough? For tortilla."

"So how do we eat this?" He reached for one and made as if to take a bite.

"No! Chris, need cook. No eat, Señor." She put her hand between his mouth and the raw dough.

"Why do you call me Señor?"

"You no Señorita." Nana snorted behind them. At least someone was being entertained.

"Señorita is what you are, no?" He quirked his left eyebrow, his blue eyes dancing with amusement.

"Yes, I Señorita. When marry—" she suppressed the urge to shudder at the thought "—I get Señora."

"Miss Ruiz to become Mrs.?"

"I no want Mrs." Especially if it meant becoming Joaquín's wife.

"Oh, come on, Vicky, a pretty lady like yourself must want to marry and have a home and family of her own."

If only he could understand. Of course she wanted to marry if the man would treat her with respect and affection like Berto treated Magda. But that wasn't her future. A man as kind and handsome as Chris would be a dream to marry. But that was all it was, a dream.

He may have said she was pretty today, but he couldn't possibly see her as anything other than a dark-skinned Indian.

Even as the words escaped, he wanted to take them back, silence them forever. Each day it became harder to think of life going back to normal once he returned her to her own people.

By the time Vicky had children, she would have forgotten all about him and his cabin in the woods. He couldn't even speak her language, and he certainly couldn't give her the life she was used to. He'd seen the hacienda's main home, a small palace really.

"Vicky," he said, watching her slow and purposeful movements. She needed to lie down before she jeopardized the progress she had already made.

She shook her head, knowing what he was going to say. "I cook tor-ti-yahs." Her words were carefully enunciated as if she were explaining something complex to a child.

"What are torti-yahs?"

"Like bread."

"So do we need to cook them in the soup for lunch?"

"No, we cook now, for eat hot with…" She searched for the right word.

"She wanted to cook something for breakfast, Master Chris. That much I can gather. The rest be a mystery." Nana gave him a look that said, "Fix this."

"So how do we cook the torti-yahs?"

"On *sartan*." With those words she ducked back down and rummaged around until she came back up with the cast-iron frying pan. At least she started to come back up. Between the weight of the pan and her hurt ribs, it looked like she might either drop the pan or pass out, or maybe both. Snatching the frying pan in one hand and wrapping the other arm around her waist, he held her upright, tucked against his side.

He felt his pulse jump and his longing for solitude dissipate like the morning fog under direct sunlight.

"This frying pan weighs more than you do. Why don't you let me take it and you direct?"

With Vicky distracted, Chris led her to a chair and had her sitting before she noticed.

Vicky nodded but then quirked a brow at Chris. "I no can cook here." She pushed against the table.

"You made the dough, Vicky. Now I will cook it and you tell me what to do," he offered, standing behind her chair so she couldn't scoot it back out. "Now, do I fry these in lard?"

It took only a few minutes for him to have a good idea of what he was doing. The round flat dough went on the dry, hot frying pan until it started to pull away or get dark spots on each side. Once he mastered flipping them over with the edge of a table knife, he started to collect them on a plate. They reminded him of flapjacks, but they didn't smell nearly as inviting. In quick order all the tortillas were done.

"No take off." Vicky ordered him around quite easily. "Now we cook...how call?" She pointed to the eggs she had been carefully cracking in another mixing bowl and had beaten with a fork.

"Eggs, child," Nana answered before he could. "Them be eggs."

"Eggs. No take off *sartan*, frying pan?" At his nod of approval he continued. "We cook eggs."

Vicky got a spoonful of lard and handed it to him. "On frying pan." She pointed and he followed her instructions. She added milk from the bucket to the eggs, then salted and peppered her concoction. It almost hurt him physically to not take the fork from her hands, but then she would just take his place at the fireplace, and bending up and down to get to the skillet would cause her a whole lot more pain than a little mixing would.

"I think I can take it from here." He stole the bowl from her before she could carry it over. "Go sit down."

"No sit down. Salsa."

"What's salsa?"

"In here." She held up one of the seven jars of soup Berto had included in their trade last year. Twice he'd tried to heat up the soup and each time, the spicy flavor almost choked both Nana and him. They'd finally left it alone, hoping to never get so hungry as to have to choke more of it down, and now Vicky wanted to heat it up for

breakfast? Could she be trying to get revenge on him
for his tasteless soups, or did she not know how spicy
the stuff was? Or was it an acquired taste? If so, would
it be something that reminded her of home?

If it meant something to her, he'd try to get some
of it down.

"I'll cook that next," he promised, hiding his grimace
and ignoring Nana's snort. She must have recognized
what Vicky had unearthed.

"No cook salsa!" The look she gave him declared
him crazy. "Salsa for tortilla."

"Sure hope the tortilla thingy makes that soup better," Nana mumbled.

"No soup, salsa!" Vicky shook her head and returned
to the task of trying to open her infamous salsa.

"Don't, Vicky. I'll open it for you." He swiped up
the jar from her. It took two tries, but he heard a click,
and the smell of onions, tomatoes, garlic and something
else greeted him.

He set it down on the table and went back to pull the
frying pan off the coals.

"I think it's ready," he announced as Vicky set a plate
down at the place he normally occupied. She returned
for the others, but he cut her off. "Go sit, woman. You're
going to end up back in bed if you don't take it easy."

He set plates in front of her and Nana.

"No need."

Vicky pointed to the cutlery he had brought with
him and the cups for breakfast. "No, no need forks."

"Well, how you plannin' on eatin' your food?"

"You see." Her tone was subdued. Was she angry or

just worn out? "Chris talk to 'Good Lord,'" she ordered but kept her eyes on the plate in front of her.

"You want me to pray?"

"*Sí*, say thank you to Dios for food." At least she had learned that they prayed before meals. Had she learned anything about God as she lived with them? He hoped so. He prayed silently that he could be a godly example of Christian charity to her.

As soon as he uttered "Amen," Vicky took a tortilla, laid it flat on her plate and served a small portion of egg right on top. Then she spooned a helping of salsa, folded one end up and rolled up the flat bread into a roll with the eggs and salsa inside. Lifting it to her mouth, she took a bite from the open end, closing her eyes in what seemed to be delight. She beamed at them as soon as she had swallowed. "This how eat tortilla."

He held his breath to see how she would react to the horrible burning from the salsa, but she surprised him by taking another bite.

"Well, I'll be. Never seen it done quite like that!" Nana Ruth shook her head at the sight but then fixed up her own with just a small dab of salsa.

"You no like?" Vicky's worried gaze caught Chris's.

"I don't know. I've never tried them before." Pulling a piece of torti-yah off, he tossed it into his mouth. Didn't taste like much of anything. Maybe flour and lard. Not as delectable as fresh-baked bread, but edible. And if it made Vicky feel more at home, for one day he could set his own preferences aside. *"No tiene sabor."* He grinned cheekily at her, remembering her words from the first time she ate his soup.

"No eat like that, Chris," the girl admonished. *"La tortilla no tiene sabor."*

"You said that about my soup. *No tiene sabor.*"

"No have…? What word?"

"Flavor. It doesn't have any flavor."

"My stars!" Nana Ruth wiped at the juice running down from the side of her mouth. "This here surely does have flavor, Master Chris. Wakes a body up for the mornin'." She took another large bite and nodded her approval at Vicky.

Vicky grinned at Nana's praise, daintily finishing off her roll without anything dripping. Chris's first roll fell apart as he bit into it. Then on the second try, it drizzled down his hand and arm. Vicky laughed at his struggle, but after a while it didn't really matter. The food, though messy as all get out, was delicious. Strange how just mixing the right ingredients could create a whole new experience. Something as bland as the flatbread mixed well with the salsa that no one could stomach on its own. Could a hacienda princess ever mix well with a humble American horse breeder?

Chapter Eight

With a sigh, Vicky set the knitting down on the table. She was dressed in her own skirt and blouse now, having had a bath the night before. Three pairs of socks, a shirt for Chris and the start of a pair of pants had occupied her hands for the last four days. She had accomplished quite a bit, but she couldn't make herself sit still any longer.

Now the sunshine peeked through the cabin windows like a young childhood friend cajoling her to come and romp with the colts. How many times had she snuck out of the house to play with Juan Manuel and José Luis? At first the boys, two years older than her, didn't want her to follow them at all, but then when the *toro* almost trampled her, they had begrudgingly let her participate if for no other reason than to keep an eye on her.

To make it up to them for having to play with a girl, she ran faster, pushed harder, tumbled and fought with as much heart as any boy, and they soon became the three musketeers of the hacienda. Of course, Mamá yelled at her for her unladylike behavior. Even if she had been the most poised, ladylike of all the young se-ñoritas in the area, her skin and hair color upset her mother. She could no more win her mother's affection or approval than she could change the color of her eyes.

Lost in her thoughts, it took a minute to realize the door had opened and Chris had entered. When she looked up at him, he grinned. "You have a visitor, Vicky. Would you like to come and see?" he asked from the doorway.

Someone to visit her? Had Papá or José Luis come looking? Joy quickly gave way to fear. What if Don Joaquín had joined the search?

"I think you miss her." Chris crossed the room and stood next to her chair, waiting.

"Who?" Her voice trembled, and she saw a flash of concern in his eyes.

"It's a good surprise," he assured her.

If she told him she didn't want anyone to find her here, would he hide her or would he turn her over to the first person who came to claim her? Before she could ask anything else, she heard a low nicker from the door he had left partially opened. A white nose pushed the door open the rest of the way.

"Tesoro!" Without thinking, she stood so quickly the room spun.

"Careful there." Chris wrapped an arm around her middle. Smells of sunshine, freshly tilled earth, horses and something uniquely him filled her senses. The world righted and she stood still, breathing deeply. The light-headedness she felt must have come from her quick movement. It couldn't have had anything to do with the handsome man who took such good care of her. "Better?" The exhale of his words teased the hair at her temple as if it were a soft caress.

"Sí."

"Then I think we should get you to Tesoro before she makes herself at home in here."

"You keep that horse outdoors where it belongs, Master Chris," Nana Ruth ordered from her perch on the side of her bed. She had been getting around better the last few days, but her knuckles were doing poorly again today.

"Yes, ma'am." Chris saluted with his free hand. Nana Ruth reprimanded him about something, but her words were too fast for Vicky to make any sense of them.

On the threshold of the cabin, Chris stood back a step and let Vicky lean her head into Tesoro's neck. *"Oh, Tesoro, I've missed you so much."*

"Not fair, telling Tesoro secrets in Spanish," Chris teased.

"No secret. I say I miss Tesoro."

"I could tell you were missing her. She's been missing you, as well."

"Does he feed you well? Are you warm and safe at night?" As if understanding her questions, Tesoro nodded her head and then nipped Vicky on the shoulder, blowing air on her as if demanding an answer for her absence.

"Someday soon we're going home, Tesoro. Rest up well because I will need you to get me there." She scratched Tesoro's darker patch right behind her ear.

When would she be able to mount up again? She missed riding and the freedom it gave her. But getting better meant leaving behind her newfound friends. Would she ever see Chris or Nana Ruth again once she returned to the hacienda? If she stayed on the hacienda and didn't marry, she might be able to convince Papá or Berto to bring her back to visit from time to time, but if she were still forced to marry... Shuddering at the thought, she forced herself to focus on Tesoro.

"Here." Chris must have felt her shiver and attributed it to the cool breeze. He slipped his jacket around her shoulders and lifted her hair out of the collar in a move as natural as breathing. Did he feel the strange tingle she felt when his fingers brushed her skin?

"I don't want you to wear yourself out, Vicky." He slid his arm around her waist and waited, standing beside her to support her weight. "I think it's time to go back in."

"I no want in," she insisted. Now that she had finally come out and felt the sun's warmth on her face and the cool breeze in her hair, she hated going back inside. "Please, *unos minutos más*."

"Fine." He chuckled and shook his head. "Let's get you settled then." Without warning, he picked her up and strode out to the barn, Tesoro following behind as if unwilling to be separated again.

Resting her against the barn wall, he ducked inside and emerged with a milking stool. Setting it out next to the corral fence, he helped her walk the ten paces and then sit down with care. "Does this hurt?" he asked, his eyes not missing anything as his gaze bore into her.

"No. I like *sol*...sun?" She pointed just in case she had the wrong word.

"I suspected as much, Miss Vicky." He stood back and then climbed the corral fence with the agility that she had taken for granted only two weeks ago. Before his feet even touched the ground, all the horses ambled his direction. He patted or scratched each of the animals, calling them by name and whispering sweet nothings to them.

Tesoro nickered and nudged her on the right shoulder, unaware of how much it hurt. Almost toppling off the stool, she gritted her teeth against the cry the sudden movement brought to her lips. Chris started to climb the fence before she could get her left arm up in a motion to stop him. "I *bien*." She shook her head at him, willing him to understand how good it felt to be outside so that he would let her enjoy the outdoors and his horses a few more minutes.

"Are you sure you're okay?" He halted his climb, his hands on top of the fence, and waited.

"Yes, I okay." Forcing a smile that hid her shortness of breath, she held his gaze. He nodded, turning back to his horses.

"Be careful with me, Tes. I can't play today, but soon," Vicky confided in her dearest friend while burying her fingers in Tesoro's mane. She watched as Chris pulled himself up bareback on one of the horses. Raising his hands in the air, he guided the animal with gentle nudges of his knees. They raced around the enclosure, turning quickly or skidding to a stop. He had trained

the animals well. They would make very valuable partners for any *vaquero* on a ranch working with cattle.

Thinking back, Berto normally bred and broke all the horses on the hacienda, but in the last few years, every spring he had added two or three to the stock that had not been born on Hacienda Ruiz. Had he been buying those from Chris each year? Had Chris had a chance to come to her Quinceañera and chosen not to? If he had, would he have vied for her hand?

Of course not. He was doing his Christian duty by taking care of her until she healed, but he could not have any affection for her. Not with her skin so dark and her lack of feminine charms.

With a sigh, she watched his herd circle the corral behind him, following him with undaunted faith. Having grown up around the stables, Vicky knew that animals had a sixth sense about people. Tesoro had never misjudged a person. If Tesoro shied away from someone, sooner or later the mean streak would show.

All too soon, Chris dismounted and hopped the fence. "It's time to get you inside for today."

"Come again tomorrow," she insisted. Her side ached terribly, but now that she had felt the fresh air on her face, she couldn't bear the thought of being stuck inside again.

"We'll see how sore you are come evening."

"Evening?" They had come to an unspoken understanding: any new word Chris said, Vicky would repeat and he'd give her a definition.

"At the end of the day. Morning is when the sun

comes up. Noon is in the middle of the day. Evening is when the sun goes down."

"Evening night?"

"Evening is when the sky is getting dark and night is coming soon."

Saving away the new word and its meaning, she stood on shaky legs and tried to stifle a moan. From Chris's frown, she might not have managed to keep it completely quiet.

"Here, let me take you back inside." He scooped her back up in his arms. Unable to help herself, she laid her head against his chest and listened to the strong beat of his heart. She knew that this man was as steady and true as his heartbeat.

Closing her eyes, she breathed in the scent of him and the pine trees that surrounded his cabin. No matter how far away her life took her, this time at Chris's ranch would be a memory she would revisit when she needed to feel safe. He might not find her lovely, he might see her skin as too dark and her hair too thick, but he treated her like a woman to be sheltered and protected. On the hacienda, everyone had wanted to keep her out of harm's way because she was Don Ruiz's daughter and Berto's *princesa*, but here, Chris took care of her because she needed the help and nothing more. Somehow that made her feel even more cared for.

Finished with the milking, Chris sat back on the stool and breathed deeply. He figured dinner should be ready by now. Truth was he had been looking for excuses to go inside and check on Vicky and Nana Ruth all afternoon. Even the horses seemed to sense his thoughts weren't with his work.

The day before, Nana had convinced him that it was time to let the lady take a soak in the washtub, since Vicky had been with them for a total of ten days. Lacking the perfumed French soaps his mother and sister would have insisted on, he had offered the cake of lye soap. She had thanked him profusely in an excited mix of Spanish and English. A person would have thought he'd given her a king's ransom instead of a tub of warm water and some privacy.

Last night he had moved his bedroll and his few belongings out to the smaller cabin that they had originally built for Jeb and Nana Ruth. The buildings were built within sight of each other, but they were far enough away that he'd be winded before he sprinted the length of the yard if anyone rang for help. Torn between propriety and keeping the woman safe, he'd waited until Vicky had gone two nights in a row without a nightmare. Surely she'd be fine. After all, Vicky could now get out of bed without aid, and if she moved slowly, with care, he noticed she barely grimaced. The girl was a power to be reckoned with.

A nudge on his shoulder brought him back to the present in the barn. "Go on, Bessy, you did a good job today." He patted the cow's side and stood, almost toppling his stool behind him. Shaking off the feeling that his body and his mind had somehow become separated, he picked up the milk pail and headed toward the house. If he were being truly honest, the moment he had picked up Vicky to take her back into the house after her visit with Goldenrod earlier in the day, something had shifted in his chest. She laid her head against him, and he hoped that she couldn't hear how she caused his heart to speed up like a horse going from a canter to an all-out gallop.

"She'll be leaving soon," he said out loud, as if the words would get his head cleared once and for all. But instead of relief that things would go back to the way they had been before, he frowned at how the prospect of that left an empty hole in his chest.

Surely once she was back with her family he would take the horses out on the trail all day like he used to and get back to his normal self. Although, Vicky would probably love to take a ride on one of the many trails he'd worn down around the ranch. In fact, it might be wise to take her on a short ride in a few days and test her endurance so that they could plan their trip back to the hacienda. If his guess was right, she'd be more comfortable on Goldenrod's graceful back with her gliding stride than on the hard wagon bench for hours on end. And since there was no way to get a wagon out to the road a few miles to their south, taking a wagon would mean days of clearing a path. Not to mention that he'd have to build the wagon.

Without meaning to, he began to form a plan. They'd take a picnic basket along and spend a few hours out on the trail that led to the small meadow across the stream overlooking his humble ranch. But what would be the point of making a trek with her that would leave permanent memories of a lovely lady in his desolate land?

His description stopped him short. His land was

breathtaking, astounding proof of a Creator's handiwork. When had he started to see it as desolate?

Since a beautiful young woman had taken up temporary residence in his cabin, that's when. Maybe she had
found a way into a corner of his heart, as well.

Chapter Nine

The light spring breeze blew a tendril of Vicky's hair across her face as she sat on a milking stool, watching as Chris slid the halter over Moonbeam's soft head.

"When go Vicky?"

The question caught him like a kick to his stomach as he cinched the saddle buckle tighter under Moonbeam's belly. Surely she didn't expect to ride a full day and a half back to the hacienda if she hadn't even been in the saddle once since her accident.

"You need to take things easy still, Vicky. If we try to take you back to the hacienda right now, you wouldn't make it more than an hour or so." He finally dared to raise his gaze to find her staring at him. "I know you must miss your family something fierce, but you need to have a little more patience. You're just not ready yet."

"I no ready go hacienda. I ready Tesoro. When Chris make Tesoro take Vicky in corral?"

A breath of relief filled his chest. His response to her words should have warned him that he had already become too attached to the woman, but he pushed those thoughts aside. There'd be more than enough time to deal with that once she returned to her life and people. "You want to ride Tesoro?"

"Si!" She clapped her hands together like a small child delighted with a Christmas gift. *"Gracias*, Chris!" In an instant she had jumped up and all but thrown herself at him, squeezing him around the middle. His arms caught and held her without his permission.

She belonged there. Right in his arms. She fit. She fit under his arm against his chest as if God himself had made her for that purpose. As if Chris had been made to protect her and hold her within the shelter of his own arms. Of course, that was nonsense. Thinking that way only spelled disaster and would lead to a broken heart in the best of scenarios. Or someone close to him dying in the worst.

God had made her to be a hacienda princess and him to be…to be a hermit. Because there was no way he could stand to live within "polite society" again and not fight against the hypocrisy that he saw everywhere. And to give her the things she deserved, he'd need to live in a large community where he'd have resources close by. No, he couldn't be her protector or anything else.

As soon as she healed he'd take her back. Back to her life on the hacienda and all her friends, for surely a woman as lovely as Vicky had quite a line of suitors waiting for her when she returned. Just the thought of some fancy Spanish nobleman holding her close for a dance or courting her caused the morning's breakfast to turn sour in his stomach.

Forcing his arms to loosen, he dared to gaze down at her and froze. Her coffee-colored eyes, wide with silent questions, studied him, then blinked slowly before she pulled out of his grasp.

"I'm sorry, Vicky. Did I hurt you?" He ran a hand around the nape of his neck to keep from reaching out and pulling her back again.

"No, no hurt me." She stood watching him. The long silence stretched out awkwardly. Finally, a horse behind them whinnied and broke their tension. "I sit on Tesoro?" She took a tentative step toward the stall and held out her palm for her horse to nuzzle her.

"Yes, you can sit on Tesoro. You can even see how you feel riding." He shook off the feeling of holding her close and headed to the tack room for her saddle and reins. A memory. That's all he would make of that. A good, precious memory that would keep him company on cold winter nights when he was alone in his cabin and she was somewhere else, married, having forgotten all about the strange American and her short convalescence in the small cabin in the woods.

Heat flooded her cheeks as Vicky waited for Chris to come back. What must he think of her? Would an *Americana* have thrown herself in his arms as she had? Surely not! The Englishman who had taught her so many years ago said that the English stood farther apart than the Spanish. He said that a proper man and woman should touch only glove to glove—never even hand to hand—much less indulge in a tight embrace unless they were betrothed. "The space between a lady and gentleman should not be less than the sum of the length of both of their forearms extended at all times." He had reminded her time and time again that if she were ever to be in the presence of a true *Americano* or English gentleman that she should act demure and mature.

Her older brother had joked that the Englishman looked like someone had stuck him in the backside with a hat pin and he feared he'd be stuck again if he dared to bend his form even just slightly. Granted, Chris had not been nearly so formal, but his remark about her returning spoke clearly about his wish to send her back as soon as possible.

Now she had gone and hugged the *Americano* like she would have José Luis or one of her younger brothers. And try as she might, she couldn't lie to herself and believe that she felt the same kind of affection for Chris that she felt for her brothers. No, he held her attention and her affections in a way no other man ever had. And now he must see her as uncouth and uncivilized.

What if he had a young lady he courted? He had never hinted about having a sweetheart, but living so far out he might be able to court her only a few times a month, and with Vicky and Nana needing constant attention maybe he had missed his chance to go. Could she, even right now, be interfering in his plans to court some Americana?

The idea should not have pleased her as much as it did. After all, he had done all he could to make sure that she was safe, comfortable and taken care of. A true Christian would want the best for him, and that would be for him to be free to court and marry a young woman of his own country.

But the heathen in her heart cheered for her to continue the interruption for as long as possible.

The port city where Spanish priests had built a monastery and mission some sixty years before, calling it San Francisco, had grown in population, especially now that the Mejican government had built a fort there. Rumors said that many of those newer residents were Americanos. Could one of those new *Americanas* hold Chris's affections?

Before she could settle her emotions, Chris came back with her saddle and quickly set to putting it on Tesoro. His movements were skilled, controlled, but he didn't meet her gaze. She moved to hold on to Tesoro's bridle, rubbing the horse's sweet spot, trying to ignore her own discomfort.

"She loves you," Chris observed, clinching the saddle and checking the stirrups once again. She noticed that her saddle had been oiled and cleaned since her escapades that brought her here. "You clean?" She waited for him to straighten up from beside the horse.

"Are you asking if I cleaned Tesoro?" He cocked his eyebrow at her waiting for clarification. Patting Tesoro's head once more, she ventured around to stand next to him.

"You clean this?" she asked, touching the saddle Papá gave Juan Manuel for his twelfth birthday. He'd been so proud of the saddle, knowing how much work the saddle maker had put into the stitching. When Juan Manuel died, Papá was so heartbroken, he didn't want to see any reminders of his eldest son and had most of his belongings burned or given away. Vicky hid the saddle in her room, and when Papá gave her Tesoro five years later, she snuck it out and insisted that only that saddle be used on her horse. Riding on her big brother's saddle almost made her feel as if he were with her on her rides.

"Yes, I cleaned it up. It is a very nice saddle." He swept a hand over the stitching and turned to her.

"It my brother Juan Manuel saddle. Papá gave Juan Manuel for birthday."

"He must miss it—" Chris again looked at her as if asking questions without saying a word "—and you."

She worked to hold back her emotions. "He no live now. He die with very hot."

"Did he get burned? Fire?"

"Fire on inside." Placing a hand on her own forehead called to mind the many times Chris had done the same while she was recuperating. "Like when I come here."

"Oh, he had a fever?" Chris's hand rose as if to touch her forehead, but then he laid it on Tesoro's side. Surely she had misread his intentions. Chris had helped with her care while she was sick because Nana Ruth had been too hindered by her arthritis to do much, but now he wouldn't need to worry about her anymore. The happiness that she should have felt didn't rise in her chest. Instead she wished that he had touched her forehead, or maybe her cheek.

"I'm sorry, Vicky."

"Why you sorry?"

"I'm sorry you lost your brother, and I'm sure that you must miss him. I'm glad you have this saddle to remember him by and keep him close." For someone who so often had trouble understanding her meanings, how could he know?

A nod was all she could manage at first. Swallowing past the lump that had formed in her throat, she tried to smile and failed. "Padre Pedro say Juan Manuel and Angelica no more pain, no more tears. I miss yes, but no want them sick."

"The padre is right. If Juan Manuel knew the Lord as his Savior, then he's in heaven now where there is no pain or tears. Who is Angelica?"

"Little sister. She live only hours. She pretty and white."

"So you had a little sister who died just after she was born?"

All she could do was nod for a moment. Would Chris have liked Angelica if she had lived? Would he have preferred the white skin and light golden eyes to Vicky's darker coloring? "You Padre Cress?"

"Are you asking about my father, or a priest?"

"You are priest?" she tried again, hoping that she'd made her question clearer this time. No one on the hacienda had a Bible nor could they read it if they had. Only Padre Pedro carried one around. When she asked to read it, he had laughed and explained that he had gone to school to be able to read it for God had written it in Greek and Hebrew. The priest read out of the Latin version that had been translated centuries earlier and the church recognized as the only official translation. Since she neither knew nor could read any of those languages, she'd have to be content with believing what the priest told her about God's Word.

"Am I a priest?" Chris looked stunned.

"Sí."

"No, I'm not a priest."

"But you have *Biblia* and you read every night at table. The night I so sick you open book and read. Padre Pedro need read Latin, or *Grego y Hebreo*."

He scuffed his boot on the ground, and his cheeks, already pink with the cool breeze, glowed redder still. "That's true. The men who wrote down on scrolls what God put in their hearts to write spoke Hebrew or Greek. Then someone who could read both wrote down the words in English so we could read it and understand it ourselves. I believe God wanted everyone to hear and understand His message. It's a message of His love. He wanted to have a relationship with every single person. When Jesus walked on earth, he treated all men equal, talking to the sinners and the leaders of the church as if they were the same." He rubbed the back of his neck and turned to look out at the horses.

Mamá had told her so many times that God loved only the noble Spanish and the white and hated the heathen uncivilized Indians. She had told Vicky it was God's hatred toward them that let the Spanish come in and conquer. Yet here, standing before her, was a man whose skin was even lighter than her own mother's and he said that it didn't matter. That God loved everyone equally. Did that mean he saw everyone equally, as well? Could he really see her as a lovely woman—not just a dark-skinned Indian? He'd said she was pretty once, but she didn't know if she could believe him. Uncomfortable where those thoughts might lead her, she caught the sides of the saddle and slipped her foot into the stirrup.

"I on Tesoro now?"

"Let me help," Chris offered as he caught her around the waist. He lifted her as if she were merely a handful of straw instead of a full-grown woman. He turned his head to the side, giving her privacy for her to settle her skirts and cover her legs.

"How do you feel?"

"Good. I good, Chris. *Gracias!*"

He finally turned and smiled up at her. Her responding smile wasn't forced this time in spite of the twinge of pain at the jarring first step. She wouldn't be riding home tomorrow or even the next day, but just to be in the saddle again was progress.

Taking the reins, he led them out the back door of the barn and into the corral. Tesoro followed him without hesitation. They managed three trips around the corral before he noticed how short of breath Vicky had become, and he carried her back into the house. Placing her on a chair, he bent low and helped her pull off her boots.

"You'd better take it easy for the rest of the afternoon. I think you've had about all the excitement you need for the day."

She felt the desire to argue, but the wheeze coming from her lungs and the way she felt like passing out kept her from saying anything. It had felt so good to be on a horse again that she would let herself be babied for a little while longer, knowing that each day a final "goodbye" inched closer.

"Well, I do declare! That girl look just plum done in. What did you do to Miss Vicky, Master Chris?" Nana Ruth shuffled over to inspect his work.

"She took a ride on her horse today. I'm not sure who was happier, Vicky or Goldenrod."

"You tryin' to kill the girl, Master Chris?" Her forehead furrowed and the glare she gave him made Vicky sit up a little straighter, but Chris just grinned, showing off his dimple again as he shook his head.

"You go ahead and try to keep those two apart. They are inseparable, and now that she's been up once, I'll give you odds that she'll be begging tomorrow to do it all again. Good old fresh air and a little exercise didn't kill anyone, Nana. You were always sending me out to run off some energy."

"'Cause you always had too much energy and not a lick of sense. She's got a broken rib. Sitting up on top of a wild beast is a sure way to get her busted up or worse."

Only after he had carried her the three steps she could have easily walked from the chair to the bed and then left with an excuse of seeing to the rest of the chores did Nana Ruth start chuckling.

"That there boy's done got it bad, Miss Vicky."

"What he have?" Vicky sat up in the bed, confused by the sudden change in Nana.

"Why, he's fallin' for you as sure as my name's Ruth. He's got it bad."

Judging from the look on Nana's face, she thought Chris cared for her. If only it were true.

"And it's 'bout time, too. He needs to find himself a good wife and start a family. Surely the Good Lord done sent you here for that. Just like He did with Adam and Eve in the garden."

Vicky felt the heat rise in her cheeks again. She was unable to meet Nana's gaze because the wise woman would see right into her heart and how much she would like the words to be true. Instead, she settled more comfortably in bed and closed her eyes. What Nana didn't know was that Chris was counting the days until he could get Vicky out of his home.

God might love all people regardless of their color and birth, but she couldn't believe that Chris did.

Chapter Ten

True to Chris's prediction, Vicky insisted on going out to the barn each day to help groom Tesoro. After that first day, he persuaded her to wait to ride again only because she couldn't stand straight enough to fight with him about it.

Instead, for the next two days, he took her for a quick visit to the horses and then brought the milking stool out to the woods.

He fell two trees and invited Vicky to keep him company while he sawed them into the right lengths to make a bench.

"What are you building?" Vicky watched his work with fascination. If he didn't miss his guess, her sore ribs were about the only thing keeping her from grabbing a saw and pitching in.

"I'm making a bench. I think it's about time you had somewhere to sit so you can enjoy the fresh air in the shade." As soon as the words left his mouth, he wanted to bring them back. She wouldn't be there by the time it was warm enough to want the shade on sunny days.

Glancing up, he started to try to backtrack, expecting her to be upset, but the look in her eyes dried up his words.

"You make for me? For me to sit and watch you work with horse while I work on sew?" The words were said with awe. "You want me here?"

"It's a better option than the milking stool." He shrugged, trying to downplay just how much he'd like to have her here come summer.

Two weeks had passed since then. Each day she had ridden better and lasted longer in the saddle with less discomfort afterward. She had also started to help with grooming all the horses. Her presence made chore time much more pleasant, and the time flew. Chris found himself with time to work on gentling Moonbeam and each day he fell one more tree standing between his cabin and the main road and every afternoon he sanded more of Vicky's bench. He tried to focus on the tasks at hand and shut out thoughts about how empty the barn would seem once he delivered Vicky back to her home.

Any day now, she'd ask to leave, and he'd be forced to face a very tough decision. How was he possibly going to take care of both women at the same time? He couldn't leave Nana Ruth here at the ranch while he escorted Vicky home, and Nana Ruth would not be able to ride a horse for five minutes, much less a day and a half through woods.

Still puzzling over what to do, he saddled Moonbeam and Tesoro, checking their hooves and their gear. The sun shone down, and a slight breeze stirred in the trees overhead—it promised to be a beautiful day for a picnic lunch in the meadow to the east of the creek. February was half-done, and March would be knocking on the door. Spring graced all the plants around him—the deciduous trees were starting to bud overhead while plants were poking their green shoots up through the ground. New life grew on the little rosebush Nana Ruth made him cut back each fall. He and Jeb had found it for her a few years back, and Nana tended it with care. It was the last gift her husband had given her.

"We go now?" Vicky's silent approach caught him off guard.

"Yes, if you're ready." Her steps were sure and her movements graceful even in old white peasant pants and a serape that hid most of her slight build. He'd become accustomed to her in her skirt and fine blouse, but somehow this outfit made her look at home here on his ranch. The sombrero that had seen better days hung down her back by the strings around her neck. How could he ever have mistaken her for a boy, even covered in mud and dressed as a peasant? A princess in disguise, but her carriage and poise gave her away. If their paths ever met again, he would not mistake her for anyone but his princess… Halting those thoughts, he vowed to enjoy the day and let tomorrow take care of itself.

"We ride all day?" She ran her hand over the bit and reins, then checked the saddle, the cinch. Warmth filled him at the sight of her with the horse he had bred and trained. They were well matched, both in spirit and temperament.

"We won't ride all day. Just for a while this morning, and then I was thinking we could picnic by the creek later."

"Picnic?"

"To take food and eat outdoors, sit on a blanket on the grass." Her vocabulary had grown so quickly he sometimes forgot to keep the sentences simple.

"Like Jesus feed many people?"

"Kinda like that." They had read about Jesus feeding the five thousand the night before. So much of the Bible that he had heard as a boy was completely new for her. She asked each night for him to read more and more, asking questions and even writing down some of the things he said. "Only we won't have fish. It'll be just cold chicken and yesterday's bread." He grinned at her and was treated to a smile of delight on her face. "And not five thousand, just you, me, Tesoro and Moonbeam."

She nodded, grasped the pommel of Tesoro's saddle and set her foot into the stirrup. He quickly caught her at the waist and assisted her into the saddle. She showed no signs of pain, no quick intake of breath like she had the first few times she'd ridden. She was almost completely healed. In fact, he'd bet she didn't need his help to mount up at all, but it was an excuse to stand close and smell the clean, fresh scent of her hair. He left his hands at her sides a moment longer than necessary.

"You gonna stand there all day or ride horse?" She grinned down at him, her sassy question laced with a touch of Nana Ruth making him laugh. The sound of laughter had become more commonplace in the last weeks. Would he find reasons to laugh once Vicky was back with her own family?

Tesoro shifted and snorted her impatience, as well. Two peas in a pod, and both of them had managed to take up residency in a corner of his heart.

Once they had headed out away from the ranch, he led them along the creek that ran from the tops of the mountains to the west. Its water was clear and cold even in the summer.

They rode in companionable silence for a time, Vicky taking in everything around them. She rode as if she had been born in the saddle. "Who taught you how to ride?"

"Berto *y* Papá carry me on horse before I walk. I have small horse—how you call?"

"Pony?"

"*Sí*, pony. I have pony when I turn four. I get old big horse when I turn seven, and you sell Tesoro when I turn fifteen."

"No wonder you ride so well."

"I love ride. I no want marry and no ride no more."

"Why would you have to stop riding just because you marry?" He glanced back at her and saw sadness in her eyes.

"A lady no ride horse. Lady make house nice, cut flowers, sew handkerchief…" She sighed deeply and looked away. What could he do to protect her from such a bleak future? She had seemed content to sew and knit while she was recovering, but once she began visiting the barn each day, she came alive. Her smile shone brighter and her laughter bubbled up constantly.

"But surely not all men expect that from their wives. Don't your haciendas have many servants who take care of your home and do your cooking?" He'd only stayed in a guesthouse next to the stables while he had been there making trades, but he'd seen the washer-women in the large side yard working on the laundry, and the house servants coming and going. It had been very much like life on his plantation growing up, the only difference being that the servants were indigenous people free to come and go as they pleased. "Surely your husband will enjoy taking rides with you."

"No, *mi mamá* say no more ride. No more outside. I black from sun. No man want wife black from sun."

Chris was stunned and hardly knew what to say. "You're…tan and healthy. Your color is perfect. And any man who truly knew you would be blessed to have you by his side." He stopped himself, wondering if he had said too much.

"*Mi mamá* say man want white wife. With green eyes and white hair."

"White hair? Like an old lady?"

"No, white like sunlight and Tesoro."

"Blond. Your *mamá* thinks that all men want to marry blondes with light complexions?"

"*Sí*, señors with blood from España want blon."

"Blondes. There's a *d* and *e* on the end."

"Blondes."

He'd like to get a hold of Vicky's mother for a few minutes and let her know what he thought about her ideas. How could a mother put her own daughter down? "I don't know about the noblemen from Spain, but I would rather have a woman who is kind and gentle, a good mother for my children and a helpmate to live beside me than a woman whose only charm was her out-ward beauty any day."

Surprise, curiosity and something else shone in her eyes for a second, and then she turned away.

"You marry?"

"I don't know. It's one thing for me to live out here all by myself, but to raise a family so remote from any-one…it's a big risk. I don't think many women would be interested in coming to live way out here in the wil-derness either."

"You ranch beautiful. You house, warm and safe. You make good house."

"Why, thank you, Vicky. I'm glad you approve." He grinned at her compliment. His chest shouldn't have puffed up at her words, but it did. Her approval meant more than he wanted to consider. "But it's too far away from neighbors if someone were to get hurt or we were attacked."

"You need make *viha*."

"Viha?"

"Vill-age?" Vicky hesitantly tried to explain.

"Village? You want me to found a town?"

"You give work to three, no, five men with horse, and they build house for they *familias*. You no live too far away if you have *viha*."

"Viha is village?"

"Sí, group of house together."

"Well, I'll think on that. It might work. Someday." But who would be willing to drag their family out to the wilderness and start a village with him? And would he want to give up his solitude? It would defeat the purpose, but maybe his purpose wasn't quite as noble as he had once thought.

Then again, if he had a village close by, he'd have been able to get word to Vicky's family that she was safe and recovering in his home. They might have sent someone to tend to her and already managed to transport her back...

It would have solved the problem of how to take her home, but it would have reduced his time with her. Their evening Bible readings, the new foods and stories that she shared with him and Nana. He would have missed out on most of those memories if there had been other families living nearby who could have cared for a young woman.

She may be someone else's betrothed and leaving in just a few days, but for the meantime, he wanted to learn all he could about her and teach her as much English as she could take in. He'd never seen someone so eager to learn before. If nothing else, she would always remember his English lessons, and maybe she'd remember him, as well. He knew he would never forget her. The laughter and the beauty she brought to his life. The excitement he felt each time he strode toward his cabin where the woman waited for him with dinner would vanish along with her, but he'd always treasure her memory.

Chris had spread a blanket out for them on the grassy slope near the bubbling creek. The sun peeked between the trees, dancing like gold dust on his hair. Vicky watched where he had told her to wait, and something caught in her chest.

He was so handsome and wonderful, and took such good care of her. What kind of man did that? And why did he choose to live out here, on his own like an outcast, when he had such a good, loving heart? Surely he could do so much for a community if he were to live among people. If he lived closer to her own brothers, she would send them to help him with the horses and to learn how to be real men by watching him.

"All set, now—careful." He took her hand and helped her walk over the uneven ground to the picnic he had laid out. He had plates, serviettes and cups for both of them. In the basket, the cold chicken that she had fried for them the night before was waiting for them along with slices of bread. Glad she had contributed to their outing, she let him help her settle on the blanket.

As soon as he sat down facing her across the basket, he took both of her hands in his, a now familiar occurrence, bowed his head and thanked God for the beautiful day, good food and the pleasant company.

Alone with Chris, she could forget that Don Joaquín waited for her somewhere and that Papá should have come looking for her weeks ago.

Pushing all thoughts aside except the enjoyment of the day, she glanced back at Chris and found him watching her intently. Her cheeks felt warm, and she wondered if she had something on her face. She swiped her face with the napkin, but it came away clean.

"Do I have food?" she finally questioned, pointing to her face after another attempt came away clean.

"No, you are perfect." But even as he said the words, he stretched out his arm and ran his thumb up her cheek and then tucked a wisp of hair behind her ear.

"Um…" Searching for something to say, she opened her mouth and words rushed past before she could stop the flow. "Why you live here, all alone? Why you and Nana no have family or friends? No villa?"

He leaned back on his arms, looking over to the running water, and the silence ran on. She almost told him not to tell her if he didn't want to when he finally turned tortured eyes back to her and, with a deep breath, began his story.

"Growing up, my father owned about seventy slaves. All the big plantations in the area owned slaves, and most of the ministers and other leaders considered owning slaves a way white men actually 'helped Christianize the heathen blacks.' But I spent more time with Nana Ruth and Jeb than I did with my own family and discovered I couldn't treat slaves like anything other than people. My father hated the fact that I treated the slaves well. Growing up, I was miserable. The lowest time in my life was when my father sold Nana's son to a neighbor. He was only a few years older than I was, and I still can remember…" He swallowed and turned back to the stream, clearing his throat before he went on. "I remember Nana crying when she thought I wasn't there." He paused for a minute, and she was afraid he would stop talking altogether.

"So when my father died, I freed the slaves. Every single one of them that very day. Drew up their papers and told them they could go with my blessing and some money to start somewhere else. Or they could stay on my plantation and work for wages just like the white men did. Most stayed, and the next year we had the best yield ever."

She could only stare as he continued, her awe growing as he spoke. She knew he was kind, but he had gone against everyone, even his own father, in defense of slaves—people who were of little consequence to those around him.

He picked up a twig and started ripping it to pieces. She doubted he realized what his hands were doing, but his intensity warned her that whatever was to follow still haunted him.

"Ezequiel, one of the younger slaves who had always had problems with authority, went to town and tried to go into the tavern. They kicked him out, but he forced his way back in and ran his mouth off about how he was as good as any of the white men there, that his money had the same value as theirs. They didn't take kindly to his words."

He swallowed hard and wiped his hand down his thigh, but she could see how it shook. She wanted to reach out and reassure him but feared he'd stop talking. "I remember when they brought his body home. They had beaten him and then lynched him. No one, no matter what they had done, should suffer like that."

"Lynched?"

"Hung from a tree. No trial, no mercy. That night, the threats started. They accused me of inciting rebellion among the county's slaves by freeing mine. They burned a few of the outbuildings and beat some of my men when they were out in the fields. Finally, I decided to sell the land that had been in the Samuels family for five generations. I sent all my workers to Canada where they could truly be free. I moved here with Jeb and Nana Ruth six years ago."

He hung his head as if he had failed, but how could that be? He had fought for what was right. Even at great cost to himself and much danger. She laid her hand on top of his arm.

"But he talk for himself. He go where only white man and he black, no?"

"Yes, he went where only white men were welcomed and forced his way in. He said things that made the men very angry. But I can't help but think if only I had gone into town that night once I heard rumor of what he was up to, maybe I could have kept him from running his mouth off. Or maybe I could have calmed the crowd—"

"Or maybe they put you in tree next to him?" Couldn't he see what mattered? He'd freed men, women and children—more than seventy human beings who had been held in bondage. One misused his freedom, but Chris had still done a good thing.

"Chris, are you God?" Her words got the reaction she was looking for. He lifted his eyes, wide and dazed, and shook his head vigorously.

"Vicky, no, of course not!"

"You just man, and no man can fix all things." Some things were just impossible to change—like the color of one's skin.

"But I was supposed to take care of them. It's my fault he's dead."

She stared at him, shaking her head. "You make Eze-quiel go and say those things?" She cocked her head and watched the wheels spin in his head.

"No, of course not, but I was supposed to protect him."

"His dead is not your fault." She wished she could convince him of her words.

"But Vicky, it was my action that freed him. It was my choice to let them stay in the area and work for wages for me, knowing that most stores would not sell to them or even let them set foot on their property. I set him up to be killed."

"You make him slave or you free him?" she questioned pointedly.

"I freed him, but I didn't give him the tools—"

"Freed mean you make own choice. You no fault for his death. No, you gave him respect and honor. He not know how white man treat slave? He not know how dangerous his actions?"

"Of course he knew." Chris sighed deeply and turned away, dislodging her hand. "But I did, too."

They both fell silent for a time, lost in their own thoughts. She had been enjoying this time with Chris, but now the mood had shattered. Part of her wished she hadn't voiced her questions, but another part of her wondered if he had ever shared his feelings of guilt with anyone.

How could he? He lived all by himself with only Nana Ruth, who had raised him and had seen him suf-fer. Maybe he hadn't believed her words today, but she prayed to the God he believed in that someday her words would echo in his ears and he'd see the truth. He was a good man. The best man she'd ever known.

Vicky took one last look at the beautiful meadow just an hour's ride from Chris's stables. From the riding path she had full view of the valley sloping down to the stream and his cabin, stables and other outbuildings sprinkled among the trees on his property up on the plateau way across the valley to the west. She had been only as far as the barn and the outhouse but not to the other buildings.

"Are you all right?" He mounted up next to her on Moonbeam and held the horse in check while he watched her. "Are you going to be able to get back to the house?"

It would have been a ten- or fifteen-minute ride if they could have crossed through the valley, but the stream was still flowing fast from the melting snow, and the other side was almost a sheer cliff. The route they would follow took the better part of an hour, but she didn't mind. With Chris taking his time to guide the horses, keeping them at a frustratingly slow pace, she didn't feel much discomfort. But now that she could ride this far, it was only a matter of time before her host turned her out. And occasions like today, a cool early spring day with the sun shining and the birds serenading them as they ate their lunch on the blanket, would be only a memory. When she returned to the hacienda, she would surely be turned over to Don Joaquín, and there would be no picnics with him. There would be no peaceful days outdoors. There would be no peace at all.

"Vicky, what's wrong?" Chris reached out and

tapped her shoulder gently. Ever since the day she had foolishly thrown herself at him when he had first let her ride Tesoro, he had been avoiding any physical contact with her. He no longer brushed her hair as he had the first few weeks or touched her hand except for when they prayed before meals. The only time he touched her now was when he helped her onto Tesoro—until today's picnic. She had missed the contact.

"No thing is wrong." She forced the words past her lips even though her heart seemed to break a little at the lie. "I no want leave. This is…" The English words escaped her, and she shook her head.

"Beautiful, isn't it? But I need to see to the chores, and Nana Ruth has been home all day by herself. I need to check in on her."

Vicky nodded, not correcting his assumption that she was talking about their picnic site. They traveled a few minutes in silence, both lost in their own thoughts, before he turned troubled eyes on her.

"Vicky, I'm sure you must miss your family, and I want to get you home as soon as you are able to travel…" His words hit her like a punch in her sore ribs. "But I can't figure out a way to do it."

He waited as if hoping for her to give him suggestions, but she had none. If she had any solutions she would not have offered them anyway. The longer she could stay in the safety and seclusion of his ranch, the better. Don Joaquín might give her up for dead and turn his sights elsewhere. Then she'd truly be free. If she told Chris everything, would he help free her? Would he see it as freeing another slave? But what if her freedom cost him something later on? Like his own solitude? Because someday, someone would find her there, and then he'd have to defend his innocent actions.

"You ride like you were born in the saddle, but Nana Ruth and horses don't mix too well."

"What *mix*?" He rode ahead so she couldn't watch his face, but she'd seen him search for meanings of words so often in the last few weeks she could imagine his brows pulling together as if by an invisible string. A double perpendicular line would appear in the middle. How often she wanted to run a finger down the creases and tell him not to try so hard.

"Go together. You *mix* flour and lard and salt to make your tortillas."

"Ya entiendo." As soon as she said the words, he turned to look at her with a bit of irritation crossing his handsome features.

"Vicky, what does *ya* mean in Spanish?" His tone of voice caught her off guard, and she hesitated for a moment before answering.

"Ya is now. *Ya entiendo, now* I understand."

"In English we say 'Yah' to the horses to make them move." He chuckled, and she saw his shoulders relax a bit. "You've said *ya* to me before and I wondered if you…" He didn't finish the thought, and it took a few moments to understand what he had been saying.

"No! *Ya* is now. I not talk you like horse!" She might easily confuse Don Joaquín for a beast but never Chris.

"Ya entiendo," he called over his shoulder with another chuckle.

Chapter Eleven

Five days had passed since their picnic. Each morning he made a conscious decision to travel no more than a few miles from the cabin, and he hadn't taken another picnic lunch even though the weather held. Doubtlessly Vicky must think he didn't want to spend time with her, and in some ways that was true. Each time they set back toward the cabin in the late morning, a look of disappointment crossed her face, but she never complained.

He hoped she didn't guess that his disappointment was as great as hers, but he couldn't take the risk of getting more attached to her than he already was. When he'd told her about his past, she'd looked up at him with admiration in her eyes. It made him feel ten feet tall. A dangerous thing—thinking he could somehow deserve her approval. She didn't know everything, though. She didn't know that he hadn't been able to find Nana and Jeb's son. She didn't know that he hadn't been good enough to save Jeb, the man who had been more like a father to him than his own. If she did, she would have had a very different opinion about him.

The day after the picnic, he'd suggested hunting, assuming the task would cause her to stay home, but instead she showed as much excitement as when they first took the horses on the trail. She even bagged three rabbits and a turkey using his extra rifle. He'd shot only a pheasant.

That afternoon, Nana had told him that four men came to the ranch and searched the place. She had seen them coming and had hidden, thinking they were looking for valuables or animals to steal. Oddly, they didn't try to make contact with her and left without taking anything. He'd not been able to sleep for more than an hour at a time since then.

Vicky's innocent trust in him made his fear grow each day. If he didn't manage to get her back to her home soon, something would happen to her. After all, she would not have been injured in the first place if she hadn't come running to his defense against the cougar. He couldn't afford to let her stay too much longer, but he still had to find a way to get her home without leaving Nana Ruth alone. Until he solved that problem, he was stuck in his own fear, fear of what he wanted and fear of what could happen to Vicky if he gave in to his heart's demands.

As he and Vicky approached the yard, he spotted a trio of horses tied to the corral. He slowed and silently held a hand out behind him to halt Vicky. Pulling his rifle out of the scabbard, he dismounted still in the cover of the trees and turned to hand his reins up to Vicky.

Instead, he found her standing next to him, his extra rifle drawn and ready. His blood froze in his veins, and terror stole his breath as he saw the seriousness in her eyes. She could be hurt or even killed if he was unable to defend them both. Then she titled her head to the side and studied the strange horses more closely. A smile spread across her face, and her eyes held an amusement that had been missing these last few days.

"*Es* Padre Pedro!" she announced, lowering her gun.

"The priest?" Chris studied the horses again and then noticed the third saddle had a red mantle under it with a white cross embroidered on the edges of both sides. He took a full breath as relief filled him. She was right. The last time the traveling priest had come through, Chris had noticed the blanket. But the man always traveled alone before. Had he come on his own power, or had he been attacked and his horse stolen? The men who had ambushed an old black man in the middle of the woods wouldn't think twice about killing a priest either. Maybe his relief was premature.

"*Sí.* The priest. He not bad man. Put away rifle." She sheathed her rifle and started to walk toward the yard, but Chris stopped her with a hand to her wrist. Despite the possibility of danger, he could not ignore the warmth that shot up his arm at the contact.

"Wait. Who do the other horses belong to?"

"I no know. I ask," she stated simply as she tried to step past him. He held her wrist firmly and didn't let her go, spinning her around to face him.

"We don't know if Padre Pedro is here or if someone stole his horse, Vicky. Wait here while I check." The stubborn light in her eye forced him to change tactics. He softened his tone. "Please."

"I stay and count ten, then I come and help. If not priest, Chris need more gun."

"I want you to stay here until I tell you it's safe, Vicky. I don't want you hurt." He fought the urge to caress her face.

"And the God you pray to, He not able to take care of me? Only you?" Her defiant eyes held his gaze.

"He's able to take care of both of us, but he made me a man. I'm supposed to protect you and Nana Ruth. I need…"

Before he could finish the thought, he saw movement behind Vicky, and he pulled her behind him and backed up a space. Then he saw the priest and two young men, also dressed as priests, walking along the corral and talking. No guns, no strain. The breath he released purged him of his fear, and he straightened even as Vicky caught sight of the men and broke out of his grasp. Hurrying toward them, she called out in Spanish. The relief he felt seconds before fled once again.

What if they were headed to her hacienda? She'd said there was some sort of a ceremony for her birthday on March third and the priest was expected there. They could take her home and solve the problem he'd been puzzling over the last few weeks.

So if they were God's answer to his prayers for provision of Vicky, why did he want to pull Vicky back and take off in the other direction as fast as his horse could carry them?

* * *

"Padre! Padre Pedro, how good to see you!" Vicky
called out, barely keeping her strides from turning into
a sprint. Even at the slower pace, she felt winded and
had a twinge in her ribs at the abuse of the still-sore
muscles, but that didn't stop her from wanting to get to
Padre Pedro as quickly as possible.

The astonished look on the faces of Padre Pedro and
his two companions caused her to laugh. She'd forgotten what her appearance must look like to them, in her
peasant clothing and big old sombrero. Every time the
elderly priest had come to the hacienda, Mamá made
sure that Vicky was suitably dressed for a young lady
of her station. Vicky lifted the sombrero from her head
and smiled. The old priest's eyes lit with affection.

"Maria Victoria, my child, is that you?" The older
man, with his kind eyes and his wrinkled face, had been
one of her favorite visitors to the hacienda. Not only did
everyone try to get along and eat together at the big dining table when he visited, but he would celebrate Mass
every morning just as the sun rose and every evening
at six for all who could attend. He loved to sit and tell
stories from the *Biblia*—stories almost too amazing
to be believed, such as Moses lifting his staff and God
parting the sea that cut off the Israelite people from
freedom, or Jesus raising a dead man from his grave.
They were the same stories Chris read to her, and he believed every word that came out of the big black book.

"Yes, Padre. It is I." She approached and bent down
to kiss his hand as he extended it to her. Then, after he
had raised his hand close to her forehead, lowered it to

her middle, to the right and to the left shoulders and then kissed his own finger, lifting the kiss to the sky, all the while invoking the Father, Son and Holy Spirit, he took her in his arms and hugged her close.

"And so good to see you, too, my child, although I never expected to find you here with the Americano or dressed..." He stepped back and once again studied her clothing with concern. Then he turned to the other men. *"These are new brothers who are helping me on this journey. They have been to seminary and are now becoming acquainted with the life they have been called to. Brother Sebastian and Brother Francisco."*

She nodded politely to each man, but their attention was focused on Chris, behind her. Padre Pedro continued the introductions.

"This is Maria Victoria Ruiz Torres, the daughter of Don Ruiz de la Hacienda Ruiz. It is her marriage and birthday that we were heading to officiate." He glanced at Chris as he continued in Spanish. *"And this is Señor Cristobal Samuels, formerly of the United States."*

Chris stretched out his right hand and grasped Padre Pedro's in greeting, and then he shook hands with Brother Sebastian and Brother Francisco. *"Welcome."*

"Thank you. I notified your slave woman that we were here. She didn't invite us in, but I understand why." Padre Pedro kept speaking, but Chris turned questioning eyes on her. She repeated in English to the best of her ability.

"Then they didn't come looking for you?" Chris asked.

"I do not know." Tesoro nudged her, ready to go back

to the barn, and she realized that the men were still in their traveling clothes and the sun stood straight above them. *"I think everyone needs to eat and rest. We go inside?"* She pointed to the cabin to confirm her intentions to Chris.

"Of course. Please extend my apology for not seeing to their comfort already."

Once she relayed the message, Brother Sebastian and Brother Francisco headed to the barn with Chris to see to the horses and store their belongings while Padre Pedro followed Vicky into the cabin, where Nana Ruth had already put a kettle on to boil and heated the tortillas.

As she helped Nana Ruth set the table, she explained to Padre Pedro what had happened to bring her out into the woods and away from the hacienda. His concern grew as he listened intently to her tale.

"But daughter, have you not sent word to your family? Do they know nothing of your disappearance? And what of your wedding? Are you planning to stay here for all of your life? You must know that God does not approve of living together outside the sacred bounds of matrimony."

"No, Father." She thought her cheeks must blaze like the fire from the heat they gave off at the priest's assumption. *"I was hurt and sick when I encountered Señor Samuels in the woods. He brought me here to help me heal and to protect me, but he has left my care to Nana Ruth and is living in the other cabin. He is planning on taking me back to my family but does not know how to do so with Nana Ruth. She is too disabled*

to make such a journey, but she is also too feeble to take care of the livestock or stay on her own here." Pausing to take a breath, she straightened her shoulders and found the courage to say the words she had dared say only to Chris and God up until that moment.

"And as for my marriage. I would rather I had been lost in the woods and perish than to have to marry Don Joaquín de la Vega Gomez."

"Child, do not even think like that, much less utter such words." The kind old priest reprimanded her with an understanding light in his eye. *"Don't you know that all things work together for God's children's well-being?"*

"I'm not sure, Father. I only know that every time I pray, God either isn't listening or doesn't care. Mamá says that the Indians have no soul, and I'm part Indian, so my prayers might not deserve the same attention as yours or those of others."

"My child, your mother is misguided. What she said is not true. God listens to our prayers, and He loves each of us, no matter our skin color or language we speak. That is the whole purpose of my visiting so many villas. But often His plans are very different from ours. And while it may not all make sense now, you must have faith, my daughter. God's ways are always better than ours."

Before they could finish the conversation, Chris and the other two men entered, carrying extra chairs. "Vicky, you need to sit at the table so Nana Ruth will feel comfortable." Chris motioned to the table.

"No, Master Chris," exclaimed the older woman, her head shaking from side to side. "It ain't fittin'."

"It's not fitting for you or Vicky to be standing while the men are all sitting, Nana. Now come and sit here at my table," he insisted, ushering Nana Ruth to the chair. It left the chair directly to his right for Vicky. Chris sat at the foot of the table, giving the spot he normally occupied to Padre Pedro. Both of the other men sat across from Vicky and Nana Ruth. It was a tight fit but they managed to get everyone around the table, and soon everyone was eating.

Everyone except Vicky. Not that she didn't try, but being the only person who understood both languages, she would barely interpret what one person asked when someone else would respond and she would be called on to interpret again.

Finally, everyone else finished their food and Nana Ruth stood to collect their dishes when she noticed Vicky's food still intact. "Well, honey child, are you feelin' poorly?"

"No, Nana, everything good."

Nana gave her a puzzled look and then turned to the men, giving them a glare. "You poor thing. You just take your time and don't pay no bother to them men jawing till you finish up your food. Go on, now," the older lady bossed, and Chris nodded his agreement, sitting back after having crossed his knife and fork across his plate. The Spaniards across the table may not have understood the conversation but must have picked up on the idea when they too fell silent until she had finished.

While everything might have been good, it tasted

like sawdust in her distressed state. Padre Pedro would be able to escort her back to the hacienda. As early as the next day she would be leaving this perfect ranch and the wonderful rancher who had come to be so much more than just her rescuer. But there would be no reprieve for her. The priest believed that her marriage to Don Joaquín was what God wanted for her. Pushing back from the table, she began to collect the rest of the dirty dishes.

For today she could pretend to still belong in this home and family.

Chapter Twelve

An hour later, Vicky and Padre Pedro sat on the new bench Chris had built, watching as Chris put the horses through their paces with the help of the two young men accompanying the older priest.

"I don't want to go back, Father. I know I should, but I am happy here. Señor Samuels respects me and would provide for my needs. He lets me ride the horses, and I can cook and keep the house. He needs me even more now that Nana Ruth has so much trouble with her arthritis. You know that Don Joaquín is not a good man." She turned toward the older man and grasped his forearm with both hands in desperation.

"But my daughter, Señor Samuels does not understand your language or customs or beliefs. Has he offered to marry you?" The priest's words dug deep into Vicky's heart.

"No, he has not mentioned marrying me. But I don't mind staying as his housekeeper. I could keep house,

*cook and help him with the horses... There is much to
do here, and he needs someone young to help him."*

"No, my daughter, he needs a wife to meet those
needs, and to give him sons and daughters. You were
born to be a noblewoman, not a washer-woman."

"But surely you see he would not consider me a wife
because of my skin."

"Now, what was this about your skin?" the kind
man asked.

"I have dark skin from my grandmother. No man
will want a dark-skinned woman who might give them
dark-skinned children. Worse yet, someone so handsome and white as Señor Samuels. You know that no
other woman would consider Don Joaquín, and that is
why he is still interested."

"My child, God sees the heart, not the skin, and loves
you for being His handiwork. Any man who can't see
your skin as lovely and love you for your deeply caring heart is not worthy of you. But as for Don Joaquín,
I fear he is primarily interested in your nice-sized
dowry."

"But his hacienda is almost the same size as ours."

"But he is not the astute man your father is and
your grandfather was, nor does he know how to barter well. His holdings are large, but he is a few days'
journey to the south, closer to Mejico and the powers
that want to strip the haciendas away from the Californianos and give them to the peasants." The priest
pounded a fist against the bench. "I do not pretend to
like Don Joaquín, but I also know it is your duty to your
father to obey his will for your life. You must go home

and let them know that you are alive and well and that you will follow whatever decision your father makes. I will be praying for you and for wisdom for your father. I will also go with you, my daughter, and speak to your father on your behalf. Your father has proved to be a very reasonable and often crafty man."

When she opened her mouth to protest, he shook his head and squeezed her fingers. *"Remember, child, God will always be with you. He loves you more than you can fathom."*

Chris leaned against the rough wood of the corral and watched Brother Sebastian ride a horse like it were about to eat him for dinner. As the priest-in-training took another turn around the corral, Chris grimaced at the stiff posture and chuckled at the way the man startled with every movement. Brother Francisco, however, showed talent and experience with handling the horses. Keeping half an eye on the two men in the corral, he snuck another glance at Vicky and the older priest sitting in the shade on Vicky's bench.

It had been pure foolishness that had caused him to build it, all the while thinking that Vicky could sit on the bench with her mending or knitting and watch him working with the horses without having to sit out in the baking hot sun in the middle of the summer. This was foolish because he'd known she'd be gone well before the summer came. Once she left with the priests, the bench would be just one more reminder of her. Would she remember him and his ranch with the same affection he had for her? At least he knew she would be safe and protected as the wife of a powerful don.

Surely she exaggerated her dislike for her intended. After all, what father would knowingly let his daughter marry a fiend? No, her father must want what was best for her—certainly more than Chris could ever offer.

It was laughable that he'd even consider offering for her hand. Not that he wouldn't cherish her for the rest of his days if she could be his, but what father would marry her off to a poor stranger when he had hacienda owners vying for her hand?

It was good that the priest had come and would be able to take her safely to the hacienda before he did anything truly foolish like believe he could keep her safe.

But the thought of letting her go with the older man and two young unknown men didn't sit well, either. What if they were attacked on their way? Would the men even know how to defend themselves or her? Would killing another man in self-defense somehow go against the vows they had pledged to become priests?

Of the four, Vicky might be the only one to fight, and she would fight. He'd seen her take out the cougar and had no doubt she would do it again if called to do so. Could he sit in his own cabin wondering if they had made it safely back to her father? But what choice did he have? Nana Ruth couldn't ride a horse, much less be bumped along on the path in an old wagon, even if they had one to use.

After all his years of working with horses, he knew he should be keeping his focus on Brother Sebastian because Chris's horses could sense his unease. But by the time he'd had the thought, it was too late. One minute the horse was prancing around with Brother Sebastian finally looking like he had settled into the saddle, and then the next minute, Moonbeam bucked and threw the inexperienced rider to the ground. Chris rushed over, putting his own body between the young man and the upset horse. Moonbeam pranced away as if saying, "That's what you get for putting a greenhorn on my back."

Vicky and the elder priest must have heard the commotion because by the time Brother Francisco had corralled Moonbeam so he couldn't do any more damage, Vicky deftly climbed over the fence. Chris started assessing Brother Sebastian for injury. Thankfully, he seemed to have only hurt his left ankle. No thanks to Chris. Once again, someone he should have been keeping safe was hurting. He shouldn't have been pining over Vicky and not paying attention to what Moonbeam was doing.

The two younger men and Vicky spoke Spanish so quickly that Chris stood helplessly to one side, picking up only a word or so here and there. The way Vicky crouched next to the man, slipped off his boot and then gently prodded his ankle gave the impression she had done some doctoring in the past. Apparently the woman was going to continue to impress and amaze him at every turn.

Once Vicky finished with her examination of the swelling leg, Chris gave her a hand up.

"Hermano Sebastian no break leg. Only make big

like coconut." Her assessment matched his but was worded in a much more endearing way.

"You mean it is swelling." He held his hands a few inches apart and then moved them further apart to demonstrate his meaning.

"*Sí*, swelling." She nodded her approval of his description. "Need to put up and put cold."

"We could bring water from the creek. It comes from the melting snow. It should be plenty cold."

Her nod and look of gratitude made him feel ten feet tall. He turned to get away before he said something he shouldn't.

"Chris? You help take back to cabin?" she questioned when he started to mount up on Moonbeam, ready to head out for cold water.

"Sure. Sorry." He dismounted and retraced his steps, fighting to keep his attention firmly on helping the hurt young priest.

Vicky said something to Brother Francisco, and the other young man drew closer, as well. Between Chris and Brother Francisco, they were able to support Brother Sebastian so that he could limp on his good leg without putting any weight on the injured one. Once in the cabin, Chris explained what had happened to Nana Ruth, and she set to helping them with the man while Chris left to fetch the water. When he returned he found the older priest standing outside the cabin, deep in conversation with Brother Francisco. Had he and Vicky misdiagnosed the injury?

"Naw, he got a real bad sprain, but it ain't broke," Nana Ruth reassured him as they wrapped the man's leg in cold, wet towels. "You know, your Vicky there is a good nurse. Yes, sir, that girl be a right smart one. She knew just what to do. Man could do a lot worse than jumpin' the broom with someone smart and kind like your Miss Vicky."

"She's not *my* Vicky," he declared. But he couldn't deny that a part of him could suddenly see their lives intertwined. She would be a wonderful helpmate. And he knew without a doubt she'd make a wonderful mother someday. Gentle and kind, compassionate and affectionate.

But he wasn't in the position to make a good husband to any woman, especially a woman who had been born into the finest things life had to offer. She was the hacienda's princess. She deserved to marry a man who could give her the best in life. Here on his ranch, there was no social life, and no one would be coming to call for tea or inviting them over for a meal.

No, Miss Maria Victoria Ruiz Torres had been born into Spanish nobility and deserved to take her place with the nobles ruling their corner of the world.

Nana Ruth had commented that Vicky had come to them for a reason. Nana had expected that reason to be to marry Chris, but he knew better. Surely God had sent her to his home to learn about the Bible. Padre Pedro could only share snatches of it for short spans of time. Even if the priest had wanted to teach each family more, his responsibility was too large and widespread to really do justice to his parish ranging over three hundred miles in diameter.

Of course God brought her into his life so he could

share the Bible with her, but Chris couldn't help wishing it was for a whole lot more. If only he could marry Vicky as Nana had suggested. But her father would laugh in his face, a stranger and foreigner with only a small cabin in the middle of the woods and no way to protect his wife and family, asking for the hand of the man's daughter. Still, if God had allowed it, marriage to her would have been amazing.

They enjoyed so many of the same things. They could take rides on the ranch and share the woods, hunt together… Married to him, she wouldn't have to give up all those things that she loved to do.

Except that he would always be terrified that something would happen to her and he wouldn't be able to protect her.

Chapter Thirteen

"Señorita Victoria," Padre Pedro started in Spanish after they had cleared the dinner dishes that night. *"We need to talk about your return home."*

She had guessed as much. Padre Pedro and Hermano Francisco had been exchanging looks ever since Hermano Sebastian's fall. If she were being truly honest, she had been a little relieved when Hermano Sebastian had been thrown. Feeling guilty, she hoped that his recuperation would take more than a week. If it did, then there would be no way to make it home on time for her party and wedding. Although, if everyone thought she was dead, and they must have come up with that assumption by now or they would have come looking for her, then maybe she would be off the hook with Don Joaquín. Maybe he had already started to court some other poor girl.

Padre Pedro had said that everything would work out. Could this be the first time that God was finally paying attention to her prayers? Had He let Hermano Sebastian fall from the horse so she would miss the ceremony?

"I understand that it will be impossible for Brother Sebastian to travel like he is, so we must wait. It is not a hardship. As I shared with you earlier..."

The kind elderly man held out his hand to stop the onslaught of her words. *"Hush, my daughter. There will be no delay if we can help it. Your family must be beside themselves with grief and worry. They deserve to know that you are alive and well."*

She nodded at the truth in his statement.

"We must leave the day after tomorrow to give you time to arrive and prepare for the ceremony."

"Must we still have a ceremony, Padre?" Vicky asked, unable to hide her desperation.

"God did not give you the spirit of fear, my daughter. He has a purpose in all of this." His gentle eyes held her gaze until she nodded in understanding. There would be no salvation from this. She would be forced to go home and face her father's wrath, her mother's disillusionment and her suitor's vulgar behavior, and then her own father would hand her over to the fiend. *"Trust God, mi' ja."* The priest's term of endearment calmed her racing thoughts. *"For we do not know exactly what the Almighty has in store for you, Princesa. We only know that it is the best for you."*

Chris froze when he heard the last of the priest's words. He hadn't understood much of the Spanish, but one word stood out. *Princess.* Of course they would call her that. He would have, too, if he had the right.

She had the grace and beauty of a princess and was the only daughter of the owner of a large hacienda, a nobleman by birth, who reigned his hacienda like the feudal lords of yesteryear had back in the old country. She belonged back on her hacienda. No matter if Chris's heart agreed or not.

"Chris," Vicky called out, and his feet took him to her side even as his head told him to go in the opposite direction. The less he interacted with her before she left, the easier it would be to say goodbye when the time came. Too bad his heart didn't seem interested in paying any attention to his head.

"Yes, Vicky?" He stood to her side, the priest studying him closely without giving away his thoughts.

"Padre Pedro want talk with you." She glanced at the priest and bit her lip.

"*Sí*, Padre?" Chris forced his eyes to stay on the older gentleman, who turned to Vicky and quickly said something to her in Spanish.

"He say we need go to hacienda day after tomorrow."

A pain rent his heart in two, but he kept his face impassive and nodded.

"Padre say Brother Sebastian no go on horse with leg like coconut."

"No, you're right, he can't ride a horse with his leg so swollen." Chris forced his voice to sound calm and reasonable. How he wished there were other reasons to keep her on the ranch. But it would all end the same. Sooner or later she'd have to leave, and if she didn't leave soon, something would happen to her on his watch. Just like his distraction had let Moonbeam buck the young priest.

"Padre ask if Brother Sebastian stay while leg get better. Hermano Francisco stay to take care of him. Padre Pedro come back after wedding." She swallowed hard after the word but continued. "He come back next week."

"They are both welcome to stay here as long as they need. But you can't go all the way to the hacienda with only Padre Pedro to keep you safe, Vicky. If Brother Francisco is willing to take care of the horses and see to supplying water and wood for Nana while we're gone, I'll go with you." This was for the best. He could see her safely delivered to her home.

Padre Pedro again leaned closer to Vicky and said something to her. His eyes closely studied Chris. Did the priest believe that Vicky had been respected during her convalescence, or did he think Chris had somehow compromised her? And if the priest doubted, what would he say to her parents? What repercussions would Vicky face due to the circumstances?

"Padre say you come with." She lowered her gaze to the ground but not before Chris caught the fear and sadness in their dark depths.

"What is wrong, Vicky?"

"I no want marry Don Joaquín de la Vega. Very bad man."

"Your father's making you marry Joaquín?" Even the taste of the words on his tongue was vile, bitter. Something clicked in Chris's mind as he thought about the name for a moment, and his stomach clenched. "Wait,

Don Joaquín de la Vega from the Vega Hacienda?" The man had approached his farm two years before. He claimed he wanted to buy Chris's stock. Chris had refused to sell him any of his own stock after seeing how mistreated the man's horse was. After their heated meeting, the man indicated that Chris should leave Alta California or face the consequences.

"*Sí*, he make me marry Joaquín." Her eyes were so large and innocent.

His throat closed around a lump that wouldn't budge. How could he take her home knowing that she faced a forced marriage? Maybe he had judged too harshly the other man at their first meeting, but the look in her eyes said otherwise. What father would be capable of marrying off his daughter to a man who caused her terror?

What if he offered for her hand, as well? The idea ran through his mind, making his pulse beat fast and his head spin with excitement, but he discarded it as quickly as it came. The Spanish nobility didn't look too kindly on marrying outside their elite group. Was the engagement already confirmed? If so, why wasn't Don Joaquín scouring the woods until he found Vicky? If Chris had been her intended, only death would keep him from finding her if she had been lost to him.

"Is there anything I can do?" he asked, finally forcing words past the emotions clogging his throat. He took her hands in his, unable to stop himself. Wanting to offer so much more and yet afraid this would end as every other time he had tried to help protect someone.

"Come with me and Padre Pedro. *Mi papá* want to

say thank-you for keep me at your house. He want to give you gift."

"Or cut off my head for not bringing you back sooner," Chris quipped, not sure he fully trusted her father or the idea of turning her over to her own family if they had caused her this much misery. But what other option did he have? He knew that God expected children to honor their parents, but to what end? This seemed extreme. Could he take her all the way only to hand her over to a fiend?

"No, no cut off you head." Vicky reached up as if to touch his face, then shook her head as she let her hand fall to her side. "He want say thank-you for save me. Padre Pedro talk with him. Tell him you good man who take good care of me. Please, Chris," she begged, a desperate tone in her voice. He couldn't have turned away from her even if Comet and Tesoro had both been tied to his legs and pulled in the opposite direction. "I no want go alone," she whispered, and she looked up at him with tears in her eyes and fear so palpable it froze him there.

"I'll go with you, Vicky. Don't cry. It'll all work out." Before he could second-guess his actions, he pulled her close, hugging her to his chest. For a minute he believed he could protect her from anything if only she could stay sheltered in his arms.

The priest cleared his throat, and Chris drew back without releasing Vicky. Padre Pedro nodded, a half smile on his lined face, and slipped away from them with a pat on Chris's shoulder as he passed. Was that his approval? If he would speak to Vicky's father, would he be willing to endorse Chris as a husband for Vicky?

"Thank you, Chris. I know you no want to leave Nana or you horses, but I no want go alone."

Pulling her just a little closer, he leaned his chin against her head. "I don't want you to go alone either." Or ever be alone again. But the last part he kept to himself. Even though he realized that for the first time in a very long time, he didn't want to be alone either.

Chapter Fourteen

Nana Ruth held Vicky close, her arms warm and comforting as Vicky stood at the threshold of the cabin and said goodbye one more time. Hard to believe it had been barely six weeks ago that Chris had carried her unconscious into this cabin for the first time. Now it felt like home. The place where she belonged.

"Go with God, honey child. I'll be prayin' for ya to come back with Master Chris. Good Lord knows that man be needin' a good wife."

"I pray come back, too." She breathed deep and forced herself to act as if she wasn't terrified of what waited for her on the other end of her journey

"God knows what He be about. You just rest in that promise and let Master Chris take care of ya."

How good that sounded, to let Chris take care of her. She trusted him with her life. If only he would marry her instead of Don Joaquín. But ever the gentleman, Chris had held her so tenderly. Even after Padre Pedro left them alone to sort out the trip, Chris had stood star ing down at her eyes. Twice his gaze had strayed to her lips, and her heartbeat had sped up with anticipation. But then he stepped back and turned away. He hadn't touched her since. Would he have stolen a kiss if she had not already been betrothed to another man?

The funny sensations stirring in her chest and setting butterflies to flight in her stomach were new to her. She remembered being about six when one of Magda's girls had talked about the excitement she felt when her intended had started to come courting. At the time, Vicky listened with some intrigue but never believed she'd experience anything remotely similar. Loving a boy had been as foreign an idea as meeting an Americano in the woods and saving his life. Now she'd experienced both.

"It's time to go, Vicky." Chris held Tesoro's and Comet's reins in his left hand, offering his right to help her climb down the steps. He wore his hat pulled down, its shadow hiding his face. Padre Pedro had already mounted up, waiting a few paces away from them as if giving privacy for their last words.

Chris dropped the reins, stepped closer to her and lifted her at the waist. He set her in the saddle, his hands lingering longer than necessary for her to find her balance. He made a show of checking the cinches and fiddling with the stirrups and her boots. Had they not taken dozens of rides together, she might have thought he doubted her ability to ride a horse. But she knew his extra attention was his gentle way of showing concern for her. With a curt nod, he handed the reins to her, mounted up on Comet and headed out.

"Goodbye, Vicky. Don't be forgettn' 'bout us, now. You come back soon, ya hear?" Nana Ruth called out from the door.

"Goodbye, Nana Ruth. I come back if God will." Oh, how she hoped it would be God's will. But as she drank in her last glimpse of the cabin and the neat yard, sturdy barn and corral, something fractured in her chest and her breath caught.

She'd always been the brave girl, tagging along with her older brother and his best friend, having to pretend to be stronger and more courageous than she really was in order to play with them. She wished she could pretend as well today. The newly built bench Chris had said he'd made for her called out to her. She had dreamed of sitting there, her knitting at hand, watching Chris work with the horses as the seasons passed. How could she leave this place? The horses in the corral nickered their farewells. She tasted the salt of her tears she could no longer hold back.

The sun stood high in the sky, peeking between the heavy evergreens. Even after six years, Chris still found the gigantic redwood trees awe-inspiring most days, but as they followed the path out to the main road, he didn't even notice them. No, his eyes kept straying from scanning the woods for danger to land back on Vicky as she rode a few paces in front of him. The elderly priest had taken the lead, an unspoken agreement between the two men to keep Vicky in between them on their travels.

How unlike any of their other rides. Vicky didn't sit comfortably in the saddle, exclaiming over the wildlife or plants that they passed by, animatedly chatting with him, learning the English words for everything. Instead, she sat rigidly, as if afraid to relax. Since leaving the yard, she hadn't made eye contact, even though she glanced quickly over her shoulder as if checking to see that he still followed.

When they arrived at the main road, Padre Pedro stopped and spoke in quiet tones with Vicky, and then they both dismounted. Chris hopped off Comet and barely caught Vicky as she stumbled. "Careful." He kept his arm around her waist as she took her first tentative steps. "Are your ribs hurting?" he asked.

"No, I not hurt," she insisted even as she leaned closer to him. He felt her breathing catch, and then as she took a few more steps, it eased a bit. He'd have to keep an eye on her for the rest of the trip. He grabbed a saddlebag with their lunch of tortillas, rabbit meat, salsa and some greens that she had found in the woods the week before, all rolled together and fried so it would stay together. She called them flautas or "flutes," and they weren't nearly as messy to eat as the tortillas.

Padre Pedro had already set a blanket out on the ground. As they approached he watched Chris and Vicky with a curious glint in his eyes, and then he held out a hand and helped Vicky sit on the ground. He took the bag from Chris, said a blessing over the food and then parceled it out. They ate, much as they had ridden all morning, in silence, each face drawn and showing concern.

"Where will we stay tonight?" Chris asked Vicky

once they had finished lunch. Padre Pedro had walked into the woods, but Chris suspected he hadn't gone far.

"We get hacienda in one or two hour, say Padre Pedro." The actual hacienda was vast enough that it took over two days to travel from one end to the other, but once they were on Ruiz land, it was just a matter of time before they encountered Ruiz men. Would they accuse him of having kidnapped Vicky or worse? And yet, even if they attempted to string him up, he would willingly give himself up rather than let Vicky face trouble on her own.

"On hacienda *mi abuelito*, *papá de mi papá*, make little houses. Cabanas? For *vaqueros*."

"Little cabins for the cowboys?" Chris clarified.

"*Sí*, for when they stay with *vacas*, cows." Vicky's face lit with excitement. She smiled for the first time the entire day as she continued. "When Berto take to hunt, we sleep in cabin. When I look for Papá—" her face clouded slightly "—I no go back to house but stay in cabin for look for Papá, but snow come and I stay two days in cabin."

"So you stayed in a cabin for two days before you came to my house?"

"*Sí.*"

"So why didn't they find you? Wouldn't they have searched for you when you didn't show up that night?" Chris watched her face for any clues as to what had happened.

"I no know." She shrugged, but he saw the masked pain in her eyes. "I tell José Luis I go with *mi papá* to meeting. Maybe he no look because think I with Papá."

"Well, we'll find out soon. If we stay at the cabin tonight, we should arrive at the main house tomorrow." He tried to smile despite the dread in his own heart weighing him down.

She missed her family and needed to be back with them. Tomorrow would be soon enough. Then he could turn around and head back to his cabin, out in the woods away from "civilization." Unlike other times, the thought of his beautiful home and the solitude he traveled halfway around the world to find didn't soothe his mind or bring him comfort.

She bit her lip and frowned. "You stay for fiesta?" Her words were softly spoken, as if she were almost afraid to voice them.

"I'm sorry, what did you say?" He crouched closer. The breeze feathered a strand of her long dark hair that had rebelled against its pins. It danced across his face. He reached up and tucked it back behind her ear, savoring the silky feel of it.

"You stay for fiesta. My birthday?" She didn't look up at his touch, but she didn't back away either.

"I don't know if your family will want me to stay. I haven't been invited," he stated simply.

"I invite you. My party. You stay," she stated emphatically, her hand slipping around his lower arm. "Please. I no want go home, but—" she paused and he waited for her words "—if I go, I want you be at party. I want dance at party with Chris. I want say thank-you for save me."

"I wouldn't have had to save you had you not killed

the cougar and gotten injured. It was my fault that I wasn't paying enough attention to my surroundings."

She shook her head fiercely and argued. "You not see puma. It want eat you for lunch. I no let puma eat any man."

"No, you didn't let the puma eat me for lunch. Thank you. I owe you my life, Vicky." He sat back and pressed his hands to the ground to fight off the urge to push her sombrero off her head and sample her beautiful lips.

A moment later—just in time—Padre Pedro returned. It should have been a relief to no longer be alone with his temptation, but the feeling that he might never have another opportunity to kiss her ate a hole in his chest bigger than any cougar's claws could ever rip open. He might never see her again after the following day, but he would do anything and everything he could to help her. If that meant staying a day or two extra to go to her birthday party, it was a small price to pay. Especially if it meant he had an opportunity to hold her in his arms once again, even under the guise of dancing in a crowded room.

"I will stay for your birthday as long as Padre Pedro thinks that Brother Sebastian and Brother Francisco are all right staying a few more days at my cabin."

"I ask him now, but I know he say yes." She smiled at him as if he had promised her the moon and stars, not just to stay for her party. "Brother Sebastian no walk for six or seven days," she added as if still trying to convince him.

Then it dawned on him. Vicky seemed to think that her birthday would also be her wedding day. Would she be married before the dancing? Surely that would be the logical way to do things.

"But I would ask just one thing, Vicky."

"What you ask?" she questioned when the silence dragged out.

"Do not ask me to stay if you get married before your birthday party."

"I trust God no marry Joaquín. I not animal to give to animal."

"No, you are no animal nor should anyone treat you like one. We will pray that God will work everything out."

The closer they rode to the hacienda, the more he prayed that God would give him a solution and a way to approach Don Ruiz. The wad of bills he had in his saddlebag from the sale of his father's plantation gave him some hope. In a moment of desperation, he had dug it up from its hiding place and brought it along. Maybe he could match whatever bride's price her intended had agreed to with her father... But he didn't even know if that was their custom or not. While Mexico outlawed slavery, the act of wedding an unwilling lady to a man twice her age if not more was just as wrong.

Chapter Fifteen

"There is the cabin," Vicky called out as they entered a clearing. She sounded out of breath even though they had slowed their pace in the last few hours to just short of a crawl.

Sure enough, up ahead, a small, weathered structure squatted in the late afternoon sun. It looked like a stiff breeze might knock it over. The size of it made his cabin look like a mansion. Even with the small roofed area off to the side of the main shack, used for stabling the horses, it would be a tight fit for all three of them.

Vicky took her time climbing down, and her disjointed movements caught his attention. Something was wrong. He hurried over to her side just as her legs buckled. "Vicky!" He caught her before she hit the ground.

"I no feel legs," she whispered, already trying to stand on her own power. "Hard to take air."

"You're having trouble breathing?" Panic seized his heart, and he lifted her into his arms as he had that first day.

"No trouble. It hurt. Ribs still not like ride so long."

In the haze of fear, it took a minute to decipher her meaning. "Oh, your ribs don't like the long ride?"

"*Sí*, rib no like long ride."

"So let's get you inside and lying down." Padre Pedro signaled to the cabin, and Chris nodded in agreement. After the priest had opened the door and checked inside, Chris carried Vicky in. Musty air met them at the door. As soon as he could get Vicky settled, he'd see to airing out the cramped room containing only two cots and a small, rough table. "Can you ask Padre Pedro to bring in my bedroll? The bed is covered in dust."

"I no *bebe*, Chris. I stand."

"No, you might not be a baby, but I'll hold you until he comes back. Just ask the priest to bring in my bedroll. I've brought you this far, I don't want to have to explain to your family how you rode all the way to the hacienda and got sick again on their lands."

She grumbled something in Spanish before turning and talking to the priest. Chris could only guess what else she might have said, but setting her down on something fairly clean was his biggest concern for the moment. Padre Pedro returned a few minutes later, having brought the bedroll attached to Vicky's saddle. As Chris set her down, she cried out in pain. Tears cascaded down her ashen cheeks as she tried to straighten her legs. Why hadn't she told him her legs had been cramping in the saddle?

Chris signaled the priest, and in tandem they each slipped off one of her boots. "I'm going to help you move your leg, Vicky. It might hurt at first, but it will feel better in a minute," he promised. He covered her legs with the edge of the blanket he'd set her on, even though she wore her peasant pants. Grasping her right leg gently, he started to rub her foot and then slowly flex it at the ankle. Her gasp of breath and the trail of tears down her face caused his stomach to clench, and he wished he could endure the pain for her.

How brave she had been. Thrust in a situation where she understood very little of what was being said around her, she had insisted on learning the language and helping instead of being waited on hand and foot. She didn't complain about the food or his humble home but looked for ways to help. So much that Chris had begun to see how she fit into his life... Even now, with pain so strong she lost all color and turned a pale gray, she let him manipulate her foot without question. She trusted him. But did he deserve her trust? After all, she wouldn't be in so much pain if he had been doing his job and paying attention to her.

Padre Pedro took up her left leg. Once they had worked with her feet for a few minutes, he moved to her calf. Finally she was able to bend her legs on her own power without shuddering with the agony.

"I have to go see to the horses and look for some wood for the fire, Vicky. Do you think you'll be all right with Padre Pedro for a little while?" He fought to keep from catching her up in his arms against his chest and pressing kisses to her face until the pain subsided completely.

Yes, outside was the best place for him to be for a while.

* * *

Three hours later, the sun was setting as Chris and Padre Pedro headed out to the lean-to where they had stowed their bedrolls. As much as it bothered him to see the elder man lie down on the hard-packed earth instead of the cot indoors, he knew it was better that they give Vicky her privacy. Soon the priest's steady breathing told him the older man was resting, but Chris couldn't settle. He'd tossed and turned, as much from the cold, uncomfortable floor and the stench of animals housed there in the past as from his mind refusing to accept that in a few days he'd be heading back home without Vicky at his side and she'd be marrying Don de la Vega.

Strange that only two months ago he'd never imagined ever wanting to share his homestead with anyone other than Nana Ruth. Now he found himself second-guessing that. But as soon as a spark of hope would light in his heart about somehow convincing Vicky to come back with him, he'd remember she had already been promised to another who could give her all Chris didn't have.

And if her betrothal wasn't enough of a deterrent, an angry voice whispered all of his failings, starting with Ezequiel's death and the mess he'd made with the plantation and then Jeb. No, Vicky was much safer far away from his ranch.

"Please, Father God, let me see her home safely. She deserves to be married to someone wonderful. She deserves to be happy and loved. Help me to do my job and get her home and then give me the strength to walk away."

He must have just started to drift off when the first scream from the cabin broke the dark night. Instantly he came fully awake and started toward the door, a few steps ahead of the priest, who moved surprisingly quickly for a man who had passed sixty. He burst into the cabin only to find Vicky alone, thrashing around on the cot.

"Vicky. Vicky, sweetheart." He stopped just short of touching her, unsure if his contact would calm her or agitate her even more. "It's all right. You're safe." He crooned other words, words that poured out of his heart. Slowly she calmed.

Padre Pedro spoke in Spanish in the same low tone and soothing cadence. Her eyes fluttered open, and she gaped at them standing by her bed. "Why you here? Why you stand and look at me?" She turned her gaze on the priest, and he quietly spoke to her again, this time resting his hand on her shoulder and helping her to settle back down.

Chris had never been one for jealousy, so the feelings stirring in his chest took a few minutes to sort out. Only after he had laid his head back down on the saddle he was using for a pillow did he figure it all out. He'd been jealous of the priest's ability to soothe Vicky while Chris had to return outside. He knew it was to protect her reputation, but he hated feeling so useless when all he wanted to do was to hold her close and help her get through the night without any more nightmares.

His frustration only grew as the night dragged on and her nightmares continued. By the time the sun had started to climb over the ridge to the east of them, he knew no one had gotten more than an hour or two of sleep all night. Staying outside and calling through the rough logs and poorly chinked walls was worse than any flaying anyone could have meted out on him. He would have preferred to take some kind of physical punishment instead of having to listen to the terror lacing Vicky's cries.

At first he dismissed her dreams as the product of the long ride, but as the night wore on, he kept hearing the words *no Joaquín* just as she had first called out in her sleep as she battled the fever and delirium after her arrival at the ranch.

By the morning he was beside himself. How could he possibly turn her over to a father who considered giving her away in marriage to someone who terrorized her so? And yet what could he do? He didn't even speak the language, much less understand the customs. And he hadn't been able to take care of a single one of the people God had put in his care yet. He couldn't risk her. Because as he fought with his thoughts, one thing became crystal clear. He loved Vicky. If something happened to her…the idea was unbearable beyond words.

Slowly, the darkness in the cabin gave way to grayish light. The awful night had passed, finally. Terror gripped her heart at the idea of even closing her eyes. Every time she did, Don Joaquín's face appeared in her mind, wearing his usual sneer as he puffed on his cigar and knocked back shots of some foul-smelling drink. During the night, she dreamed that he had transformed from man to beast, a puma waiting to devour her. He'd come at her, claws outstretched, ready to kill her when Chris would step in the way, defending her but getting clawed instead.

When she woke from the first dream, Chris had stood there, just out of reach, his eyes sad and full of… something—she'd almost convinced herself it was longing to hold her, but he didn't reach out, didn't so much as touch her shoulder. Not like Padre Pedro did, placing a reassuring hand to her shoulder.

After the first time, Chris stayed outside. She could hear his voice through the cabin's decrepit walls, but he didn't come back in. Instead, he left Padre Pedro to take care of her. He might have done so to protect her reputation, but her battered heart felt rejected.

If only she could be heading home to marry Chris. She'd dream of happily-ever-after, of contented picnics, of sitting on the bench in the yard and watching him work his wonders with his horses… She'd wake to the sight of his dear face. But dreaming would only make her reality that much harsher. Chris could never come to love her, a dark-skinned Indian, and dreaming of it only made things worse.

Scrounging up what little faith and courage she still possessed, she forced herself to get up and get ready for the day.

Chapter Sixteen

"Well, it's time to go, Vicky." Chris had stalled all he could, taking his time finding firewood and then heating up coffee and tortillas with salsa and beans. Then they had taken a long walk to get the circulation going in her legs, but finally there was nothing else to keep them from the last segment of this journey. He'd never dreaded anything more.

She nodded without looking him in the eye and then quietly mounted up. Padre Pedro spent most of the morning reading an old, frayed book. Before breakfast, they'd read from Chris's Bible with Vicky trying to translate the story as they went for the priest.

After watching Vicky carefully, Chris saw no evidence of her being uncomfortable this morning. He'd be stopping them every half hour or so and making sure she took time to walk, holding her arm tucked around his as they strolled. The last thing he wanted was to have her suffer another bout of those cramps today. Especially if it happened in front of her family.

He distracted himself from the reality of his destination by admiring the landscape around them. The Hacienda Ruiz had some of the best lands for cattle in the area. Not only had they been blessed with the land, but they had maintained it well, the shack from the night before notwithstanding. Although, Chris knew that many of the huts the slaves back home lived in were no better and sometimes even worse for wear.

If only they had met back in South Carolina. He would have known how to court Vicky and approach her father for her hand. How could he do it now, with her already promised to another? And yet, he knew after hearing her terror last night he couldn't walk away without trying to give her another option. She might not love him, but surely she didn't fear him like she did Don Joaquín.

"So, Vicky, how do I greet your father?"

"Mi papá?"

"Yes, how do I say 'nice to meet you' in Spanish?" he prompted, and he waited as she seemed surprised by his request.

"Chris say, *'Mucho gusto,* Don Ruiz.'" She sat up straight and waited, watching him with a little gleam in her eye. He did the best he could at repeating the sounds and trying to remember what words went in which order.

The morning sped by too quickly. The priest often corrected his mispronunciations and chuckled at his mangled Spanish, commenting from time to time to Vicky, saying something that made her cheeks glow.

"What did he say?" Chris finally asked.

"He say I good teacher but job easy when student like teacher."

"He's right. You're a good teacher, Vicky. I should have asked you for lessons instead of being content to teach you English. You're a good student. Much better than I am."

"I have good teacher and I like teacher." Her blush darkened once she said the words, and they warmed something in Chris's chest. They had become friends, if nothing else, during her stay. He knew that *like* was too mild a word for the feelings he had developed for the amazing woman who had crashed into his quiet world, disguised as a peasant boy, saving his very life from a cougar. Only God could have orchestrated something so convoluted. But even as he could see God's hand at work, he didn't understand the point.

Why bring a woman into his life to steal his heart and give him a longing for things that could never be? Why give him a glimpse of what love could look like only to rip it all away and expect Chris to be the gentleman and face the biggest test of his faith by taking her back to where she belonged?

Abraham's trip up the mountain with young Isaac couldn't have been much more heartbreaking than the feelings coursing through Chris's heart as the sun reached its zenith. He hadn't even read that story with Vicky. He should have. Truth was, he hadn't gotten through the Gospels with her. There were too many new things to explain to her. If only they had more time. Temptation to turn the horses around and head for the hills, literally, caught him so hard he could hardly swallow.

"Let's take a break," he announced. *"Time to have some lunch."* He tried his new Spanish and got a nod from Vicky and a chuckle from Padre Pedro. If only they knew more of each other's language, they might have become fast friends.

Lunch flew too quickly, and once again they were back in the saddle. He'd noticed that Vicky's movements were slower at lunch, and even though she claimed she was fine, he still feared something was wrong.

They'd been riding in silence for less than twenty minutes when she almost slipped out of the saddle. He called out to Padre Pedro even as he pulled up alongside her within seconds to see that she had a sleepy look on her face. "You're too tired to be riding."

"House is still two hours," Vicky mumbled, and he couldn't help chuckling at her sleepy determination.

"And you won't get there at all if you fall off Tesoro." He debated his next step. As much as he wanted to keep her with him as long as possible, they were too close to try to stay another night on hacienda land without arriving to the main house. They just had to keep going. "Come here." He held out his arms, unsure if she would let him carry her, but not seeing any other option unless they stopped completely and waited for her to take a nap. It was a cool day, and there didn't seem to be any structures around that she could have used for shelter.

"I no *bebe*," she insisted, but something in her eyes made him wonder if she didn't long to be in his arms as much as he longed to have her there. Surely that was just wishful thinking on his part.

"No, but you do need to rest. I will hold you, and you

can sleep. I promise to keep you safe," he pledged, wishing he could promise the same for a lifetime instead of just a few hours in the saddle. He cocked his head and sent a smile that had convinced Nana Ruth more than once to give him a snack before dinner.

Nodding, she handed Tesoro's reins to him and then lifted her arms so he could catch her around her waist. Once the transfer was done, he settled her close to his heart, wishing she could stay there forever. After all, the muscled organ in his chest would continue to beat long after he left her at the hacienda. But his heart, the part that loved, she'd be keeping with her whether she knew it or not.

"Thank you, Chris." She curled up even closer, her breath tickling the bottom of his chin.

He continued heading east when everything in him cried to head west. "Go ahead and rest, Vicky. You need to be bright and chipper when we get you home. Can you imagine how excited everyone is going to be when you arrive?"

"Hmm." She nodded again. He transferred the reins to his left hand, which supported her back. Using his right hand, he caught a tendril of hair that caressed her cheek when it escaped her sombrero. He played with its silkiness for a moment before pushing it back up under the rim of her sombrero. Her skin was soft and smooth as he ran his thumb down her cheek. He held his breath even as he cupped his right hand on her shoulder and pulled her against his chest. Would his familiarity be offensive to her? As if sensing his concern, she smiled slightly against his collarbone and snuggled even closer.

Within minutes, her even breathing told him she had fallen asleep. He tried keeping half an eye on the trail, but Comet and Tesoro were content to follow Padre Pedro's horse. Chris found himself paying more attention to the beauty in his arms. After all, in a few days, he'd be able to look his heart's content at the fields when he left Vicky. Today he wanted to memorize the feel of her breath against his neck and her warmth in his arms. He tightened his arm around her, hoping that she was warm enough.

Close to an hour later, movement to the south caught his attention at the same time as Padre Pedro pointed in that direction. The field, unlike so many of the others they had passed, had a herd of cattle and men patrolling the edges. Even as he watched, one of the men on horseback, sporting a sombrero and a serape similar to Vicky's, pointed to them. He started toward them, his rifle coming into view although he was still well out of range.

"Vicky, wake up. There are cowboys, *vaqueros*, coming." He couldn't reach his rifle without jostling her, and he would struggle to sight down much less shoot it with her in his arms, but he didn't want to walk into a situation without being able to defend them. He didn't want to have the cowboy start shooting and hit Vicky either. There was no telling what he might do if that happened.

"Vicky," he tried again, and this time she shifted but didn't wake. Instead she said something he didn't quite catch.

Stealing a glance down at her beautiful face, he knew

these were the last few minutes he'd ever have to be close to her. The thought nearly killed him right there on the spot.

"*Te quiero*, Chris." She sighed and turned her face closer to his chest. *"Te amo."*

What? What had she just said? Had she just said *I love you*? *This* was the moment when she would choose to utter those words? When he couldn't do a single thing about it?

She was asleep. It didn't mean anything. She was probably dreaming of someone else. Probably.

He wished she would open her eyes and repeat those words to him while fully awake. He might actually believe her if she did that. With the assurance that she loved him even in some small way, he'd do whatever her father deemed necessary to win her hand. "Vicky, you need to wake up. The cowboys have spotted us."

Her eyes finally opened, and he watched as the smile on her lips bloomed when her eyes focused on him. "There are some men coming our way." He nodded his head in the direction of the field. She shifted in his arms, sitting up a little taller and pulling away from his side. He ignored the ripping feeling in his chest as if she had somehow sewn his heart to her.

Shifting her once again in his arms, he pulled his rifle out of its sheath and slowed the horse down even more.

Vicky had been dreaming that Chris had come to her hacienda and swept her up into his arms as he sat atop Comet. He'd kissed her like she'd seen Rosita, one of Magda's daughters, kiss her husband in the shadows of the barnyard. She didn't want to wake up. She'd told him that she loved him. Obviously she was dreaming. But part of the dream was true. She did love him.

Then she'd heard Chris's voice laced with concern. Something about a cowboy. Opening her eyes, she found it hadn't all been a dream. Chris held her close to his chest as he rode Comet! But then reality stole her smile. Instead of leaving her father's land, they were on the trail that led to the main house. And when he nodded in the direction of the field to the south, she saw José Luis cautiously approaching, rifle pointing to them as he called out in Spanish.

Scrambling to sit up, she told Chris who it was heading their way and then called out to her self-appointed big brother, *"Put that gun down, José Luis."*

"Vicky? Is it really you?" He lowered his gun and kicked his mount into a full gallop even as Chris kept Comet at a steady gate, his arms tightening around her slightly.

"Sí. Tell the men to put their guns away!" She saw the others in the field sighting down on them. José Luis turned in the saddle to signal the men but didn't slow as he flew over the last couple of hundred yards.

"Vicky. We thought you were dead!" he shouted even as he came alongside and reached out to take her from Chris. For a second she lifted herself as if to be transferred, but Chris's arms locked her closer to him.

"Come here, Vicky. Who is this Americano and what has he done to you?" José Luis's midnight-black eyes

sized Chris up, and she saw him calculating how to get her out of the stranger's arms without hurting her.

"He saved my life and brought me home once I had healed enough to travel."

"I thought you had gone with your father until he came back and you weren't with him. We looked for you. We even found your rifle next to a puma. Your necklace was there, too. Then we found your canteen farther downstream. We had given up hope of ever seeing you again! We even went to the Americano's cabin, but no one was there. We searched all over the rancho, the barn, everything. We were there only ten days ago."

"Well, I'm alive." She grinned at her childhood friend and then glanced up to find Chris's face as serious and stoic as a statue. Switching to English, she introduced the men. "Chris Samuels, this is José Luis Galván. He work for *mi papá* and teach me fish, hunt and play like boy. His pants." She grinned as she pulled her skirt up high enough to show the cuff of her white peasant pants that had weathered the trip but were stained and threadbare due to her adventures over the years.

Chris tucked her even closer. *"It's nice to meet you."* José Luis nodded his greeting, his eyes pinning Chris, and some communication went on between the two men. Comet sidestepped as the tension started to build.

Padre Pedro chose that moment to greet José Luis just as some of the other *vaqueros* arrived. Each and every one wanted to know if the "Americano" had mistreated her. To a man, she knew they would defend her honor if she so much as indicated that he'd been rude.

He seemed to sense the protective nature of their questions because he sat up straighter but didn't release her.

"We need get Vicky to hacienda," Chris called out in his broken Spanish as the men continued to gather around. The second time he said it, the men backed off and nodded.

"What happened to Tesoro? Why is the American carrying you?" José Luis now sat to her right and Padre Pedro to her left.

"When we stopped for the night last night she had terrible cramps, the poor child," Padre Pedro answered for her, sending her a kind look even as he continued. *"Now, had she told us she had pain earlier, I'm sure Señor Samuels would have insisted we stop and she could have avoided all that since he's been coddling her from the beginning of our trip, but it's beside the point,"* he reproved gently.

"So why isn't she riding today?" José Luis didn't look convinced.

"She did for most of the morning, but about an hour ago she almost fell off because she was so sleepy. He insisted on carrying her so she could arrive home directly and well rested."

"Well, I can carry her now," José Luis stated, once again reaching out to take her in his arms. He'd carried her more than once as children. But as much as she trusted José Luis, she wanted only Chris to hold her. The day after tomorrow she might find herself forced to marry Joaquín and never be held or cherished again, so she'd stay in Chris's arms until she absolutely needed to get down. At least one more hour to memorize the

feeling of this man she'd come to love caring for her, holding her close.

"No," she and Chris answered at the same time. He looked down at her with emotions she'd never seen in his gaze before. His dimple and smile made an appearance for two beats of her heart, and then he turned his attention back to José Luis. *"He can carry me home. You have cattle to tend to."*

"Your papá would skin me alive if I didn't look after you first. I'm seeing you to the house like I should have done that awful day." His last statement caused her to feel a touch guilty. Knowing him, he would have personally felt responsible for her disappearance. For the first time, she considered how her decisions might have affected the people on the hacienda who truly cared for her.

José Luis called to the men and then sent them out to round up the animals. Apparently they were bringing in all the herds closer to the hacienda so the men could attend the service the priest would celebrate. Just as she had guessed, since there was no way to communicate to Padre Pablo, they had waited until he was expected to come to have a funeral on her behalf. José Luis sent one of the younger *vaqueros* off ahead, presumably to warn the stables and the house of their arrival. They'd be having a birthday party instead of a funeral.

"Vicky, is he your intended?" The words sounded strange on Chris's lips as he struggled to get his tongue around them. He'd asked her to teach him many words earlier in their ride that morning. Some that made sense, like how to greet her father and mother, and others

that he'd probably never need to worry about, but she'd taught him all the same.

"No! He's my father's foreman. He good friend with Juan Manuel, then Juan Manuel die. He been my good friend, like big brother." She smiled and watched the other *vaqueros* start to round up the herd. "José Luis loves Maritza, not me."

"So you do not love him? And he does not love you?" Chris asked again. Turning in his arms, she studied his face. His eyes carefully watched José Luis and the other men, then he turned his gaze to hers and seemed to probe into her very heart. "You do not *amo* José Luis?"

"No, he promised my brother—" She paused, because he had used the word she'd dreamed. Surely he didn't know how much she'd come to love him if he could even ask about her loving José Luis. "When my brother sick, José Luis promise to take care of me."

"So he promised to take care of you like your older brother would have if he had lived?"

"Yes. We go hunt, fish and ride horses. I love José Luis like love my brother." Something flashed in his eyes, but he continued to quiz her as if it were very important he understand her relationship with José Luis.

"But you'd rather marry Joaquín?"

"Rather?"

"Want to?" Chris looked down at her, and she noticed that he seemed different somehow. There was a question in his eyes, a question that she couldn't quite read.

"No!" How could he even think that? "I no want marry Joaquín. I want stay on hacienda and no marry." Unless it were Chris offering. Then she would marry him in an instant and follow him to the ends of the earth, or at least back to his wonderful, peaceful *rancho* in the woods.

"You don't want to marry? You don't want a man to love you. Say *te amo*? Have children?" He'd used the word twice. Had he read her mind? She never believed she could be happily married until she met Chris.

"If man good and love me, yes. I want marry. But I no want marry Don Joaquín. They say he kill other wife when no baby, and I no want him to..." She stopped. Even to say the words out loud made her nauseated. To be touched by such a man after knowing someone like Chris existed and would have treated her so differently!

What great sin had she committed that God would punish her in such a way? At least before she had been lost in the woods, she had been ignorant of the way a man could hold her and make her feel safe. But to go from Chris's care to the misuse of Joaquín... Maybe she could run away before the wedding. It was the only way. Even as she began to plot her escape, the lines of worry and sadness that she had never seen before on José Luis's face reminded her others would be affected by any action she took.

But then if they had believed she was dead, maybe Don Joaquín had turned his interest somewhere else. Even as hope grew in her heart that maybe she had been spared, she prayed for God to protect any other poor woman whom Joaquín happened to fancy. The questions nagging her about what she might find when she reached the house would be answered within an hour. In the meantime, she vowed to enjoy the time she had left in Chris's arms.

Chapter Seventeen

As they rounded a curve, the Hacienda Ruiz's main building came into view. Chris had seen it before, but it still impressed him. Maybe even intimidated him. The large, cobblestone plaza with a fountain in the main yard gave plenty of space for visitors to hobble horses, park buggies or wander by the gardens in the warmer months before actually reaching the entryway. A large black steel gate, built into the whitewashed adobe outer wall, stood open most of the time and led to an inner courtyard that had a lush garden most of the year leading to the large veranda of the home, two wide steps of flat river stones, the long covered porch and then the massive wooden doors.

Chris had seen similar architecture in many of the Spanish ports they had docked in during the long journey around South America, which brought back memories of drawings of castles in Europe. Every time Chris visited the palatial Hacienda Ruiz, he'd always been impressed with the neat appearance and the grandeur of the landscape. He'd always felt like he was encountering nobility when he came to this palatial home—and it was where Vicky had grown up. Why did Vicky seem so down-to-earth when she really was the princess of this vast estate?

"They come," she whispered into his shoulder, and he found his gaze drawn back to her. Even with her jet-black hair pulling out of its pinnings, hanging in tendrils close to her cheeks, framing her dark brown eyes ringed with fatigue, and her nose smudged with travel dirt, he found her breathtakingly beautiful. In that moment, in front of her people, he had to fight the urge to kiss her. He was in dangerous territory here in more ways than one.

He raised his gaze to the three men charging toward them, their horses eating the distance between them. He recognized the cowboy whom José Luis had sent out ahead of them. The other two men, both bulkier and older, rode with the ease of years in the saddle.

"Papá and Berto," she whispered. Within minutes the two men rode up and slowed but didn't dismount. He recognized them once she said their names.

The younger of the two, Vicky's father, was in his forties at least. He had a lighter complexion and a longer, thin nose and chin. His sombrero hid most of his hair, but he sat at least four or five inches taller in the saddle than the older man.

"Vik-ee-ta!" Berto called out, emotion choking his voice. He spoke in rapid Spanish as he made no attempt to hide the tears sliding down his sun-weathered face. He reached out and caressed Vicky's face with his work-worn hands.

Berto was in charge of the horses and barns on the hacienda. His words were too fast for Chris to pick up much, but he heard *Vik-ee-ta* and *princesa* a few times over. How that man must love her to respond so. And yet, who could resist loving Vicky? Chris certainly had tried and failed. It made sense that the family she grew up in would be devastated by her loss, and he could only imagine their relief at having her back with them.

All the while Don Ruiz, Vicky's father, spoke in low tones with José Luis. Once José Luis apparently had his instructions, he came alongside Comet and said something to Vicky in a hushed tone, catching Chris with a look that said he'd better treat her like a princess or else. Chris held his eye contact without flinching.

Don Ruiz reached out as if to receive Vicky, but she shook her head, clinging to Chris and explaining something about her middle as she pointed to the area of her still-healing ribs, and settled back against Chris. Her father narrowed his eyes at him. There'd be some explaining to do when they arrived at the hacienda, if they let him get that far. But then again, he had a few questions of his own.

"They not shoot you, Chris," Vicky whispered as the whole group made their way toward the hacienda.

"I would hope not, but I've got the hacienda princess on my horse and only your word and Padre Pedro's to defend me. How do we know that the minute I put you down, they won't string me up for kidnapping?"

"What kidanappting?"

"Stealing a person."

"Steel, like metal?"

"No, steal, *s-t-e-a-l*, to take something that does not belong to you."

"Oh, *robar*."

"Yeah, to rob or steal. They might think that I stole you from them."

No doubt about it. The burning of Don Ruiz's gaze was prickling his skin even as they rode along. The man may have let Chris carry his daughter, but he wouldn't let them out of his sight. Probably a good thing, since Chris still fought the temptation to wheel Comet around and head for the hills with her in his arms.

Seeing how tired Berto, Papá and even José Luis looked caused Vicky a twinge of guilt. They had been worried about her. Enough to search off hacienda lands. And they'd been saddened when they had found her rifle and necklace in the creek. They'd brought her things back to show her family. It must have been the day they went hunting. Nana had told Chris some men had come to the cabin once they came home from the hunt.

Her thoughts came to a halt. *Home.* The grand, cold stone palace awaiting her with open arms after almost two months' absence no longer felt like home. A small, cozy, one-room cabin in the woods to the west of her father's hacienda now was the home of her heart.

Would she ever be able to forget Chris once he rode away as if nothing had happened between them? Had he not felt anything? Even now, as he supported her in his arms, she felt his every breath through the strong solid chest that supported and protected her hurt ribs. Each time he looked down on her with concern, she wanted to beg him to take off, help her escape. She would rather go back with him to his home. Maybe she could convince Padre Pedro that he should marry them instead. That way, her father couldn't protest and she would be free. Free to live at Chris's cabin and cook his food, ride his horses, and maybe someday, he might come to care for her and they could have a family of their own.

But her fear kept her silent. She knew he cared about her well-being, but maybe he saw her as just a girl. Or worse yet, a sister. He had told her many stories about his own sister and their escapades growing up. He might see her as a sister, but she could never confuse him for a brother.

No, if she were to be completely honest with herself, she'd have to admit that she had finally learned what Maritza had giggled about when she had said how she had fallen in love with José Luis. Or why Magda, even after all these years, paced the kitchen floor when Berto was late coming in from the fields or a hunt. Hadn't she begun to do the same thing at the cabin in the last few days? Keeping an eye out the window for his return and not feeling settled until he had retired to the safety of the other cabin for the night?

Ever since she could remember, her parents barely managed to be civil to each other and looked for ways to avoid contact, but she had seen other couples in love on the hacienda. She just hadn't believed that she would ever feel that way for anyone. She had believed that because she was of noble blood, mixed with indigenous, she would never know the strength of emotions like that. Love seemed to be reserved for the poor while the ruling nobility had to be content with their position in life and the relative ease that brought without ever experiencing the grand feeling of loving and being loved.

Maybe love was only for the poor, but she had somehow managed to sample it in passing. Surely she could never have such emotions for Don Joaquín.

At the thought of the dreaded man, she cast another look around the outbuildings. While the yard was designed for carriages and wagons to pull up around it, most of the lands surrounding theirs were too densely forested or too wild to have navigable roads. Even the main road around the mountains and out to the port where the Franciscan mission had been was more a horse trail that the cattle trampled down on their way to the coast once each year.

Had Don Joaquín arrived for what he had declared to be their marriage only to be informed she had been killed by a puma? Had he already left the hacienda, or had he stayed to pay respects at the service to be held on her birthday? She didn't see any sign of him in the barnyard or on the veranda where her brothers now vied for the best view.

"Vicky! Vicky!" they both cried out as they saw her coming. Juanito, at age nine, should have already been helping in the stables, but Mamá had not wanted to take any chances with her remaining boys after having lost her two other children.

"Your brothers?" Chris questioned in his stilted

Spanish. She nodded, her heart climbing into her throat at the sight of them and keeping her from getting any words past it. She hadn't realized how much she had missed them until she saw them again.

"Juanito is big?"

Again she nodded. "They are happy to see you." He had switched back to English.

"Sí, they are happy." She repeated the words in Spanish so he would learn a new term and then looked up into his eyes, the light blue like a cloudless day in summer, and saw concern and understanding.

"I'm happy you home, Vicky. I not happy you not at my home," he whispered in Spanish, but before she could ask what he meant or even if he knew what he had just implied, they were at the gate. Papá slid out of his saddle and pulled her into his arms, still as strong as ever for a man of forty-eight.

"Mi' ja." His use of the *Mejican* term of endearment Berto and Magda used for her and their own children touched her heart and brought on the tears she had held back for the last few minutes. *"We thought you were gone forever! You don't know how much we all missed you."* He held her close and then let her feet sink to the ground. *"I trust the Americano treated you well."* He kept her close but sent a look over her shoulder to Chris. The creaking of his saddle and then the sound of his boots landing on the cobblestones gave her a sense of where he was even with her back to him.

"He was wonderful and kind and generous and always a gentleman," she rushed to reassure her father,

only to have him hold her out at arm's length and study her with a knowing look.

"Don Ruiz. Good to see you again." Papá turned her toward Chris but kept her tucked under his arm. Chris shook her father's hand, keeping his gaze on him. *"Vicky have long ride and need sleep."* Chris spoke in a soft, respectful voice. He motioned to the house as if wanting to herd them in like the cattle in the fields.

"What happened?" Papá kept a protective arm around her shoulder as he guided her up the steps and into the shade of the veranda.

"I'll tell everyone once we're inside, but please invite Señor Samuels in. If not for him, I would be dead. You owe much to that man, and I told him that he would be welcomed into your home." She had never dared to tell her father what to do before now, but she would not abandon Chris to the *vaqueros* while she went inside.

"Of course, we have many questions for him, daughter," Papá responded but didn't turn to invite Chris. She stopped walking. Papá stutter-stepped before bending down toward her. *"Are you hurt? Do I need to carry..."*

"I asked you to invite Señor Samuels inside, and yet he stands by the gate. Your men won't let him come any closer," Vicky accused her father and then turned, looking past Padre Pedro to the men blocking Chris's progress. *"Let him past, men,"* she called out in the voice she used to break up her brother's fights.

Berto and José Luis gave a quick look at her father before stepping aside and motioning Chris ahead. It didn't escape her attention that they followed at only two steps behind him. The stable boys had already started to collect the horses and take them to the barn.

"We need to talk, hija." Papá's voice held a warning in it, but before she could question him, Juanito and Diegito threw themselves at her, hugging her around the waist and almost knocking her down in their excitement.

"With care." Chris stepped closer, creating a barrier between them while he shifted down into a crouch to eye level with her brothers. *"She need care. Got hurt. But she miss you much when not here."* His words slowed her brothers down but didn't keep them from asking a million questions at the same time.

"We will talk inside," she insisted. Papá held the door open as Chris and her brothers followed her, and they headed toward Papá's office. She had just crossed the threshold of the room when she came face-to-face with her worst nightmare.

Don Joaquín slouched in one of Papá's horsehair chairs, his cigar dropping black ash on the polished wooden floor and his shot glass empty on the walnut side table. He didn't stand when they entered but grunted like a stuffed pig.

"About time you came back!" he huffed out, his eyes sweeping down her form from her head to her feet, lingering too long on places no gentleman would stare. She turned, ready to flee the room, but her escape was blocked by the others entering behind her. *"Don't you turn your back on me, girlie. We had an arrangement with your father. Did you think I wouldn't find out about your little trick?"* The man had come up behind her,

his heavy breathing sending shivers of fear racing up her back. His odor of unwashed male, stale cigar smoke and alcohol, wafted over her. Her knees turned to liquid and she almost collapsed, but Chris caught her elbow and kept her upright.

"Look at me, woman, when I'm talking to you!" the foul man yelled as he spun her around. *"I'll teach you never to try to escape…"*

An arm flew past her and caught Don Joaquín's wrist as he swung to slap her across the face. Chris's grip tightened on Joaquín's arm, and she saw a grimace of pain flash in his eyes, then anger and hatred like she had never seen before. Fear, no longer for her own safety but now for Chris's, froze her in her place.

"We no touch woman like man." Chris's voice came out low, clear and menacing.

"Let me go!" Don Joaquín yelled, but Chris didn't flinch. Instead he stepped closer, putting himself between Vicky and her tormentor. At the same time, Papá stepped around her on the other side.

"Go have a seat, Vicky," Papá whispered before turning his attention to his guests.

José Luis and Berto linked arms with her and helped her cross the floor on shaky knees. She sat and her brothers came around, hugging her from both sides and watching with wide eyes as their father and Chris walked Don Joaquín out of the room.

Chris paused only long enough to glance back and catch her eye. His gaze swept over her, but instead of making her feel dirty, she saw only concern for her well-being. He nodded to José Luis and Berto, who came to stand at the door.

"You have overstepped your place here, Don Joaquín," her father growled in a tone she had never heard before. His growl continued, but as they moved away from the room, his words were too low to hear. Her heart beat in her chest with panic. She couldn't stand to be in the same room with the beast for more than a few minutes—surely Papá would see that a marriage between them would be torture, for if he dared hit her while her father stood there...

Magda appeared, tears streaming down her face as she sniffed and placed a tray with glasses and a crystal pitcher on the side table. She enveloped Vicky in a hug that calmed her racing heart. While Don Joaquín might have much power outside the hacienda, he wouldn't be able to reach her again with Berto and José Luis now standing guard at the door and Magda fiercely protecting her.

And Chris. While her father had not physically intervened for her, Chris had. If only she could count on his protection for the rest of her life instead of only a few more days. But even as the warmth of security filled her at the idea that he had stepped in, the memory of hatred on Don Joaquín's face caused her blood to freeze in fear. What would he do to Chris in retaliation?

Chapter Eighteen

Chris didn't release the grip he had on Don Joaquín until they were well down the hall and the man could no longer insult Vicky. The disgust rose like bile in his stomach at the idea of this man having the opportunity to lay a finger on Vicky. If he openly tried to hit her in the presence of her father and other men while they were only betrothed, what would he do once they were married and in the privacy of their own home? Praying for the strength to keep from killing the man then and there, he pulled air into his lungs and tried to understand the low, menacing words Don Ruiz spoke as they marched through the hallway. The stench of the man didn't help his swilling emotions.

He had expected to head to the main door and throw the piece of trash out into the yard, but Don Ruiz led them to a staircase, and only then did Chris understand that even after Don de la Vega's rough handling of Vicky, he was still a visitor in the Ruiz home. As much as it chafed, Chris would need to tread carefully if he wanted to help Vicky. On the heels of that realization came the thought that by manhandling a Spanish nobleman, even to protect Vicky, he might have just signed his own death warrant, or at least his own eviction notice.

Don Ruiz waved upward and seemed to dismiss Don Joaquín. The obscene man, who had to be years older than Vicky's father, shot Chris one more look of pure hatred before turning and huffing his way up the stairs. As he climbed, his steps became less sure and his pace slower, his breathing labored. The man might be powerful among his peers, but if he ever tried to best Chris, there would be no competition. However, he'd have to watch his back and from now on patrol his ranch more carefully. The hatred he saw in Don Joaquín's eyes was nothing short of diabolical.

Vicky's father continued to watch the stairs until the echo of a door slamming cut the tense silence. *"Come, we have much to talk about."* His words were soft and slow so Chris could understand. At least he wasn't showing him the door. As they headed back to the office, Vicky's father placed his hand on Chris's shoulder for just a minute, causing him to pause.

"Thank you for bringing Vi-kee-ta back to us. We will always be..." Chris didn't understand the rest of the words, but the look on the man's face and the tears in his eyes said enough. His gratitude shone brightly. But if that was his reaction to having his daughter brought back from what he had thought was the grave, why let a man who would hit her still stay under his roof? Was Vicky's father anything like his own—cold and

so self-absorbed he didn't notice or care about the suffering of those around him? On their first encounter, he had believed Don Ruiz to be a fair, kind gentleman. Had he been fooled?

"I am pleased to be of service." Chris grimaced at his mispronunciation of the words Vicky had tried so hard to teach him. The older man's smile proved his message had been understood. Was he truly what he appeared or just a charlatan?

"You didn't speak Spanish before," Don Ruiz commented as he began walking again.

"Vicky teach me some. She speak more English," he admitted.

"She's a smart girl." The older man glanced at Chris. Something in his gaze said his comment wasn't just a flippant remark.

"She is," Chris confirmed, *"more than me."* Her father nodded as if Chris had passed a test and once again patted his shoulder. Hopefully it was a vote of confidence and a step in the right direction toward winning her hand. In the few seconds after he had laid eyes on Don Joaquín, he'd come to the overwhelming realization that he wouldn't be walking away from Vicky, not for anyone or anything, especially not for a monster like Don de la Vega. How that would play out was anyone's guess, but he would do all he could to win her heart and her father's approval. First he needed to determine if her father had made this agreement with de la Vega out of duress or financial trouble or if another option just hadn't been found.

Chris paused. Should he say something to Don Ruiz?

Before he could form a question, much less try to translate it for Don Ruiz, the other man caught his gaze and held it with his own midnight-black one.

"Señor Samuels, you have questions? Yes?"

"Yes, I have questions. Why Vicky marry bad man?"

The serious look on Don Ruiz's face did not bode well. Chris tried to swallow past his suddenly dry throat.

"I do not want my daughter married to Don de la Vega." Don Ruiz did not break eye contact or fidget. Yet they had not removed the man from the house, just the room where Vicky was. It didn't add up.

"There is much in California that you do not know, Señor Samuels. Watch out for Vicky and keep her safe. Trust only Berto, José Luis and myself."

With those cryptic words, he entered the office where everyone was gathered around Vicky. Chris took a deep breath and followed.

Did Don Ruiz actually trust him and was looking for a way out of the marriage or just trying to get him to play along until he could somehow separate Vicky and Chris? Would he be shown the door in the near future? And if they did, how would he possibly help Vicky? They found Vicky embraced by an older woman, running a hand down her shoulder and across her cheek as if making sure she was real. Assuming the woman was Vicky's mother, he smiled and reached out to shake her hand when she turned to acknowledge the men, but Vicky subtly shook her head. Remembering she had said something about giving a kiss in greeting to the women, he stepped closer still and bussed the woman's weathered cheek. She stepped back in surprise, her eyes taking him in, and then caught him in a warm hug.

"Thank you, thank you, Señor, for bringing our Vi-kee-ta back to us." Her tears flowed freely again, and he fished out his handkerchief and offered it to her.

"Señor Chris, this is Magda, wife of Berto," Vicky spoke up as the woman took his handkerchief. It took a moment for her words to sink in. This was their housekeeper not Vicky's mother. Had he made a cultural misstep?

"Nice to meet you." Chris managed to get out the Spanish greeting. The woman smiled, pinched his cheek and then said something to Vicky that made her turn a darker shade of pink. Vicky glanced his way, bit her lip, then looked away. Was that longing he saw in her eyes? What had the woman said? From the grin on the older lady's face and Vicky's blush, he could hazard a guess.

After a moment of awkward silence, Don Ruiz invited Chris to have a seat, and they offered him lemonade and some sweet bread. Vicky began telling the story of what happened to her in Spanish to those gathered around while Chris sat back and watched the interaction of her family.

True affection shone from Don Ruiz's eyes as he pulled his chair closer to his daughter's and patted her shoulder. What did his actions mean?

Magda came and went, seeing to everyone's needs. She shooed the boys off their sister's lap, only for them to return there as soon as Magda left the room until Don Ruiz said a few stern words and both boys settled on the floor at her feet. Vicky's father asked her question after question. Chris followed some of the conversation, picking up on words here and there.

Where was Vicky's mother? She hadn't come to greet Vicky yet, and surely by now the entire hacienda had to know about her return. Was the woman ill? Bedbound? But if so, why hadn't Vicky asked to go see her mother?

"Chris?" Vicky caught him as he pondered her family.

"Sorry, yes, Vicky?"

"We go make clean now. We eat in one hour. You go see you room?"

"That would be fine," he answered in Spanish even though she had spoken English to him. If he could communicate in their language, he might win more favor.

Don Ruiz led them all back to the staircase where Don Joaquín had gone before. At the top of the staircase, a balcony ran the length of the foyer with large windows looking out onto the courtyard that sat in the middle of the structure. They went down the left hallway, where Don Joaquín had gone to the right. At least Chris could hope that Vicky would be safe in her room, but then again, she should have been safe in her father's office with her father, her father's foreman and her would-be rescuer. They stopped at a door where Vicky and Magda entered. Don Ruiz continued on but Chris faltered. While it wasn't his place to take care of her or see to her protection at the hacienda, he couldn't seem to stop thinking of himself as responsible for her. He wondered if that would ever change, no matter how far away she was, or whom she was married to.

"Señor," Vicky's father said over his shoulder, *"your*

room." He pointed to the door across the hall but still Chris hesitated.

"Can you see?" He pointed to Vicky's door, frustrated with his inability to communicate. "No Don Joaquín?" The older man's eyes lit with understanding and something else. He nodded and returned to the door the women had just shut. Knocking, he entered without letting Chris in behind him, not that Chris would attempt to enter Vicky's room unless they needed his help ousting an unwanted guest. Quickly the other man returned with a smile.

"She's with Magda. They are..." His words were lost on Chris but not the meaning. They were safe and he'd be staying across the hall. He entered a guest bedroom about as big as his whole cabin, with light streaming through the windows overlooking the side yard that led to the stables. A finely appointed double bed, set of dressers and a wooden chest at the foot of the bed with no personal effects except for his saddlebags confirmed this to be a spare room. In the corner was a screen for changing behind, and he could see the corner of a table behind it where he assumed he would be able to clean up.

"Bath." Don Ruiz pointed to the tub that sat behind the screen as well, steam curling up from it. At Chris's nod, the man withdrew from the room. He took a few minutes to soak the travel dust off and wash his hair. He shaved and dressed in the dark blue chambray pants and shirt that Vicky had sewn for him during the weeks while she convalesced. He checked his image once more in the long mirror and sighed. He had once been a genteel Southern gentleman who owned a plantation worth over a hundred thousand dollars, but even so, he had never been of noble blood. Would that be the deciding factor against him?

"Dear God, I don't know the language, the customs or even if I stand a chance, but I know nothing is impossible with You. Just like Gideon went into battle with few men against a multitude knowing he would come away the victor because You had promised, help me to see the way I can help Vicky. Protect her from that vile man and use me to do it if it be Your will. Thank You, Father, for bringing us this far and lead us on until we reach home, either here, on earth or with You."

He heard movement out in the hall and quickly crossed the room. Swinging the door open, prepared to face either the object of his affections or his new enemy, he surprised Berto, who was about to knock. *"Dinner is ready,"* the man said slowly, as if coaching Chris to learn.

"Vicky?"

"Vicky in room." He pointed to the door across the hallway.

"I wait for Vicky," Chris explained, crossing his arms and standing with his legs spread apart.

"You good for her." Berto clapped him on the shoulder and moved away, down the hallway toward the stairs. Chris stood a little straighter and felt his chest rise.

Berto's approval of Chris caused hope to grow in his chest. Would Don Ruiz pay any attention to Berto's opinion of him?

* * *

Dressed like she were ready for a ball, Vicky snuck one more glance in the mirror and couldn't believe it was really her. She had been forced to get dressed up for a few events since her Quinceañera four years before, but she hadn't been worried about impressing anyone with her appearance. In fact, if she were truly honest, she had intentionally leaned a little too much to one side and slouched, trying to disguise her developing curves. If she had acted like she didn't have a sane thought in her head and accidentally spilled food down the pure-satin gowns just to have an excuse to leave early, her only defense was that none of those men had ever been kind to her like Chris.

But tonight, for just tonight, she wanted to be the princess for Chris. If only she had paid attention to Mamá's lectures about how to attract a man's attention. Maybe if she had, not only would she be able to impress Chris, but Mamá would have cared that her only daughter had returned. Magda had whispered earlier that Mamá's head had been pounding terribly so she had taken to bed earlier in the day. She wouldn't be able to help Vicky get ready for dinner. Not that it was a change from the normal. Mamá hadn't taken any interest in Vicky in years.

"Beautiful." Rosa smiled at Vicky's reflection in the mirror as she rearranged another curl. Magda had been up and down the stairs a number of times to check on her progress but had not left her alone, insisting that her daughters stay to help her. Rosa and Margarita had helped her to bathe and wash her hair, and then they

had helped her into her fitted silk fuchsia bodice with elaborate lace around her low-cut collar and matching skirts with four petticoats underneath.

She felt more like a fool than a princess. After all, no matter how much she tried to pretend to be beautiful, she was just a half-breed, half Spanish noble and half savage Indian, and her Indian characteristics all but eradicated the Spanish in her features.

"Thank you, Rosa, Margarita." She ran a hand down her dress from the neckline to the middle of the skirt and then pulled it out to the side, showing off her petticoats and slippers underneath. She would never be graceful or feminine. No, she should have been born a cowboy, comfortable only in peasant pants and old serapes to hide the girl underneath. She could wish all she wanted to, but she would never be white or tall or beautiful. She would never be elegant like Mamá.

"You are our princesa." Rosa fluffed a flounce and smiled at her in the mirror. "Princesa" had been a nickname Berto had given her. The *vaqueros* teased her that a princess shouldn't ride horses or be seen outside of the "palace" without their tiaras. Their teasing had egged her on to try to beat them in roping or jumping competitions that they had while out watching the cattle. Papá or Berto would have skinned her alive to see some of the stunts she had pulled out there, but José Luis had always kept an eye on her mischief and kept her from getting caught.

"No, I was never a princesa," she whispered to her reflection. *"Princesas are graceful and winsome."*

"No, Vicky, you are our princesa. And I know some-

one else who thinks so..." Rosa teased even as Margarita finished pinning her hair into place. Her hair swept up off her head in intricate braids with tendrils hanging down to grace her neck and forehead, she looked at the stranger in the mirror.

"Don Joaquín," Margarita answered with a wince. *"And he won't let that Americano steal you from him. He said something about not being able to have a child with you until after nine months so no one confuses an American dog with a noble-born Californiano."*

"I won't marry him. I'd rather die than to be wed to that...that pig!" she exclaimed.

"I don't blame you, but I don't know how your papá can back out of an agreement now. Don Joaquín said something about bringing him up on charges of treason." Rosa shook her head as she helped to put the dressing table to rights.

"But how could he possibly say that?" Vicky asked, incredulous.

"He said if your papá allowed you to consort with the enemy then he himself had become an enemy of California."

"But Chris is not the enemy of Mejico. He lives here in Alta California and has a wonderful home. He is a good man. He is not the enemy." Vicky stomped her foot in frustration.

Rosa smiled knowingly at her. *"I see you have fallen in love with the Americano. How well does he kiss?"* She raised a brow and studied Vicky closely. Vicky felt the heat color her face, and she looked away from her friends. Picking up the small hand fan that Papá had gifted her a few years before, she fanned her face and shook her head.

She only wished she knew the answer to that. But he had never kissed her. Never given her any reason to think he saw her as anything other than his temporary charge that he could now turn over to her father.

"It is time to go to dinner," she announced, unwilling to say anything more about Chris.

"Must have been some kiss!" Margarita stage-whispered to Rosa with a wink. *"Either that or it was boring."*

"What was boring?" Magda came charging back into the room just in time to save her from having to respond to Margarita's taunts.

"Kissing the Americano," Rosa answered her mother with a shrug. *"Vicky doesn't seem to want to talk about it, so it must have been a horrible experience."*

Magda chuckled as she came up and surveyed the work Rosa and Margarita had done. Placing a kiss on Vicky's forehead, she smiled down on her. *"I suspect it was just the opposite. That first kiss of true love is something to be kept private and secret. You don't go around sharing that with anyone. No, you remember it for when you are waiting for him to come home at night. And when he finally comes in, you remind him again how much he likes to hold you close and kiss you until you both no longer can breathe."*

"Aye, Mamá!" Margarita scolded. *"I don't want to imagine you and Papá. I was imagining that handsome young Americano."*

"You have your own husband to run home to and

kiss, young lady. I suggest you go there, before you put too many ideas in Vicky's head." Magda shooed the others out of the room. *"It won't be too much longer before you'll be chasing young bucks with their serenades from your own daughters' windows."*

Rosa and Margarita fled from the room after groaning at their mother's warning.

"Oh, I'm sorry. Excuse me," Margarita exclaimed in the hallway. They twittered like birds in a bush. Their giggles carried back into the room, as did Chris's quiet response to their attention, the cadence sounding like he was attempting to speak Spanish though the words were not clear. They giggled louder this time, just before the door closed and their conversation was cut off.

"You look lovely, Vicky. Don't worry about a thing. I'm sure between your papá and your handsome Americano, they will work everything out. Neither one wants you to be saddled with that vile man." She cupped Vicky's chin and forced her to look at the lady who had been more of a mother to her than her own had.

"Then why did Papá agree to it in the first place?" Vicky asked the one question that had bothered her most. Why had her father, whom she had always adored, been willing to turn her over to a monster? She would have understood if Mamá had somehow…

"Your papá and your Americano will take care of this. Don't you worry."

"But how can I not? Don Joaquín is not a strong man who could challenge Chris to a duel or even a fight. No, he would be the one to wait in the bushes and shoot him in the back without warning."

"Then your Chris will have to grow eyes in the back of his head and watch the bushes carefully, but it won't matter to him—he loves you, mi' ja. And nothing but death will keep him from marrying you, Vicky."

"Do you really think so?" Hope sparked in her heart at the idea of Chris loving her like she loved him. But Magda's words struck fear, too. Would it cost him his life or his *rancho* to defend or even be associated with her?

"I don't think so, I know so. Otherwise he wouldn't be standing outside your door waiting to take you down to dinner."

"He just can't speak the language and feels comfortable with me." She explained away Magda's words to keep the seeds of hope from burrowing deeper into her heart.

"If you don't believe he loves you, then at least pray to God to protect you. Surely you trust God even if you don't trust your Chris and your father."

"God has never answered any of my prayers before. Why would He listen now?" Vicky replied harshly before she could stop the words.

Magda shook her head and frowned. *"God always listens and always answers. You may not like the answer He gives, but He listens. He cares. He loves. He sent Chris to save you."* She lifted Vicky's chin once more.

"Mamá said that God only listens to civilized ladies and gentlemen, and we both know I will never be a lady much less civilized..." Magda placed her fingers over Vicky's lips, her look stern.

"Your mamá may be the mistress of this hacienda

*and so I must show respect, but her tongue and her
heart are filled with poison, worse than any serpent.
She kills the soul with her words. Mi'ja, God loves all
and invites you to talk to Him."*

*"Chris says the same thing. Did you know that he has
a Bible in his own language? He read from it to me."*

*"And what did Chris say about prayer? Did he say
it was only for the white, civilized rich? What about the
slave woman you said lived there? Did she believe in
God and pray to Him?"*

Thoughts of Nana Ruth gave Vicky pause. Nana Ruth
prayed day and night, talking to "the Good Lord" and
"Jesus Christ" and "Father God" all the time, as if He
were right in the room and part of the conversation.

*"And you came back with the priest. Have you heard
Padre Pedro ever tell anyone that God wouldn't listen to them because they are 'dirty Indians' like your
mamá says?"*

Magda's words set her mind to reeling faster than a
spindle when they were spinning wool into yarn. All
this time she had feared to trust God because He hadn't
listened to her prayers. But if He had heard her prayers,
why had He let Angelica die and left her to listen to her
mother's words of rejection time and time again? Why
had He let Juan Manuel die and leave her without her
older brother whom she adored? Why had God let her
find out what it felt to be loved only to bring her back
to the hacienda and be forced to marry Don Joaquín so
that Chris would be safe?

Yet, could she do it? Could she find the strength to
marry that beast? Only God could give her that kind

of courage. Bracing against the feeling of impending doom, she straightened her spine and hugged Magda for a long moment, cherishing the feel of safety and love. If she ended up married to Don Joaquín, she might never have the opportunity to do it again. Would she survive a marriage to such a man? Other women before her had not. What would make her any different?

"Te quiero, Magda, mi vida." She kissed the older woman's cheek and then pulled away while she still had the strength to do so. Squaring her shoulders, she headed to the door and to her doom.

"I love you, Vicky. As if you were my very own daughter, Princesa. Do not give up hope."

Chapter Nineteen

When the two women left Vicky's room giggling and blushing as they stole looks at him, he had thought she would be out soon. As the time stretched out, he began to wonder if she was still in there. Maybe she had left before and their laughter had been about him lingering at an empty room. But then he heard the soft voices inside and resumed his patrol of the five feet on each side of her door.

Surely he looked silly, besotted even, but he didn't care. He hadn't been successful in protecting anyone before, but Vicky wasn't just anyone, she was the woman he wanted to spend the rest of his life with, share everything with, create a family with, raise children... the possibilities were endless. Of course, they couldn't start that life together until he found out from her father just what was expected of a suitor, and then he'd need to build a home worthy of her.

That in itself would take a year or more, and he'd need to hire a number of men to get it done. The stash of money he had brought with him should get him started. Would she wait for him to build them a home? And honestly, with almost a ten-year difference between them, did he even have a chance? Would she even want him to court her? Or did she have a younger man whom she fancied? If she did, what would he do about it?

He knew that he would never force her to accept him as Don Joaquín was attempting to do. No, he wanted to marry her but only if she wanted him. He loved her. He hadn't said the words to her yet, but it was true. And she hadn't exactly said she loved him either. At least not while she was awake. Was it just a dream or had she meant the words? Had she truly been talking to him?

Even if she didn't care for him in the same way, he could woo her and convince her to trust him. He knew what she wanted—to ride horses and live a simple life. Somehow, despite growing up in this palatial hacienda, she had not become a princess who dressed regally and turned her nose up at hard work. After all, she had made meals, cleaned the cabin and started to do the wash before Padre Pedro had arrived. Even the clothes he wore were proof of her diligence. The woman extolled in Proverbs 31 didn't do anything more than what Vicky did. He'd noticed her hands were already work-roughened when she had arrived. His sister and mother would have had an attack of vapors if their hands had been calloused or their faces bronzed by the sun. Vicky was happy with who she was and fit perfectly in his life. As if she were designed to fit him.

But if she didn't care for him in the same way and she accepted his proposal anyway, he'd spend his life knowing that she would rather be somewhere else, with someone else. What kind of life was that?

He'd been so lost in thought that when the door opened he almost knocked into the lady who emerged. She wore a long, satin evening gown in the color of one of the native flowers he'd seen on the coast, bright and cheery, too pink to be red but too dark to be pink. The woman's hair had been caught up in wave after wave of intricately laced braids.

"Excuse me, I didn't see…" His words died in his throat as the lovely woman's gaze raised to meet his. Deep sorrow shadowed her gaze, but then a spark of happiness illuminated the pools of dark coffee when she looked at him.

"Vicky?" He couldn't believe the transformation. She nodded, her forehead starting to wrinkle in uncertainty. She looked down as if embarrassed. His heart flipped over in his chest. He was surprised the walls of the hall weren't vibrating with the pounding since it beat so loudly in his ears. "You're beautiful. Truly exquisite."

Finally, all his mother's lessons in comportment kicked in and he caught her gloved hand in both of his, knelt on one knee before her and brought her hand to his lips to kiss it lightly. "Would you do me the honor of letting me escort you down to dinner?" He waited with bated breath. He was completely enchanted with the brilliance of the woman who stood before him, and yet doubt came into his head. There was no way this vision of loveliness could possibly want to live in the backwoods on his ranch, even if he spent the next six or seven years building her a home to rival the grand one she had grown up in.

"Why you on floor?" she asked, the cute little line between her eyebrows appearing as she tried to puzzle out what he was doing. There, in that half frown, he saw the young woman he'd fallen in love with. Could they ever go back to their simple life again? And yet, admittedly, he didn't want to go back to that. She had been a friend, a charge, a responsibility but not his wife. He didn't want to have to hold back from holding her close as he walked his lands. He wanted to live with her, grow old with her, share a life and a family with her. Did she want the same? And if she did, how did he go about asking her father?

"Chris?" She squeezed his hand and brought him back to the present. "Why on the floor?"

"Because a gentleman should take a knee when in the presence of a princess." He punctuated his words with another kiss to her hand. "Will you let me escort you?" he asked again. "Accompany?"

"Oh, *acompañar*." She beamed a smile at him that could have blinded him if he hadn't still been in shock. She pulled on his hand and he stood, turning to tuck her arm under his and threading it through his elbow as they started to walk down the hallway. Movement at the door caused him to glance back as Magda exited the room, an approving nod and smile encouraging him. Nana Ruth had always said he could charm the women. If Magda's vote counted, and he hoped it did, then he was pretty sure she'd cast it in his favor.

Juanito and Diego came charging up the stairs, shouting their greetings to Vicky.

"Good evening, gentlemen." He tried for the voice Nana Ruth used to stop him from his mischief. He purposefully stepped in front of Vicky.

Her brothers stopped all right, midstride, to stare at him with wide, black eyes just like Vicky's. They even had the same furrow in their little brows as they tried to figure him out.

"How are you both tonight? Juanito?" He turned to the older, sticking out his hand as if the boy was a grown man. Juanito glanced up at his sister first, gauging what his response should be, before placing his hand in Chris's. He gave a quick squeeze and then reached to do the same for Diego.

"Diego, you look very handsome tonight." The lifting of both boys' shoulders and their glances back and forth caused him to smile.

"You sister hurt. No touch this way." He struggled with the words. Shaking his head, he pretended to push Juanito, who stood on the same side of Vicky, and then rubbed his own ribs. They seemed to understand his meaning. Dieguito lifted his arms to Vicky in the universal sign of "lift me" but Chris stepped in. He reached down and caught him up. Then he took Vicky's arm and relinked it to his. Juanito went to Vicky's left and, after studying how Chris had linked their arms, did the same with his sister.

It felt right. Not only to be linked with her but to be in the middle of a family. A vision of them growing closer as the boys grew up and visited the ranch circled his head as they slowly made their way to the formal dining room. The doors to the room had been closed before but now had been flung wide open, and inviting smells of something savory and spicy reminded him just how long it had been since he'd had a warm meal.

Chris set Diegito down, and her brothers tore off down the hall. He turned to Vicky just as an older woman approached them from across the hallway.

Dressed in black from head to toe, contrasting her tawny-looking skin and odd orange tinge to the whites of her eyes, she might have once been beautiful, but the years had not been kind. Her sunken eyes and papery-thin skin gave an aspect of someone with little time left on the earth. Her elaborately done hair had as much white as black, and deep groves on both sides of her face and her forehead hinted at a permanent frown. At least twenty years older than Don Ruiz, she must be Vicky's grandmother. Odd that Vicky had never mentioned her grandmother.

"Hija." The older woman came closer, an overwhelming scent of sickly sweet perfume and something else overwhelming his senses. Chris was puzzled for a moment as he watched her with Vicky, who tensed and drew closer to his side, as if bracing herself for an attack. What kind of relationship did she have with her grandmother? The woman stopped just at arm's reach but didn't reach out or touch Vicky.

"Mamá, let me present you with Señor Chris-to-fer Samuels." He loved the way even his plain name sounded more exotic when she said it. *"Chris, this is my mamá."* For a second, the words didn't register, and

then he fought to keep the shock from showing in his face. This old woman was Vicky's mother? The woman Vicky never wanted to talk about?

"Pleased to meet you, Señora." Chris concentrated on the words and gave her a kiss on each cheek.

"A pleasure," the older woman said, though her glare told him far more about what she actually thought than her words did. As her breath rushed past his face, he almost jumped back for fear of being pickled. She reeked of alcohol. Was that the reason she hadn't come to greet her daughter earlier in the day? Had she been too inebriated? Did she need alcohol for pain, or had she been drowning her sorrow at losing her daughter? But no, Vicky had tried to convince him that this woman did not miss her and wouldn't care if she ever returned. Perhaps it was another kind of sorrow she was drowning.

She looked him over from head to toe and then latched on to his other arm, wobbling slightly as they continued toward the table. He glanced down at Vicky to find her eyes bright with unshed tears and her face drawn.

"Vicky," he whispered softly as he paused, supporting her mother with a firm hand under her elbow. "Sweet, sweet Vicky, don't cry." His heart broke for her as he thought about how she had been so affectionate with everyone, even the cowboys and her little brothers, and yet her mother had not touched her. Not even when she had been brought back from what they all believed to be the grave.

She shook her head, but those tears didn't fall. She closed her eyes and breathed deeply. He squeezed her hand between his arm and his middle to try to give her some kind of comfort. When she opened her eyes, she didn't look up at him but started forward, leading him to the table. The picture of a woman in control of her emotions. Poised and ready for a formal dinner. A true princess.

Dinner felt endless to Vicky. Juanito and Diegito bickered and squabbled over every little thing. Papá sat at the head of the long table, Mamá at the foot with the boys on each side of her. Don Joaquín and Padre Pedro were on the opposite side of the table from Vicky and Chris. Don Gonzalez, Don Castillo and Don Hernandez and their wives sat closer to Papá. They had all arrived in the last couple of days to participate in the wedding that Don Joaquín had announced at Don Gonzalez's daughter's wedding last fall. Instead of their presence keeping Don Joaquín from making a scene, it seemed to egg him on. He continued his diatribe about why they needed to take over Alta California and revolt against Mejico's corrupt government.

"This is exactly why we need to push out all the Americanos immediately!" Don Joaquín had been very vocal about his opinions throughout dinner, ignoring Padre Pedro's suggestion that the conversation was not suited to dinner with ladies and children present.

"They have no culture, they come in and sweep our children away! They steal our lands and corrupt the next generation. They are uncivilized and barbaric! They don't even speak our language." He paused only long enough to pull a long draft from his glass of wine.

"And they are heathen. They do not respect the Holy Roman Church or its representatives. Isn't that so, Padre Pedro?" He gazed hard at the priest. Padre Pedro didn't seem intimidated.

"Actually, I find it interesting that you have not built a chapel on your hacienda in all these years nor have you invited me to conduct Mass for you except for your marriages, not even a Mass in celebration of the lives of your dearly departed wives, and yet you claim to know about the spiritual state of another man's soul. A man who has made me feel welcome in his home despite our language and religious differences. He shows true Christian charity." Padre Pedro returned an equally hard gaze. *"Have you asked Señor Samuels if he is a devout man of God or the heathen you claim him to be?"*

"No, I can see it in the ridiculous clothes he wears and the fact that he kept Vicky with him for so long before you went and saved her. I can only imagine what she must have suffered at his hand."

Enough was enough. Before Vicky considered what her words might do, she interrupted his rant. *"He's behaved as a gentleman at all times. His elderly servant cared for my needs when I was too sick to take care of myself."* Her indignation at the words Don Joaquin hurled about Chris made her forget whom she was talking to. Had she been thinking clearly she would not have been so easily baited.

"So I see he has already bewitched you, girl. What else has he done to you while he had you trapped in his little hovel?" the man sneered.

"He's not bewitched me! He's been a gentleman.

And that's more than anyone can say about you. You've intimidated and mistreated our people here on many occasions. That's why I left..." She paused but not before enough had been said to condemn her. What had she done? Had she just made Chris Don Joaquín's next target? She could survive just about anything but that.

"So you admit you left here with a purpose? Did you think I wouldn't eventually find you? And I would have found you sooner had I known the Americano had lived. I heard that he had been killed along with his slaves last summer." Don Joaquín turned a dismissive glance at Chris before retuning his glare to her. *"Don't be a fool. Your father is a wise enough man to know not to cross me, especially for a worthless daughter no one else wants. No, wench, you'll be my wife and bear me a son or wish you had."*

Her father was on his feet instantly, followed by Chris, who she could see was struggling to understand what was happening. *"Get out!"* her father raged. *"You dare to speak like that to my daughter at my table!"*

Don Joaquín made a show of wiping his mouth with his serviette. *"I think you may want to rethink your words, Manuel. Surely you are too wise to show me such disrespect."*

"You miscalculate your own worth and power, Joaquín. I had many misgivings from the start with this arrangement, but you have now confirmed my worst suspicions. Get out now or I will remove you myself." Papá pushed his chair out from behind him.

Chris stared at Don Joaquín, clearly ready to remove the man at the first sign from her father. As quickly as they were talking, she knew he hadn't been able to understand the words exchanged, but she could see that he now understood what was happening.

She wanted to pull him back down and insist he stay out of all this. But she'd already caused trouble by opening her mouth, and now her father and her rescuer were going to pay the price. She gripped the arms of her chair as if hoping they would hold her wobbly legs up, but Chris put a hand on her shoulder and stilled her movements, a silent warning to sit quietly and not intervene. For a moment, she was concerned, hoping that no one else noticed his familiarity with her. But she also thrilled at his defense of her, his willingness to put himself at risk on her behalf without even thinking about it.

Don Joaquín's face turned an alarming purple color as he finally pushed his chair back with such force it toppled with a loud thud. *"Well, you both just signed your own death warrants,"* he shouted. Pointing to Chris, he shook his head. *"They'll pay for not having done their job last time. You won't be spared again, American dog. I'll make sure you're dead myself."*

Vicky couldn't help the gasp that escaped her at the unveiled threat. The men who had killed Jeb...

Turning haughty eyes on the others at the table, Joaquín raised his nose and sniffed. *"Once we are free from the Mejican rule, I will be 'El Presidente.' You will all answer to me. Make certain you choose your friends carefully."* Reaching for the priest's arm, he took on a civil tone. *"Padre, I'll escort you out so you don't have to associate with the likes of these traitors."*

Padre Pedro pulled his arm free. *"I'm perfectly ca-*

pable of choosing when and with whom I travel, and I think I'll be staying a while longer, Don Joaquín de la Vega. I would not threaten so many men at one time and then turn your back. The Almighty says 'Vengeance is mine,' but He just might choose to use one of the men here to bring about His wrath."

With a snort, Don Joaquín left the room, his gait unsteady. Surely he'd been drinking most of the day. If he were able to saddle, much less mount up, Vicky would be surprised.

"Berto," Papá called out. Berto, José Luis, Alfredo and Guillermo from the stables appeared at the door, cutting off Don Joaquín's escape. *"This man needs an escort to his horse. Please make sure that he is saddled, mounted and leaving in the correct direction. Then we will post guards like we had spoken about for the duration."*

Papá's words brought a mix of relief and concern to Vicky. He'd been planning to say no to Don Joaquín and had started to prepare for the backlash before this dinner.

"No, don't leave without her!" Mamá screeched. *"She is a reminder of my disgrace and misery!"*

Papá pivoted from where he stood watching José Luis and Alfredo, the two biggest men on the hacienda, crowd Don Joaquín out the door. *"Woman, don't try my patience!"* he roared, and Vicky wondered just how her parents had ever survived all these years together.

"Why her? Why not take her and leave me Angelica? Couldn't God have left me a beautiful child instead of her?" Mamá turned her glare to Padre Pedro.

"Why does God hate me so?" She punctuated her wail with the crash of her crystal decanter against the wall where it smashed into a thousand pieces, its golden liquid spilling down.

Vicky wasn't aware of standing, but suddenly Chris had an arm around her shoulders and was leading her out of the room, up the stairs. He stopped at the top of the balcony, as if catching his breath, and then pulled her toward the windows that overlooked the courtyard in the middle of the building. He wrapped his arms around her shoulders, sharing his warmth and taking some of the sting of Mamá's words away. His voice, soft and reassuring, soothed something deep inside. The roaring in her ears subsided as he bestowed a kiss to her forehead before he released her and she found herself wrapped in the loving arms of Magda. Magda led her the rest of the way to her room.

"Don't let her words poison your soul, child. She's bitter and hurting, but you are not what she says. You are a gift from God. A princess." Magda had always been the one to comfort her when her mother's words had devastated her. Her arms still had the strength of a woman many years younger and the ability to soothe, but she missed Chris's arms around her. She feared he would leave, as well. After all, she had gotten him into this mess. He didn't deserve to be caught in the middle of a war between the noblemen of Alta California. It would change the way life had been. No more would she be free to ride and go out with the men. And what about Joaquín's threat? Would he go back and kill Chris as he had vowed?

While she might have gotten a pardon from having to marry Don Joaquín, he'd still effectively taken away her freedom. And now Chris's life was in danger, thanks to her. It was no way to repay the man for all the kindness he had shown her, for everything he had done on her behalf. For a moment, she wished she'd never laid eyes on the man she now loved. Because she could cost him everything.

Chapter Twenty

Following as Magda led Vicky to her room, Chris forced his hands to his sides and stayed a few paces behind only by sheer willpower. Everything in him wanted to take her back into his arms and see to her comfort. She had stilled in his arms, and there had never been a moment in his life when he felt more confident of what he wanted and who he had been created to be—Vicky's husband and protector. But he'd also never felt more frustrated and out of his element than he had tonight. Out of the whole meal, he'd picked out only a handful of words, and they didn't even begin to explain to him what happened.

Before he let the women enter the room, he went in and searched, making sure no danger lurked there. "Keep the door locked, Vicky. I don't want anything to happen to you." He stood at the doorway, torn between the need to find her father and the need to stay with her. For the sake of their future, he needed to speak with her father as soon as possible.

Vicky's eyes were still full of worry. Surely after what had happened at the table, Don Ruiz had sent the awful man packing, but then why did Vicky still look so scared?

"Stay with Magda, she'll keep you safe." Again he forced his hands to his sides instead of reaching out and clutching her to him. She looked so forlorn he almost gave in to his impulses, but he needed to find her father before he withdrew into his own chamber.

"I need to speak with your father. If you need anything, please have someone find me, Vicky. Please?" She nodded and Magda closed the door. "Lock it," he insisted. He didn't move until he heard the dead bolt slide into place.

The downstairs hallway was eerily quiet. Chris retraced their steps back to the dining room where a woman who looked similar to Magda but younger cleared the table. As he paused at the threshold of the room, she looked up from her work, and he recognized her as one of the two who had exited Vicky's room earlier all giggles. A knowing look and a half smile lit her eyes when she saw him. *"More food?"* she asked slowly, watching his eyes for understanding.

"No, no more food. Want talk Don Ruiz." Chris put the words together and smiled his appreciation when she bit her lip to keep from laughing at his mispronunciations.

"In the office." She set her tray down and led him down the hallway to the room they had gathered in upon their arrival. The door was partially closed, and

as they approached, Padre Pedro's voice carried out to them, his tone somber.

"Gracias." He nodded to her and half bowed, not sure what was customary, then turned and knocked on the door.

"Pasa." The voice was Don Ruiz's. Praying that God would help him to understand and communicate in Spanish because his future depended on it, he pulled open the door and found himself back in the study. Leather-bound books filled the shelves along one wall, and two large fainting couches and overstuffed horsehair chairs sat at angles by the two long windows at the far side of the room. A fire roared in the fireplace under a large portrait of a man resembling Don Ruiz but who had lighter skin and startling blue eyes. He took a moment to take in the room as he gathered his thoughts and prayed silently once more.

"Mi papá." Don Ruiz stood and gestured to the portrait. *"King of España sent him here,"* he continued in slow, clear Spanish. Of course, Vicky had already told Chris that much, but to see the man, or at least his likeness, and then to see how closely his son resembled him in stature and build was interesting. He assumed Don Ruiz resembled his mother in coloring. Chris stood and studied the likeness and then his prodigy.

They both had given Vicky the small furrow in her brow when she concentrated. Both men also shared the same oval-shaped eyes and long, thin nose, but Vicky's nose was much flatter and her eyes were more almond in shape. She had a unique beauty, a beauty all her own.

"Please, have a seat." Don Ruiz indicated a chair

next to Padre Pedro. None of the other guests from dinner were present. At least he wouldn't have to endure an hour or two of small talk he didn't understand before he could corner Don Ruiz about his proposal.

Don Ruiz sized him up with a calculating look as he settled on the chair opposite Chris and next to Padre Pedro. Chris sat staring at his hands for a moment, the silence heavy, before he cleared his throat and lifted his gaze. If Chris hadn't known better, he'd believe those were tears that glazed Don Ruiz's eyes.

"Thank you, thank you, Señor Crestofer Samuels, for returning our princesa to us." The man cleared his throat again and sniffed. *"We expected to have a misa for her with Padre Pedro because we thought she…"*

The words came too fast. Even after the older man tried twice more, Chris felt the frustration building. If they couldn't get even simple things ironed out, how could he ever convince her father he was the man to take care of her forever? How could he find out what was expected of a suitor and begin to try to fulfill those requirements?

Don Ruiz must have had the same thoughts as he sat back in his chair and ran his hand through his curly jet-black hair. At forty something, only a few gray hairs stood out in his sideburns, and his stature hinted of a strength hidden under the extravagantly embroidered suit. He fingered the mustache that covered his upper lip.

After a moment of concentration, he conferred in low tones to Padre Pedro. *"Mi Inglés,* no *muy* good.

Many years and no practice." His words were halting and heavily accented but English. Chris smiled.

"Don Joaquín de la Vega no *es* good man. He want fight Mejico and say no more Mejico. Alta California new country. I not want Vicky marry him, but he say he marry her at wedding last year. Her *mamá* say words that hurt Vicky and send letter in my name to him to marry Vicky. Vicky need family and home for Vicky away from her *mamá*."

His words were hard to piece together. Did Don Ruiz also want to revolt against Mexico's rule? Was that why the noblemen of the area had met? Had Chris somehow fallen into a conspiracy and, if so, what side was he on? Would he even get a chance to decide, or had his presence already sealed his fate?

"We no like Mejico tell us land no more ours. But we no want fight. We want send *delegados*—how say man who speak for others?"

"Delegates?" Chris offered, smiling slightly at playing the same game of deciphering words with Don Ruiz as he had often done with Vicky.

"*Sí*, delegates. Don Joaquín no want delegates. Want to rule Alta California. We—Don Gonzalez, Don Castillo *y* Don Hernandez—made plan. Send letter to Mejico General for come and get Don Joaquín. He no come on time." Don Ruiz paused.

So they had been setting a trap for Don de la Vega but the Mexican General had been late. From what Chris had gathered, it was a pattern throughout Mexican history.

"We want no fight. We want live in peace," Don Ruiz stated.

"All men should live in peace and enjoy freedom."

"Even *esclavos*?"

"Slaves?" Chris clarified.

"*Sí*, even slaves?" The man watched him closely. Somehow he knew the question was some sort of test. The only response he could give was the truth.

"I believe that slavery is bad, it's a blight to mankind and we will be paying the price for the sin of putting one man in bondage to another for a very long time, even if someday it ceases to be practiced."

Don Ruiz nodded his head even as Chris realized that half his words would have been unfamiliar to the man. "Why you come to Alta California, Señor Samuels?" The change in topic caught Chris off guard.

"My father had a large plantation, or hacienda if you will. When he died, I inherited it." At the frown across Don Ruiz's forehead, Chris reworded his explanation. "When my father died, no longer live, the hacienda in South Carolina now mine." He tapped his chest and received a nod to continue. "My father have many slaves. I no want slaves." He paused, grimacing inwardly at the way he was starting to mistreat the English language. "I let them go free. I offered to pay them to stay and work as free men and women. But other haciendas did not like my people to be free. They were worried that their slaves would revolt."

"So you let you men go?" The man's dark brown eyes seemed to look into his heart and see more than he wanted anyone to see.

"Yes. But most stayed. Then the other plantations started to hurt my men while they work. They kill one when he went to town. I told my people to go to Canada, no more slaves in England and Canada. Only Nana Ruth and Jeb, her husband, stayed with me and made the voyage to Alta California."

"Who Jeb and Nana Ruth?"

"They were slaves for my father. Jeb was killed last year. Nana Ruth is at *ranchito* with student of Padre Pedro."

At the mention of the priest's name, Don Ruiz turned and asked him a few questions. The priest regarded Chris with speculation for a moment and then answered quickly, a nod of his head ending their dialogue. He sent Chris a smile.

"What you want here? Do you have family? Will you go back to South Carolina?"

"I will not be going back. I sold the plantation and have come here to stay."

"Will you take wife?" Don Ruiz focused his attention on Chris, and it was all he could do to sit still. He had been praying for a way to introduce the topic, and here Don Ruiz brought it up on his own.

"I would like to now. God has changed my heart in recent days, and I would like to marry and have a family of my own."

"Can you give wife a house that safe and warm? Give her and children food and clothes?"

"Yes. I can provide all those things for my wife and children. I have planted crops of corn, wheat and had a large garden. There is an abundance of wild game in the woods around our home, and we would never want for meat. I work hard and would protect…" He stopped. He needed to be honest, even if it cost him Vicky's hand. Her father would know just how unsafe the wilds of Alta California were without the protection of a community like the one the Ruiz family had created.

"Don Joaquín say he think you dead. You say Jeb dead. When did Jeb dead?"

"Last summer three men came and attacked while Jeb and I were in the fields. They shot him before we could even react. I got back to the cabin and defended it from them, hitting one, killing another, and the third one ran away." He could still see the blood on the ground when he went back to help Jeb.

"The men speak Indian or Spanish?" Don Ruiz's question brought him back from his dire thoughts and into the present only to have to return to the memories again. He had been so focused on protecting Nana and himself he hadn't paid much attention to what they might have said. Then an image came into focus in his mind. The third man, mounted on a strong, fast horse with a Spanish saddle, had raised his fist in the air and shouted in Spanish, *"Go home, Americano dog."*

"Spanish." The memory collided with the more recent one of Don Joaquín saying nearly the same thing at the dinner table.

"*Sí*, you are *inteligente*. You now know Don Joaquín send men to kill you. He will do the same now Vicky no marry him."

Dread washed over him with Don Ruiz's words, and his body went numb. An image sprang to mind of being attacked at the cabin again, this time Vicky and a baby cuddled in her arms being shot at as they sat on the bench by the cabin while he worked in the fields. He couldn't take that risk. He would never be able to live with himself if something happened to her. Her father had to know it, too. As any good father would, he was making his position clear as to why he could not accept Chris's proposal. He couldn't blame the man.

"You have no villa close to you?" Don Ruiz questioned as if he could read Chris's racing thoughts.

"No." He had wanted to be alone, isolated from the horrors of humanity, but what about those who helped? The isolation he had so longed for became the very reason he would miss out on the most important things in life. A wife, a family. To show love and kindness to someone and have it shown to him in return. To belong.

"Why no make one now?" Don Ruiz's question was simple and yet profound. Could he build a village close by? Could he give up his solitude for a chance at a family? Or maybe it was time to move. If Don Ruiz would let him lease some land on his hacienda, he could move his horses and *ranchito*. He'd miss the valley and the woods he'd worked so hard to tame, and he'd need a few months to get everything together. He'd have to talk Nana Ruth into the move, but she'd come along. He'd find a way to convince her.

But whether he built a village close by or moved to one, it was the answer he'd been looking for, the way to have the life he'd come to want.

Straightening, he sat up and looked Don Ruiz in the eyes. The man's gaze was solemn. "Don Ruiz, you said Don Joaquín is not going to marry Vicky. Is there someone else who has spoken for her?"

"You ask if someone want marry Vicky?"

"Yes, sir. Has someone else asked for Vicky's hand?" Chris reworded the question and waited. "Does she love someone else?"

"No. No other man ask for Vicky." Chris felt his breath rush out with the answer. Did Don Ruiz notice his nerves? The man sat completely still, as if waiting for Chris's next move. Did he know what Chris was going to say? Did Don Ruiz know that Chris was in love with his daughter?

Chris took a deep breath and spoke the words he'd been turning over in his mind for a long time now. Probably longer than he even realized.

"I do not know the way Spanish or Californianos ask for a woman's hand. What must I do to ask for Vicky?"

"You would ask to marry Vicky?" Don Ruiz shot a glance at Padre Pedro, who nodded in return.

"Yes, sir. I want to marry Vicky." His voice caught at the end with the emotion of it all.

"I will make arrangements. You will make *viha*?" Don Ruiz looked excited, as well.

Astounding! He closed his eyes for a second and thanked God for having given him grace and granting him the desire of his heart.

Now, for the arrangements. "I must build a bigger house, and yes, I will need to find men and families who are willing to build their homes close to mine so we can create a village." He'd pondered and prayed about asking for her hand, but now that her father approved, he had so many other things to plan.

"I send men. I have many *vaqueros*, they not all need to work here," Don Ruiz stated. "I send them to make *viha* and live on your land. You give them work in field and with horses and watch for no attack. Marry on Vicky's *cumpliaños*."

Don Ruiz held out his hand as if to conclude the deal, but Chris hesitated. He needed to understand what was expected of him. Was there a bride's price to pay? Would they take American dollars, or would he need to find a way to exchange his money and gold for pesos or pesetas?

"What must I give you?" he asked, prepared to give everything he had after calculating the cost of building a large home and paying the workers. Much of the materials would be found nearby, the trees and rocks and such, but glass for the windows was a specialty item that he'd have to go to the coast to order and wait for months if not over a year.

He still couldn't quite believe this was all happening, that he was worrying about glass windows for the house he was going to build Vicky.

Don Ruiz quirked his eyebrow almost exactly like Vicky did when she was puzzled by something.

"You not want for wife? You buy like slave?" The man's countenance grew stormy like a thunderhead over the sea.

Quickly Chris waved his hands as if to dispel the words from the room. "No, not buy like slave. Some countries make the man pay father to marry the daughter. Do you have this custom?"

"No, I give you money for marry my daughter."

"That's not necessary. All I want is to marry Vicky," he answered, this time stretching out his hand toward his future father-in-law. But when their hands clamped together, he realized one very important thing: she had not been involved in the process. What if she would not have him? He would not force her to marry him as Joaquín had tried to. Maybe it was good that he had so much work to do. The time would afford him opportunities to get to know her family and visit her at her home. Bring her flowers and take her on picnics, woo her in ways he hadn't considered before because she had been his charge and promised to another.

She had told him she did not want to marry and move away from her beloved hacienda. Would he need to relocate? He'd do it in a heartbeat if it ensured her sharing his life and becoming his wife. But what if she felt for him the same sisterly interest that she felt for José Luis?

"Don Ruiz, before we make any more plans, we need to ask Vicky if she will have me. I do not speak Spanish or know your customs and ways. She might not want to live with me. She may love someone else."

"She will marry you, Señor Samuels. She cannot hide the way her heart love you when she at table today. She never let man carry her on horse. She not want Papá to carry. She want you." Don Ruiz shook his head once more. "She want marry Americano." The older man stood, and Chris followed his example. Don Ruiz clapped Chris on both shoulders and then pulled him into a hug. "You will marry day after tomorrow," he stated jovially as he let him go. The shock of the announcement left Chris speechless.

"Que vive mi yerno!" Don Ruiz called out in a loud voice.

Padre Pedro rose to his feet and answered, *"Que vive!"* He also held out his hand to Chris. As their palms met, someone slammed the front door and started shouting. Chris caught only the words *Don Joaquín* and *José Luis*. It was enough to turn his heart to lead. He followed the others out of the office and down the hallway, trying to keep from running them over in his hurry. Where was Vicky? Was she safe? Had he been a fool to think a dead bolt could keep Don Joaquín from doing her harm?

Chapter Twenty-One

"Good evening, Magda." Vicky entered the kitchen. Magda had left her when they assumed the danger had passed and she had grown restless with her worries for Chris' safety.

"Vicky, mi'ja. I thought you would be resting by now." Magda wiped flour off her hands on her apron. *"Is everything all right, mi'ja?"*

"I fear for Chris and Papá. What if Don Joaquín..."

Magda shook her head and tsked her tongue at her as she kneaded the dough she was making. *"I have prayed for this day, my child."* Then she left her work and squeezed Vicky close, her warm, strong arms having sheltered and comforted Vicky so many times in the past. *"Do not fret. Your Chris is strong and smart. He loves you and will do whatever he needs to in order to protect you. I knew it, I just knew it the minute I saw him standing next to you and his gaze so protective. He would have killed Don Joaquín to protect you. He is a good man. I liked him the first time he came to sell*

Tesoro. Berto said the same thing. You could not find a better man, save my own Berto, if you searched all of Mexico and España. You'll have to settle for second best." Magda laughed and pinched Vicky's cheek.

"I know. I've always been envious of you, Magda. You and Berto are so happy. You love each other." Even she could hear how wistful her voice sounded. How she wished she could have been born to a simple *vaquero*, then she would be loved by someone humble and kind like Chris.

"And you and your Chris will have a love that lasts a lifetime."

"It is true that I love him," she finally admitted out loud. *"He is such a good man and wants to protect me from Don Joaquín, but that does not mean that he loves me."*

"And you're telling me that man who can't keep his eyes off you doesn't love you? Did he tell you that?"

"I'm too dark skinned to be loved…"

"Now, you bite your tongue right now, young lady." Magda held a hand to her lips.

"Your mother has planted seeds of doubt in your heart for years, and it has to stop. God doesn't have favorites. Ask Padre Pedro. He comes and speaks the Misa for all of us. Not just your father and mother or even just your family. He insists that we all attend because he says that God loves all men and we will one day all be in heaven with Him. Now, if God loves me, a humble Indiacita with no noble blood, then surely He can love you, too. And so can your Chris. He loves you, Vicky, my princesa. I have seen it shining in his eyes."

Could it be true? Did God really love her as she was? Chris, Magda, Nana Ruth and even Padre Pedro had said similar things… Could it be true? And if it were, then she could pray. She could try to trust. Maybe He did answer but she just hadn't understood His message.

She needed to go somewhere and think. Maybe even try to pray.

"I want to take a treat…"

"Out to Tesoro. Yes, I imagined you would. I will wait for you to come back before I go home. Do you want me to start some tea?"

"Yes, please." She took two apples and two carrots from the pantry and then gave Magda a quick hug on her way out the door. *"Thank you for everything, Magda. I know I don't say it enough, but I love you."*

"Aye, mi'ja. Hurry back."

With a nod, she slipped out the kitchen door and headed for the barn. Standing in the middle of the yard, she stared up at the night sky. The same stars had winked down on her at Chris's cabin when she stood in his yard. *"Thank you, God. I know Chris talks to you all the time. He said that You wanted to hear from me, too. Thank You for saving me from having to marry Joaquín. Protect Chris and Papá from the schemes that evil Joaquín is planning. I don't trust anyone but You to keep us all safe."*

She crossed the rest of the yard, pausing as a shiver ran up her back. She should have grabbed a serape on her way out, but now that she was almost to the barn she'd just ignore the cool night air. She'd soon return to the warmth of the kitchen and sit with Magda while they sipped tea and caught up on events around the hacienda.

Pulling the large door open, she paused—something didn't feel right. The door wasn't latched. Odd. None of the *vaqueros* would have left it open. Berto demanded that everyone be careful for the protection of the animals under his care. Reaching for the lantern on the peg inside the door, her hand closed on only thin air. No lantern. Odder still.

A whinny from the stalls caught her attention.

"Just a minute, Tes. I'm looking for the lantern." Another noise, this time as if someone had bumped into something, sounded close to Tesoro's stall, and then Tesoro snorted again. Picking up a shovel, Vicky cautiously stepped a little farther into the barn. *"If someone is here, you'd better come out and stop messing around in the barn. Berto won't take kindly to your mischief,"* she called out, proud her voice didn't shake the way her hands did.

"Don't care what Berto thinks of my mischief," a voice snarled at her in the dark. Don Joaquín. Her blood froze like ice in her veins. How would he have gotten away from José Luis and Alfredo? They wouldn't have let him get away. Had he killed them? *"By the time anyone finds out that I didn't leave as quickly as they had expected, we'll be long gone and they won't want to cross me again. I came for what's mine. No one denies me anything!"*

"Mi papá never promised me to you. He said he would consider the match, but he didn't commit. You

*were the fool who announced it last year. Mi papá
would not do that to me!"*

*"You foolish girl. I don't need a commitment from
him. I always get what I want. Learn that now and
you'll live a bit longer. We could even get along just
fine if you'd learn to keep your mouth shut and do what
you're told."*

"I won't..." She stepped back, aware of every rustle
of her skirt that gave away her movement.

*"I don't want to kill you now. But I will if you run.
And as for your lover, he's as good as dead already.
He won't see morning light."*

If she fled, Don Joaquín would go after Chris and
Nana Ruth. She couldn't let him hurt the very people
who took her in and showed her love. They saved her
life. She would not be the cause of them losing theirs.
She'd rather die.

"If you leave Chris alone, I'll go willingly." After
all, if she had to die, she now knew God would take her
to live in heaven. But to know that her escape caused
harm to her friends would be living torture.

She set the shovel aside, wishing she could see the
man so she could use the implement to knock him into
the next world. She walked blindly toward the back
of the barn, knowing that each step took her closer to
her doom.

The odor of Don Joaquín alerted her to his presence an instant before his clammy hand clamped over
her mouth, his other hand holding something hard and
cold to her back. *"Now, don't make a sound and don't
do anything foolish."*

As if giving herself up to the whims of this man was not foolish? But she bit her tongue. No need to antagonize him more.

"Now, get on that horse of yours you can't be without. I've got her saddled and ready. At least you saved me from having to retrieve you from the house."

She shuddered at the thought. There was no way he would have reached her room without someone having encountered him first, and in the frame of mind he was in, she was sure he would have killed them to get to her.

"Get moving!" He shoved her forward. He caught Tesoro's reins and then faced Vicky, his foul breath causing her stomach to threaten to revolt. She clenched her teeth together. *"Get on that horse!"* he roared, slapping her across the face. Without waiting for him to do anything more, she ducked around him and settled as quickly as possible on the saddle. Her dress didn't lend itself to riding, but she'd stay in the saddle. Her ribs were already burning like someone had set them on fire, and she hoped he would be too drunk to last long. Maybe he'd doze and fall off his horse.

"Now, don't go getting any ideas about getting away from me. I'll come back and kill that Americano and your family if you do."

The other man who had left with Don Joaquín and José Luis stood at the threshold of the house, his face puffing on one side from what must have been a blow with something blunt. The men all spoke at once, and Chris didn't understand anything. Frustrated, he ran up the stairs and pounded on Vicky's door, unconcerned about the amount of noise he was making or whether she was asleep. He needed to see she was safe, whole and untouched. No one answered his persistent knocking even as others came up the stairs behind him. A glance over his shoulder reassured him it was only Don Ruiz and Padre Pedro.

Don Ruiz just threw the door open. The fact that it was unlocked made Chris's blood freeze. Had it been forced? For propriety's sake, he stepped aside even when every fiber of his being wanted to follow the other two men into her room. As they made a quick search and came up empty, he went to his own room and grabbed his handgun, praying it wouldn't be needed.

They made a quick search of the other ten rooms on that hallway, and then Don Ruiz sent a few of the *vaqueros* to check on the other wing. Padre Pedro led the rest back down the stairs as Chris went straight back to the kitchen. Its strong, thick door had been closed. Magda turned at his arrival, looking startled to see him there with his gun drawn. She must not have heard the noise at the front of the house.

"Magda, where Vicky?"

"Go see Tesoro."

"Don Joaquín escaped." He repeated the only words he'd understood at the door. All color drained from her face. Chris slid a stool under her just as her legs gave way. "

Go! Go mi Vicky," she ordered and motioned him away.

He crossed the kitchen and had his hand on the door when she called to him. *"Señor Chris. Go with God and bring Vicky back."* He nodded and then slid out the door, pausing with his back against the wall to let his eyes adjust to the dark night. The barn door stood open, but no light flooded out. Dread squeezed his heart again. If Don Ruiz's man looked that bad, what would Joaquín do to Vicky when he had her alone?

He ran to the end of the house, and then crossed the yard at an angle so that he wasn't in sight if Joaquín looked out from the barn. The moon and stars afforded a little light, but the pitch-black inside the barn would give Joaquín the advantage for a minute or two. He stood just to the side of the door and waited, trying to hear any movement over the pounding of his own heart.

"God, please keep her safe. I've failed her once again. I don't know if I can bear it if she's..." No, he couldn't say the words, couldn't think them. He would get her out of the barn safe and sound. Or die trying.

He heard muffled voices in the barn. He ducked and entered, keeping to the right side. If only they were in his barn, he'd know the place blindfolded. But he remembered seeing shovels by the entrance on his last visit here. Keeping low to the ground and close to the wall, he holstered his gun and let his hand explore until he found what he had been looking for.

A stall door creaked, and Tesoro snorted. Something, or more likely someone, wasn't to her liking. Good horse. If Joaquín tried to ride double to keep Vicky close to him, there would be no way that Tesoro would be able to carry that much weight and make good time. That would be to Chris' advantage if he couldn't keep them from leaving the barn. If Joaquín was thinking straight, he'd choose the fastest horse and take it. Comet was the obvious choice unless Berto had bought some other horses from someone else in the last year.

A second stall door creaked open and then thudded shut. That would mean Don de la Vega was using two horses. If he could somehow get them separated, he could disarm de la Vega. His guess would be he'd be carrying a pistol. Creeping across the alley so he was on de la Vega's right, he crouched low and bid his time.

De la Vega hissed instructions to Vicky. Chris could see her silhouette as she climbed up on Tesoro. Slowly, they made their way toward him. He nickered like one of the horses and made a snorting sound. Vicky's head cocked in his direction, and then she faced front while Tesoro nickered in response. De la Vega followed. The second horse also snorted, and Chris knew it was Comet by the sound. He silently promised Comet sugar cubes for the rest of his life if he tossed the heavy man on his head.

As Vicky passed, she looked directly at him for an instant. Even in the dark he could see the look of relief followed immediately by pure fear and sadness in her eyes. Was she saying goodbye? She shook her head as if trying to dissuade him from rescuing her. But there was no way Chris was going to let her leave. Not like this. Not for Don de la Vega.

She glanced once more at him, and the longing in her eyes called to his heart. For a second he could read her thoughts as clearly in her eyes as if she had said them out loud. She cared for him. Not just a little. She was going with the monster in part to protect him.

Not on his watch. She would not have to sacrifice for him. *No*—he would protect her, no matter the cost. Determination filled his chest, and his blood thrummed through his veins.

He'd come for her. As soon as she heard the horse nicker by the door even though there was no stall there, she knew it was Chris. He'd risked his own life and come to save her. If only she could warn him away! Her life wasn't worth him taking such a risk. But the look on his handsome face said there would be no reasoning with him even if she could have stopped to talk with him. So she had no other option than to ride right past, praying that God would protect him. At the very last moment she let her fear and longing show in her eyes. He gave her a strange expression, then looked past her, determined.

Maybe she should have prayed for Joaquín's soul. The look on Chris's face showed none of the kindness, none of the gentleness she had come to expect from him. He looked capable of killing with his bare hands if necessary. Don Joaquín deserved no less for having gotten away with killing his other wives. And there was no doubt in her mind that he either caused their deaths directly or created such despair that death was better than being tied to him.

Just as Tesoro carried her over the threshold, hands reached out of the darkness and plucked her out of the saddle, whisking her away from the door. *"Shush, Vicky,"* Papá's voice whispered as he set her down by the outside wall of the barn. Then a thud sounded, and a gun went off. A scream followed as Comet neighed in rage and stomped. Images of Chris being trampled in the upheaval made her legs threaten to give out.

"We need to go and help Chris!" She tried to pull away, but Papá held her fast. *"Please, he might get hurt."* She'd beg if she had to.

"If you go in there, you'll distract him and he will get hurt. Let your man handle Joaquín. There isn't much of a chance Joaquín will come out the victor."

Even as she fought her father, she heard the sounds of something hitting hard against the wall. Though her father tried to hold her, Vicky managed to escape his grasp. She fled to the barn, desperate to see Chris, to make sure that Don Joaquín had not taken away her future.

Once Vicky passed him, Chris could see the pistol Joaquín held in his right hand pointed directly at her. He lifted the shovel and waited until Tesoro carried Vicky over the threshold, praying that they would flee as quickly as possible and be clear of the shot if he couldn't get the gun away from the other man. Then he leaped at Joaquín, bringing his shovel down across the man's arm with all his might.

The scream of rage and pain was drowned out by the report of the pistol. Joaquín dug his spurs into Comet's flanks as he dropped the gun and cradled his right forearm, which was hanging at an odd angle, obviously broken. Chris had never used spurs on any of his stock, and Comet, unused to the painful sensation, bucked, intent on throwing the tyrant off his back. It took only two tries.

Don Joaquín flew backward. A resounding crack filled the air when his shoulder and head slammed into the stone wall, and then the man slumped to the ground.

"Whoa!" Chris held out a hand and caught Comet's reins, keeping an eye on the man who remained deathly still. Chris whispered words of assurance to calm the horse and catch his breath. Between the fear of something happening to Vicky and the absolute fury he had never felt before tonight, his own body shook in the aftermath.

He dropped the shovel and pulled his revolver from his holster, tightening his grasp on Comet's reins in his left hand as he crossed the dark room to stand over the slumped form.

Vicky dashed into the barn as her father called out behind her. Berto lit a lamp. Chris stood over Joaquín, who was against the wall, his right arm obviously broken and his left shoulder dislocated. His eyes were closed. Even in the lamplight his color looked ash gray. The rise and fall of his chest confirmed that Chris hadn't ended his life. Relief for Chris mixed with frustration. Would Don Joaquín come back looking for revenge? Would they ever be free of his terror?

Berto relieved Chris of Comet's reins, and Chris holstered his gun.

"Chris," she called, and he spun around just as she ran into his arms. He caught her to his chest and held on tight.

"I thought he had already taken you or…" He paused and held her at arm's length as he looked her over. "He didn't hurt you?"

She knew the exact instant he saw the red welt across her cheek. His jaw twitched, and his eyes grew hard. He started to turn away from her, back toward the unconscious man on the floor.

"You've punished him enough from the looks of it." She laughed at his confused expression and tried again in English. He shook his head when he understood her meaning.

"He hit you and tried to take you from us. He doesn't deserve to still be breathing."

"But you saved me, Chris."

"I won't let him near you ever again," Chris promised, hugging her close, but she felt a change as he stood there. Even with his arms around her he was pulling away from her.

"What is it?" she asked.

"Let's go inside. You need to rest." He slid his right arm over her shoulders and hugged her to his side as he led her past the growing crowd. Señor Gonzalez, Señor Castillo and Señor Hernandez all stood behind them, watching everything with guarded eyes. They had been part of the meeting Papá had gone to. They had also heard the threats Joaquín had yelled earlier at the dinner table. If it came to a feudal war, would they side with Joaquín or with Papá?

The barn filled with *vaqueros*. Everyone must have heard the gunshot in the otherwise calm night. For a moment, Vicky worried that Don Joaquín might still meet his maker that night. After all, he had tried to steal two horses and Don Ruiz's daughter. The horses alone would merit a hanging had he been a plebeian.

Because of his station in life, if one of the *vaqueros* were to take matters into his own hands, he might end up in prison or worse. But with the other dons and her father there, having witnessed everything, Papá and the others would determine how to mete out justice.

When Vicky and Chris reached the steps to go into the kitchen, he leaned down and looked into her eyes. She saw something in his face that caused her fear to grow. Something was wrong. He was saying goodbye— even though he'd promised only the day before to stay until her birthday. Now that there would be no forced wedding with Don Joaquín, they could celebrate her birthday with joy. Surely he would keep his word and stay for that.

The door opened before she could ask him any questions, and Magda swept her up in a strong embrace. *"Mi'ja. I was frantic. I thought surely that animal would kill you for standing up to him."*

"He tried to take me away, but Chris saved me." She glanced at Chris but didn't see the tender expression he normally had for her. Instead he looked sad, forlorn, as if the world was ending.

"I told you he's a good man. God was looking out for you, Mi'ja. He gave you a hero for your very own." Pulling Vicky with her into the kitchen, Magda pushed her into a chair at the table and then pointed to the one next to it for Chris. He sat down heavily as if he had aged fifty years in one night.

"Chris, are you hurt?" She turned her attention to him as Magda went to bring the tea.

"No, I am fine," he said, but his voice lacked conviction. He sat with his forehead leaning in his palm.

"Chris, you no talk the *verdad*."

"Verdad?" He didn't turn to look at her.

"When words are yes. Real. Not *mientira*."

"Mientira?"

"Mientira—when you see sky blue and say it red or say snow is green or grass is pink…"

"Not true? A mistake?"

"No mistake. When you know grass is green and say it pink."

"You're asking if I'm lying?" He turned his face to her, and she could see the deep sadness written in his eyes and etched in the lines of his forehead.

"You lie. You say you fine, but you not fine." She bit her lower lip and ducked her head so he wouldn't see the tears starting to form. It had been a long and eventful day, and for a few minutes, not even an hour, she had believed that someone as wonderful as Chris could want her to be his helper and mate for life. She had begun to let Magda's words spark hope in her lonely heart. How foolish. A tear slipped past her eyelashes, and she sniffed. "You no want stay for my birthday. You want go to home. No want dance with me."

"Hey, Vicky, it's not that at all." His voice softened. He turned in his chair, catching her chin in his palm and forcing her gaze up to meet his. The look of concern and tenderness had returned. He slipped a finger across her cheek and caught the stray tear. "You have no idea how much I want to stay. I'm just… I almost lost you."

Magda set a cup of tea in front of each of them, placed the sugar bowl and honey between them and retreated. *"I must go home and rest for tomorrow. You go get some sleep soon, mi'ja. Señor Chris."* Magda left out the back door.

Vicky waited only until the door closed behind Magda. "You no have to lie, Chris. I not want you to dance with me if you no want." She'd find a way to forget about him. She'd live the rest of her life trying to help her father on the hacienda. No one would ever compare to Chris, so there would be no more dreaming of romance or finding someone to love, to form a family with. Ever. But before meeting Chris, she had never dreamed that could be her life anyway.

"I'm not lying, Vicky. I promise you I'm not lying. I failed to take care of those who depended on me most. Ezequiel, Jeb, you… You deserve someone who can keep you safe."

"You came and save me. You risk for me. You good man."

"But I didn't protect you from Don de la Vega. I shouldn't have left you alone. If I had been with you when you encountered him…"

"You be dead," she stated even as a chill ran down her spine. It was true. Even as she said it she knew it to be the truth. Chris opened his mouth as if about to argue but then stopped and looked at her, his eyes widening with realization.

"He would shoot you and then take me. He bad man.

God sent you to save me, Chris. He let you be safe so you could save me. You good man." She swallowed and bit her lower lip to keep more words from pouring out. He was the man she wanted for a husband. No one else.

He pushed a tendril of hair off her forehead, tucking it behind her ear. His touch caused a tingle to run from her cheek, down her neck to her chest. Her heart sped up as his gaze shifted from her eyes to her lips and then back to her eyes again, asking her something. He could ask of her just about anything and she would comply—knowing that he would never intentionally hurt her. He leaned just slightly closer, and she did the same. Then his lips covered hers in a tentative kiss. Sweet and gentle like the man himself. He sat back, but she wanted another taste of him, of his concern for her and his caring.

"I shouldn't have done that. It will be harder," he muttered and moved away.

"Why?" She had heard Rosa's and Margarita's stories about *vaqueros* stealing kisses. She'd even seen Berto steal some impassioned kisses when he returned from the fields and he and Magda thought they were alone. At the time she had wondered if she would ever be kissed by someone handsome and worthy. Now she had, and he'd regretted it immediately.

"It will be dangerous out on my ranch. What if de la Vega had come across you there?"

"God would save me. And if He hadn't, it would have been for some purpose." Nana Ruth had said those words more than once when Vicky had paced from one window to the next watching for a sign of Chris's return when he had been out all day.

"But I thank God you save me, Chris. We safe here now. He use you."

"But as your husband I should protect you. I don't know if I can. What would happen if someone else came and attacked?"

Her breath froze in her throat, and for a moment she couldn't quite find any words to argue. He'd said "as your husband" as if he wanted to marry her! Her dearest and most vivid dream come true. Did he really mean it?

But then he'd come for her in the barn and fought a man armed with a pistol and a noble at that. Yes, he did care for her. He might even love her, but he feared that love. Maybe that was why he'd been living out in the woods all this time.

It clicked, like one of her brother's wooden puzzles when the pieces fit together. He feared not being able to protect her and losing her... He hadn't wanted to bring her here to marry or even to keep her out of his home, but because he'd already lost Jeb on the ranch and he feared something similar would happen to her.

Well, he had taught her a lot about the Bible and about English, but maybe it was time she shared the lesson she had just learned, as well. She asked Father God to give her the words as she squared her shoulders and looked deep into his wonderful, kind blue eyes. Eyes she'd like to look into every day for the rest of her life.

Chapter Twenty-Two

"Chris, why you think you could stop bad men from being bad?"

He shook his head, refusing to listen. "I couldn't protect Ezequiel. I couldn't protect Jeb. I couldn't even protect you the day we met. You would never have gotten hurt if I had been paying attention and shot the cougar on my own."

"And I would have been too lost in the woods and too sick that night to find shelter. I be dead by morning."

Something about her words stopped him. His body stilled. His breath stayed stuck in lungs that refused to work. She nodded. "I sick when I see you by water. I not want talk. Not know if you good or bad. Then puma try eat you. By getting me in water, God save my life, and you take care of me. Cristofer Samuels. You a good man, and I thank you for save my life then and tonight again. You not God to keep everyone always safe, but God use you to help."

Could her words be true? Had he been relying on his

own power and thinking he was responsible for everyone and everything?

"You very good man. One man, Ezequiel, die because of his own words and his foolishness, but many family free today because of you. You a man I trust with my life. Why you live with no *viha*?" Her gaze was too probing. As if she already knew more about his answer than he wanted to admit.

"I wanted to show that I can make a living without relying on anyone else's labor. I was going to do it all myself, and I didn't want to be responsible for anyone else's safety."

She sat still for a minute, her gaze on the teacup as she concentrated. He sensed she was forming an argument, but he wasn't willing to battle with her anymore. As soon as her father had given his blessing, all he thought about was finding her and proposing, but then the threat of Don Joaquín interrupted their discussion and reminded him once more of all his shortcomings.

She turned to face him, her eyes full of question. "You say that name Cristofer mean one like Christ. Yes?"

"Yes, it means 'Christlike one.' Someone who tries to be like Christ."

"Jesus live all by himself in desert? He not have any friend? He not talk to God in the early morning? He do it all himself?"

He didn't understand her logic. "No, Vicky. Surely you remember what we read. Jesus regularly went off by himself to pray, to talk to God the Father, but he lived with his friends, the disciples."

"So he talk with God the Father because he need friend?" she asked haltingly, as if puzzling out her questions.

"Yes."

"And when he go from town to town? He go alone, yes?" She sat up and grinned at him as if she had just solved a puzzle.

"No, Vicky. He took his disciples. He had many people who followed him. He taught them as they went. He told the stories or parables to large groups of people. He had the twelve disciples who were always with him, helping him and learning from him."

"You not like Christ." Even as she spoke, she laid her hand on top of his, as if softening the words she said. "He live with friends. He let others work with him. How you tell others who no have Bible about Jesus if you never talk to them? How other men feed family if you no give them job?"

Could it really be that simple? Had his intentions to avoid people been wrong? Then he remembered the "great commandment"—to go and make disciples of all the nations. He hadn't shared the Bible with anyone other than Vicky for all the years he had been living in Alta California, content to let Padre Pedro try to teach the whole of Alta California on his own.

He bowed his head and whispered a prayer. "Sorry, Father. I put my agenda ahead of Yours. I went where I could avoid the pain and responsibility, but that wasn't what You created me to be. You gave me blessings, but You expect me to be responsible with those gifts and blessings. Thank You for bringing Vicky to my life.

She's taught me more than I could ever have taught her. Amen."

When he lifted his head, he found Vicky sitting closer to him, tears in her eyes. She leaned in, touching his face for the first time, skimmed her finger up his cheek, her index finger exploring his dimple, then she framed his face and pulled him to her, kissing his lips. Her kiss was innocent and pure.

He held back for a second and then gave in to the need to be close to her. She smiled even as he kissed her. But there were things he needed to say, a very pressing question that needed an answer before he could indulge in kissing Vicky any more. Still, breaking the kiss was one of the hardest things he had ever had to do.

"I love you, Vicky. I can't imagine life without you. We can have half the hacienda move and make a *viha* by us or we can ask your father for some land to rent here and be closer, safer. I just want to spend the rest of our lives together. No more being alone. Vicky? Will you marry me? Your *papá* already gave me permission." He leaned back to look at her closely. He should have waited for just the right moment. He should have gotten down on one knee, should have had a ring or flowers or…

"Yes. I marry you, Chris." A tear escaped and raced down her cheek even as her lovely smile bloomed across her face. He reached out and smoothed the teardrop away.

Relief filled his lungs with a breath of air, laced with the scent of her hair and her floral perfume.

"Chris, *te amo*." She smiled tentatively and then leaned in for another perfect kiss.

For a while, they sat in silence. He watched as she sipped her tea, unable to believe that the beautiful woman next to him was truly going to be his wife. Then he realized she was exhausted, the emotions of the day catching up with her. As soon as she finished her last sip, Chris stood and pulled her chair out for her. Helping her to stand with his hand supporting her elbow, he led her up the stairs to her door. When they arrived, they found Berto sitting there.

Vicky seemed surprised, but Chris wasn't. If the older man hadn't taken the post, he would have himself, whether it was proper or not. Berto made eye contact, and Chris wondered if there was a second reason he had chosen to sleep in the hallway that night.

"The room is safe?" he asked Berto.

Even with Berto's assurances, Chris entered, leaving Vicky waiting out in the hallway. He opened her cabinet doors, checked the windows and made sure that the built-in steel bars were all secure. Then he came out and kissed her sweetly on the cheek, hugging her against his chest and whispering, "I love you, Vicky, my sweet."

"I love you, Chris."

With her words in his heart, he pulled himself away. Waiting while she entered her room, he heard the dead bolt slide into place before he opened his own door. Making a quick sweep of his own room to reassure himself no one was waiting to cause any more mischief that night, he readied for bed. Kicking off his shoes, he went back to the door and opened it. Berto sat up straighter and gave him a fierce look.

"I door open. I..." He paused and then held his hand to his ear to try to show that he just wanted to be able to hear if anyone should need him during the night. What if she had more nightmares? After coming face-to-face with Don Joaquín and being kidnapped at gunpoint, she had reason to have night terrors.

The older man smiled and nodded, then pointed to the door, signaling to Chris to go back inside by flicking his wrist and fluttering his fingers. Then he pantomimed laying his head down. Chris nodded and returned to his room, sure that he was too keyed up with all that had happened to be able to sleep. So he would spend some time talking with God, learning to turn over those he loved most and felt responsible for to God's watch, care and protection. He'd have to pray daily for God's strength and wisdom and the peace to rest in His omnipotence and might.

And he also planned to thank God for bringing Vicky into his life.

Chapter Twenty-Three

The next day her father announced at breakfast that they had a little over twenty-four hours to prepare for not only her birthday but also her wedding day. Mamá had chosen to sulk in her room, ignoring Vicky's request for her to come out and take part in the preparations.

Magda had called in many of the women from the hacienda for assistance. They came to the main house to help prepare the food, clean the house and sew Chris's suit and put the finishing touches on Vicky's dress.

As the day flew past, she caught only glimpses of Chris. She still could hardly believe that he had asked her to marry him. That he would make room on his land for a village so that they could be protected. Could he have become even more handsome overnight? She thought he might have. Or maybe it was the gleam in his eye that hadn't been there before.

The grief and weariness she hadn't noticed until it was gone no longer kept his smile from reaching his eyes. He looked deep into her eyes, and she felt the connection in her heart. He openly played and laughed with others now, no longer afraid of creating connections and even showing affection.

"He's so handsome." Margarita had come to help sew the last of the jacket pieces together as they worked in the late afternoon.

"And strong. I heard he subdued Don Joaquín last night and didn't even get hurt!" Rosa commented as she finished Vicky's veil.

"Papá has had him working out in the corral with the new horses this afternoon," Margarita reported. *"All the young women are gawking."*

"But of course you didn't, Margarita," Rosa, the older of the sisters, teased. So that explained why Chris hadn't been up to talk with her or check the window or a dozen other things he had found as excuses to be nearby earlier in the day.

"No, I didn't stand around with my mouth hanging wide open like I'd never seen a handsome young man before. After all, I have Cente."

"Well, Vicente is very handsome and I'm glad you have him," Vicky admitted, *"because I'll be keeping my Americano."* She couldn't quite crush the urge to run downstairs and out into the barnyard to chase away all those girls who were admiring her soon-to-be husband. But before she could do more than set her sewing aside, someone knocked on the door.

"I wonder who that could be." Rosa batted her eyes at Vicky and clasped her hands at her chest and sighed exaggeratedly.

Throwing a pillow at her friend, Vicky scrambled up to see who was at the door. *"Quien?"*

Standing in the corral, watching the horse stomp and snort, Chris concentrated on keeping his voice low and his movements slow. He was aware of the men and women standing around watching him work. The colt didn't like his presence in his corral any more than Chris liked the idea of someone still on the hacienda who had taken a shot at José Luis the night before. Two men had ambushed José Luis, Alfredo and two other *vaqueros* as they escorted Joaquín off the premises. The first of Joaquín's men had been killed in the gunfight, but a second one had escaped. Joaquín was tied up and guarded in one of the *vaquero*'s cabins.

Finally the colt stopped prancing and Chris held out his hand for the animal to sniff his scent. It was the first step. Before he could move to touch its muzzle, someone shouted from the back of the gathered group.

The colt bucked and started to rear. Knowing there would be no more progress today, Chris backed away, climbed over the fence and saw what the commotion had been about. A man with a bloody cloth wrapped around his midthigh, hands bound behind his back, was being dragged toward the cabin that served as the lockup. As the man was hauled away, he looked behind him, and his gaze landed on Chris. Fear and then pure hatred, the kind he'd seen only a few times in his life, glinted like steel in the man's dark brown eyes. Then he spat at Chris and said the same words he had heard twice before. "Go away, you American dog."

It was the man from the attack. One of the three who had tried to kill him and had shot Jeb in the back with no warning.

Fury straightened his spine, and he was halfway to the man before he almost ran over a child. The red in his vision cleared slowly as he stooped to help the small girl. Her eyes were as big and dark as Vicky's, filled with fear of him. It halted him in his tracks. He could not let the anger he felt toward Joaquín and his men turn him into an animal who mistreated others.

Crouching down to her level, he made eye contact. *"I'm sorry, small one."* He uttered the phrase he'd heard Vicky use the day before while talking to her brother. He picked up her rag doll from the ground and wiped the dirt off. He handed it back to her, but she paused a moment before reaching out and taking his offering.

The little girl stepped back, giggling. As she raced off, he heard her call to her friends, *"The Americano talks funny."*

At least she wasn't running off in terror.

He went as far as the steps of the small cabin where they were keeping the prisoners. Don Ruiz stood just inside listening to an animated account from the *vaqueros* who had apprehended the injured man. The man in question hung from the arms of the two who had brought him in. The length of his pant leg was soaked in blood. If they didn't get the bleeding stopped and the wound cleaned, they'd only need a pine box for him.

"Don Ruiz, man need doctor," Chris called out from the doorway. All heads turned to look at him. Joaquín

twisted on the cot where he was bound and began shouting in a menacing voice.

Don Ruiz shouted over him. *"This man shot José Luis last night! He not man..."* The rest of his words were unfamiliar, but Chris understood the gist of them. By attacking men on the hacienda, these men relinquished any rights to be treated humanely.

He stepped back, away from the cabin. He needed to pray. Was it right to let a man bleed to death? While he waited, Berto hobbled over and entered the place. Soon most of the other men exited except for the guards and Don Ruiz. Chris wandered back, still debating and silently praying for wisdom.

The door had been left open, and from it he could see Berto slit the bloodied pants of the wounded man who now lay on the cot. Joaquín had been tied to a chair in the far corner of the cramped cabin, and a *vaquero* stood at the ready with a pistol in hand. Berto prepared a cloth to treat the injured man's wounds. With the first splash of some sort of alcohol, the wounded man screamed and bucked almost completely off the bed. Chris entered the room and hunkered down at the foot of the bed, holding the man's legs still so Berto could continue his ministrations. Before they were done, the man passed out.

"Thank you for your help, Señor Samuels." Don Ruiz slapped him on the back of his shoulder as they finished washing up at the pump by the barn.

"You're welcome, sir. And I'd like you to call me Chris." He finished toweling off his hands and looked about the yard. Men and women hustled here and there, and he glanced up at the second-story window. What was Vicky doing now? He'd been up to bother her a dozen times earlier, and all he wanted was to run back up there again.

"Fine, Chris." Don Ruiz paused for a moment, but Chris knew that he had something on his mind. "My English no good to tell you what I think. My Vicky have good man. Man who take care of her and protect."

Chris met Don Ruiz's gaze and nodded, confirming what was said without words. "I love your daughter, sir. I will do everything I can to protect and cherish her."

"You know that man who we fix?"

"Do I know who that man is?" Chris clarified.

"Sí. You know?"

"Yes. He and two other men attacked my *ranchito* last year. They shot Jeb, the man who worked for me, in the back while we were working in the field."

"Joaquín say he kill him for not doing job of killing you. We need him to live to tell El General what Joaquín pay him to do. But that not why you want doctor?"

Chris heard the question in the man's voice and knew he needed to be honest. "A part of me wanted to kill him when I recognized him. He killed a defenseless old man and shot José Luis, as well. He needs to be punished. But to let him bleed to death is not the Christian way. He needs to go to court and have a judge listen to his case. He needs to be tried for his crimes. And if he can testify against Don Joaquín, all the better."

"Chris, we live in middle of trees and mountains. No many court or judge here. We make justice. But Joaquín *es* don with big hacienda. He need to go to army so can take land from him. He need to go to *presidio*—how you say? Fort? I take him day after you marry Vicky. He no send more men to attack Americanos. You and you *rancho* and you *villa* be safe."

"Thank you, Don Ruiz."

The older man settled his hand on Chris's shoulder even though he had to reach up a good three inches to do so. "You now part of Familia Ruiz. Take care of *mi princesa*."

"I will, Don Ruiz. I'll take very good care of our *princesa*." Vicky's father nodded his approval and pushed him toward the house.

"Go talk with Vicky. She think you forget her." A glance at the sun riding so low on the horizon gave credence to Don Ruiz's words. Hurrying to the house, Chris took a deep breath and exhaled, thanking God for the way all things had worked out.

"I." His accent hadn't gotten any better in the last day, but it was music to her ears.

Swinging the door open, she stepped out into the hallway, closing the door quickly behind her before he could catch a glimpse of her dress or his new suit.

"Are you all right?" he asked as he slid his hand down her arm, linking their fingers together.

"Yes. And you?"

"I'm great! I've got the prettiest bride who will become my wife tomorrow, and I've just spent two hours playing with horses. The only thing that could have been better is if you had been playing with the horses with me."

"It more fun than sewing all day." She tried to keep

the pout out of her voice, but his look of compassion said he knew she would have rather been outdoors.

"I'm sorry, honey. I know today isn't much fun for you." He leaned closer and kissed her forehead.

"It no important. You will look so *guapo* in your suit tomorrow." She promised and hoped he would like the charro suit that they were making for him. Most of the time the ladies from the hacienda would take anywhere from a few weeks to a few months to put together the special-occasion suit because the embroidering that was required and all the fancy stitches took hours and hours of patience. But they didn't have that kind of time.

"Is there anything I can do for you?" Chris asked as he began to lead her down the hallway toward the stairs.

"Hmm." She grinned. "How good you sew?"

"As in needle and thread?" The look on his face was priceless. "You saw those tattered clothes I was wearing when you first came to the cabin. That should give you a clue."

"Clue?" A new word. Would she ever get to a point where she understood everything he said?

"Clue. Hint."

"Hint?"

He nodded and then explained as he slid an arm around her shoulders, pulling her into his side. "Listen, Vicky. I wanted to talk with you about our time here." Chris led her to a bench with a view overlooking the patio. He paused as he waited for her to settle her skirts, and then he took a seat next to her. He lifted her hand and, after kissing the back of it, kept it clasped loosely in his own.

"I know you have been gone for a while from here, and I'm sure all your friends want to see you and have a chance to talk, but I'm worried about Nana Ruth. I don't know the *hermanos* very well who are staying with her. They don't speak English, and she doesn't speak Spanish. I can't leave her alone for too long. I also have to start to get the fields ready for the spring planting and the..."

"Chris," Vicky interrupted, knowing his worry would be resolved quickly. "We leave the day after we marry. We leave day after tomorrow."

"Oh." It stopped him short, and he turned to gaze fully at her. "Did you already talk with your father?"

"Yes. He say no stay too long. He want to take Don Joaquín to the *presidio*. Papá want take Joaquín before he try escape again. The other dons here, they go with Papá and then go home to their haciendas. Papá say sooner I go, sooner he come to visit." She grinned at the look of relief that washed over Chris's features.

"But what about packing? I'm sure you will want more clothing than the last time you stayed with us. Not that there is much room for all your pretty dresses in our little cabin just yet, but we will build you a house this summer. It won't be nearly as big as this one, but it will have at least five bedrooms, a living room, dining room, study and kitchen."

Disappointment caught her unaware. She had hoped to go back and settle into housekeeping for the two of them with Nana Ruth in the cabin, as well. Something about the cabin made her feel safe and secure. Would she feel the same in the new home Chris planned to build for her? He squeezed her hand in his, bending to see her face better.

"What are you thinking? Do you want the house to be bigger than that?" His forehead creased in wrinkles of concern.

"No, I not want big house. I like cabin. It where I met you and Nana Ruth and learned to love…" His smile came back in full bloom.

"I like my cabin, too, but we need a bedroom for ourselves, honey. And when your parents come to visit? Where would we have them all sleep? Your brothers would end up in the barn."

She had to concede his point, but she didn't want to give up his cozy cabin either. "But I like cabin. It like home for bird or rabbit."

"It has birds?" Chris looked out at the patio. "I can imagine this one might have bird nests, but mine doesn't."

"No, you house like nest." He had inadvertently given her the word she looked for. "It warm and nice and *perfecto*."

He grinned and hugged her into his side. "It's too small for us and Nana Ruth."

"No, we all stay in cabin like before."

"Vicky, someday, I hope, you and I will have children. They'll need a place to sleep."

The idea of having children with this man she loved filled her with more happiness than she could express. "Oh, yes. Need bigger house!"

Chris laughed and then leaned toward her, pressing a kiss to her temple.

* * *

The day had arrived. Chris stood at the front of the chapel and nearly had to pinch himself to make sure it was all real. Things had happened so fast. Not that he had any doubts.

God had blessed him above and beyond anything he could ever have imagined, sending Vicky to him when he had determined never to open himself up to anyone. And she herself had surprised him over and over with her hidden abilities, intelligence and wisdom. She had taught him a valuable lesson about his responsibility to take care of those around him. He'd do his job to the best of his ability and rely on God to be God.

When Vicky had presented him with the new suit that morning after breakfast, he had been astounded, humbled and amazed. When had she and the other ladies had time to finish such elaborate stitching? The suit looked very much like one of the outfits Don Ruiz wore but tailored to fit Chris exactly. He'd never seen the colorful charro outfits until he'd come to Alta California.

Before he could contemplate any more, movement from the doorway caught his attention. The rustling of fabric and the sound of footsteps on the wooden floor announced the arrival of the bride. Finally, Don Ruiz led Vicky into the chapel on his arm. She looked like a princess. White gauzy skirts flowed like a cloud over colorful underskirts and accented her trim waist, and her bodice had lace and who knew whatever else. His eyes caught Vicky's gaze and stayed there.

She took his breath away. She was radiant. Her shy smile as she waited at the entrance of the chapel touched something deep inside his heart. For all her beauty and courage, she was still young in so many ways. He'd find ways to cherish her every day for the rest of his life. He touched his heart with his right hand and hoped his admiration for her was as easily read in his eyes as the love shining in her own. He'd remember this day for the rest of his life. The room, the other people, the day—everything else disappeared and they were alone.

Time stopped as Vicky came closer. With one last kiss on the forehead, her father slipped her hand into Chris's. He reached out with his free hand, unable to stop himself, and brushed the back of his fingers across her cheek. "You're beautiful." He choked out the words because the emotions of the day had settled like a lump in his throat. *"Bella."*

"You are so beautiful, Chris." She smiled even as a tear formed in the corner of her eye. He'd have to teach her another day that men were *handsome*, not *beautiful*.

"Hey." He swiped a finger under each eye, collecting her tears and then kissing her cheek. "There will be no tears on your wedding day. This is a happy occasion."

"They happy tear. You no have happy tear in South Carolina?"

"Well, I was raised not to cry, so I wouldn't really know. But I can tell you my heart is ready to beat out of my chest, and my throat feels like I have a lump of tortilla dough stuck in there." She giggled at his silly words as they turned to face Padre Pedro, who began the ceremony.

As Padre Pedro went back and forth from Latin to Spanish, Chris wasn't able to understand much, but he knew, by the love that shone out of Vicky's eyes as she studied him, that they were both making a vow of a lifetime.

"I came to Alta California to be by myself, but God had other plans for me," he began when it was time for him to speak. "His plans are always best. My love, I promise from this day forward to be faithful to you and you alone. To protect, provide and support you in every up and down life brings our way and rely always on God for His protection, providence and sustenance. I will love you always and forever. Even when God calls us home, I will always love you."

A tear escaped and slid down her smooth cheek. He let her hand go long enough to gently wipe it away, and then she smiled her most brilliant smile, and he wondered again at the grace that had led her to his land and had saved his life that day. Now she had saved his life in a very different way. He no longer wanted nor needed to be a hermit, paying a penance for the failures in his life. Now he could enjoy his new life, new community and new family. His greatest success as a man would come from building a community that worked together.

"And I love you, Chris. My *bello* Cristofer Samuels. I be your wife, love you every day, make your food, clothes, house clean and give you many sons." She blushed slightly with those last words but continued to look directly into his eyes. "I have no other husband and never leave you, in sick or *salud*. I obey you and pray with you every day."

Not the traditional vows but in so many ways, better. Heartfelt with a slight nod to Nana Ruth's influence on Vicky's English. If only Nana Ruth could have been with them on this day.

At Vicky's pause, Padre Pedro slipped a white ribbon in the shape of a figure eight over Vicky's shoulders and then Chris's. As the priest prayed over them, Vicky whispered, "This show we tie together like rope. Not take tie out."

Nodding in understanding, Chris concentrated on praying for their bond. That God would bless it and protect them through the years to come. Neither one had grown up in homes overabounding in loving relationships for them to use as role models, and they would need to figure out how to be the husband or wife the other needed.

Then he considered Berto and Magda, sitting off to the side of the chapel. The older man had his arm wrapped affectionately around his wife's shoulders, and she sat leaning into him as if he were her pillar and support. Jeb and Nana Ruth had a similar relationship. Nana might have fussed at Jeb often, and he had enjoyed getting her riled up, but Jeb had once confessed that he loved seeing the spark in her eye when he teased her. After almost fifty years, there had still been a spark. He could only pray that God would grant them the same blessing.

Sighing deeply, Vicky looked deep into Chris's eyes as he led her around the dance floor. Their first dance as husband and wife. Until now, she had never thought much about dancing. Had dreaded it most of the time, but now, it became an excuse to be held close to Chris.

There might be over a hundred people in the room, and yet while they danced, it was as if the world ceased to exist.

"You look so lovely today," he whispered to her.

"And you, Chris, very handsome?" He'd taught her the word while they were eating at the banquet.

"Sí, mi vida. Mi reina." She smiled at the new words someone had taught him. No longer the princess, someone had told him to call her his queen.

"Te amo, mi rey."

A few minutes later, Papá took Chris's place and led her around the floor. Ever since she was small, he had danced with her, but after her Quinceañera she felt disconnected from him. Like he was putting space between them, or maybe it was her perception. But this dance was different.

"Hija, I can't tell you how happy I am that you found Chris. He is a very good man. He already makes you happy. It shows on your face and in your eyes."

"He is wonderful, Papá. I love him."

"Don't forget to visit your family here, too, child. I'll miss my princesa, but this is as it should be. You will have your own home, where you are respected and taken care of." He glanced up and narrowed his eyes slightly. She followed his line of sight and caught sight of the edge of Mamá's black dress as she swept out of the ballroom, probably to retreat to her room.

"Do not fret, Papá." She held his gaze and met the unspoken apology there with a new confidence. *"I know now that God made me beautiful for Chris. I don't need to be what Mamá wanted me to be. Only what God made*

*me to be. She is very sad and lonely and makes every-
one else miserable because she is hurting. Please, find
a way to be more kind to her. I know there are things
that have hurt you, just like she has hurt me, but we
must show compassion."*

"Aye, mi'ja, how wise you have become." He kissed
her forehead once more and then led her back to the
side of the room where her groom stood waiting for her.

Magda intercepted her before she reached Chris and
pulled her into a warm hug. *"Mi princesa, you are so
beautiful. I couldn't be prouder."*

*"Aye, Magda, you've been like my mother in so many
ways. I can't thank you enough for all that you do. The
wedding, the food, the dress...you organized it so perfectly."*

*"It was a joy to perform any task to see you happily
married to a good man. And a handsome one at that."*
Magda drew her closer once more and then let her go.
*"Now, go dance with that man who can't keep his eyes
off you. And don't forget to come home for a visit from
time to time."*

*"I'll come and visit. And I expect you to come and
visit our villa once it's built. After all, I'd like to convince Rosa's or Margarita's family to join us there."*

"We will see what happens here." Magda stepped
back and let Chris claim her.

"You must come visit," Chris insisted. He had surprised Vicky with some of the things he had understood
over the last few days. *"Vicky missed you when she was
with us before. You are Vicky's family, too."*

"*If God permits and Don Ruiz can make do for a few days, it would be nice to visit your new home,*" Magda answered with a smile.

Epilogue

Vicky patted Tesoro's neck as her horse leaned over the cool stream. She admired the wildflowers and tufts of green plants all around them. Chris sat astride Comet a few feet from her. From here they could see the work on the addition they were making to the cabin. She'd soon discovered she agreed with Chris's desire for privacy but couldn't turn Nana Ruth out from the cabin. Adding a two-story house to the cabin and leaving the original structure for their bedroom had been Chris's idea, but she loved it.

"Hey, *bella*, what are you thinking about?" Chris asked, pulling her down from the saddle and into his arms.

"How good God is to us. He saved us both here, at this spot." She pointed to where he had been standing just a few months before.

"I'm so glad He brought you here to save my sorry hide." Chris kissed her before she could answer. By the time he gave her a chance to speak again, she'd almost forgotten what they had been talking about.

"He save me, too, Chris. He had Tesoro bring me home. Home to you. I never leave again," she announced, pulling his head down for a kiss of her own.

He grinned down at her when she finally pulled back. "Really? So you don't want to go to the hacienda next month? José Luis finished his cabin today, and he's going back to the hacienda tomorrow."

At her look, he held up a hand. "I've already reminded him to stop by and see you before he goes. And yes, his arm is much better. Nana checked his wound today. He and Maritza plan to get married next month and hoped we could attend." Shaking his head as if disappointed, he shrugged, pulling her off the ground with her arms wrapped around his shoulders. She loved the strength of those wonderfully broad shoulders. "I'll just have to tell them…"

"No, we go! We go!" Excitement filled her at the idea of going to visit everyone at the hacienda. "I learn now. I take long journey home."

He looked puzzled at her words, so she explained. "I leave hacienda looking for Papá without know that I looking for love and home. I go on long journey, brought me to Americano in woods and cabin with Nana Ruth. *Mi* Tesoro bring me home to my love and my new life."

"It's true, Vicky, this is your home. And it took a long journey to get here, but you made it. We both did."

"I home here, with you." She slid a hand to his cheek and caressed it and then tapped his chest. "This my home. We stay here or you take me to hacienda, to South

Carolina or *España*. If I can come here—" again she tapped his chest above his heart "—I home."

He pulled her in tight. "You are my home as well, Vicky. I love you."

"*Te amo*, Chris." She sighed and wrapped her arms around his waist, knowing he truly loved her. And had shown her that God had always loved her, too. She'd found her earthly home with Chris and had certainty that someday she'd go to her celestial home now that she had learned that God loved her and accepted her exactly the way He had made her.

But before that happened, she intended to live a long and happy life with the best man she had ever known.

* * * * *

*Don't miss the other heartwarming
historical romance from Bonnie Navarro:
INSTANT PRAIRIE FAMILY*

Find more great reads at www.LoveInspircd.com.

Dear Reader,

Thank you for coming on this journey with Vicky and Chris. They have a special place in my heart and hopefully in yours now. Growing up, different cultures and languages fascinated me. The church I attended actively supported many missionaries, and I would pepper them with questions about their foods, languages and customs. In high school, I became involved in tutoring students newly arrived to the United States. Charades and a lot of pointing became a way of communication.

When I went to college, I met a man from Peru, and although he spoke English, he promised to help me learn Spanish by speaking only Spanish with me from then on. This June we will celebrate twenty-four years of marriage, and he still speaks "only Spanish" to me. I guess he's kept his word. There have been times in our marriage where we have had issues with communication, sometimes because of the language, but most often because men and women are wired differently—for which I am extremely grateful.

As I've met people from all over the world or right around the block, I am constantly reminded that we are all God's princes and princesses. And despite our differences we are all so very much the same. We all have fears, we all need to be loved and to love. We need community. We all want a hero who loves us enough to risk his own life to save us. I thank God that He is our hero. He loves each and every one of us regardless of our race, background, language, economic situation or education. And actually, He loves that we are diverse. After all, He designed each and every one of us and declares His creation "Good."

I'd love to hear what you think about Vicky and Chris's journey, or you can share your own. You can email me at bonnie12navarro@gmail.com.

May God keep you and bless you on your journey.

Blessings,

Bonnie Navarro

WED BY NECESSITY
Smoky Mountain Matches • by Karen Kirst

Caught in a storm overnight with her father's new employee, Caroline Turner finds her reputation damaged. And the only way to repair it is to marry Duncan McKenna. But can a sophisticated socialite and a down-to-earth stable manager put their differences aside and find love?

THE OUTLAW'S SECRET
by Stacy Henrie

When Essie Vanderfair's train is held up by outlaws, the dime-store novelist connives to be taken hostage by them, seeking material for her next book. But she doesn't anticipate falling for one of the outlaws...or that he's secretly an undercover detective.

THE BOUNTY HUNTER'S BABY
by Erica Vetsch

Bounty hunter Thomas Beaufort has no problem handling outlaws, but when he's left with a criminal's baby to care for, he's in over his head. And the only person he can turn to for help is Esther Jensen, the woman whose heart he broke when he left town.

THE RELUCTANT GUARDIAN
by Susanne Dietze

On the verge of her first London season, Gemma Lyfeld accidently stumbles on a group of smugglers, catching them in the act...and they think she's a spy. Now she must depend on covert government agent Tavin Knox for protection. But how will she protect her heart from him?

LIHCNM0117

REQUEST YOUR FREE BOOKS!

2 FREE INSPIRATIONAL NOVELS
PLUS 2 FREE MYSTERY GIFTS

Love Inspired HISTORICAL

YES! Please send me 2 FREE Love Inspired® Historical novels and my 2 FREE mystery gifts (gifts are worth about $10). After receiving them, if I don't wish to receive any more books, I can return the shipping statement marked "cancel." If I don't cancel, I will receive 4 brand-new novels every month and be billed just $4.99 per book in the U.S. or $5.49 per book in Canada. That's a saving of at least 17% off the cover price. It's quite a bargain! Shipping and handling is just 50¢ per book in the U.S. and 75¢ per book in Canada.* I understand that accepting the 2 free books and gifts places me under no obligation to buy anything. I can always return a shipment and cancel at any time. Even if I never buy another book, the two free books and gifts are mine to keep forever.

102/302 IDN GH6Z

Name _____ (PLEASE PRINT) _____

Address _____ Apt. # _____

City _____ State/Prov. _____ Zip/Postal Code _____

Signature (if under 18, a parent or guardian must sign)

Mail to the Reader Service:
IN U.S.A.: P.O. Box 1867, Buffalo, NY 14240-1867
IN CANADA: P.O. Box 609, Fort Erie, Ontario L2A 5X3

Want to try two free books from another series?
Call 1-800-873-8635 or visit www.ReaderService.com.

* Terms and prices subject to change without notice. Prices do not include applicable taxes. Sales tax applicable in N.Y. Canadian residents will be charged applicable taxes. Offer not valid in Quebec. This offer is limited to one order per household. Not valid for current subscribers to Love Inspired Historical books. All orders subject to credit approval. Credit or debit balances in a customer's account(s) may be offset by any other outstanding balance owed by or to the customer. Please allow 4 to 6 weeks for delivery. Offer available while quantities last.

Your Privacy—The Reader Service is committed to protecting your privacy. Our Privacy Policy is available online at www.ReaderService.com or upon request from the Reader Service.

We make a portion of our mailing list available to reputable third parties that offer products we believe may interest you. If you prefer that we not exchange your name with third parties, or if you wish to clarify or modify your communication preferences, please visit us at www.ReaderService.com/consumerschoice or write to us at Reader Service Preference Service, P.O. Box 9062, Buffalo, NY 14240-9062. Include your complete name and address.

LIHIS

SPECIAL EXCERPT FROM

Love Inspired HISTORICAL

*Forced to marry her father's new employee after
being caught overnight in a storm, can Caroline find
love with her unlikely husband?*

Read on for an excerpt from
WED BY NECESSITY,
the next heartwarming book in the
SMOKY MOUNTAIN MATCHES series.

Gatlinburg, Tennessee
July 1887

As a holiday, Independence Day left a lot to be desired.
Independence was a dream Caroline Turner wasn't likely
to ever attain.

The fireworks' blue-green light flickered over the sea
of faces, followed by red, white and gold. She schooled
her features and made her way along the edge of the field
to where the musicians were playing patriotic tunes.

"Caroline, we're running low on lemonade."

"Then make more," she snapped at eighteen-year-old
Wanda Smith.

"We've misplaced the lemon crates."

At the distress in the younger girl's countenance,
Caroline relented. "Fine. I'll look for them. You may
return to your station."

It took her a quarter of an hour to locate the missing
lemons. By then, the last of the fireworks had been shot
off and attendees were ready for more food and drink.

The celebration was far from over, yet she wished she could return home to her bedroom and solitude.

A trio of young women approached and engaged her in conversation. As usual, they wanted to know about her outfit, whether she'd had it made by a local seamstress or her mother had had it shipped from New York. Before they'd exhausted their talk of fashion, a stranger inserted himself into their group.

"Excuse me."

Caroline didn't recognize the hulking figure. Well over six feet tall, he was as broad and solid as an oak tree and looked as if he hadn't seen civilization in months. He was dressed in common clothing, and his shirt and pants were clean but wrinkled. Dirt caked the heels of his sturdy brown boots. His thick reddish-brown hair was tied back with a strip of leather. While he appeared to have a strong facial structure, his mustache and beard obscured the lower half of his face. His mouth was wide and generous. Sparkling blue eyes assessed her.

"Would you care to dance?" He spoke in a rolling brogue that identified him as a foreigner.

Don't miss
WED BY NECESSITY by Karen Kirst,
available wherever Love Inspired® Historical books
and ebooks are sold.

www.LoveInspired.com

LIHEXP0117

Turn your love of reading into rewards you'll love with
Harlequin My Rewards

Join for FREE today at
www.HarlequinMyRewards.com

Earn **FREE BOOKS** of your choice.

Experience **EXCLUSIVE OFFERS** and contests.

Enjoy **BOOK RECOMMENDATIONS**
selected just for you.

PLUS! Sign up now
and get **500** points
right away!

Earn
FREE
REWARDS
Join
Today!
HarlequinMyRewards.com

MYR16R